D1569677

HONEST MONEY

Also by Erle Stanley Gardner available from Carroll & Graf:

Dead Men's Letters and Other Short Novels
The Blonde in Lower Six

ERLE STANLEY GARDNER
HONEST MONEY
AND OTHER SHORT NOVELS

Carroll & Graf Publishers, Inc.
New York

"Honest Money," *Black Mask,* November 1932
"The Top Comes Off," *Black Mask,* December 1932
"Close Call," *Black Mask,* January 1933
"Making the Breaks," *Black Mask,* June 1933
"Devil's Fire," *Black Mask,* July 1933
"Blackmail with Lead," *Black Mask,* August 1933

This Carroll & Graf edition is published by arrangement with
Argosy Communications, Inc., in cooperation with Thayer Hob-
son and Company, representing The Erle Stanley Gardner Trust,
Jean Bethell Gardner and Grace Naso, Trustees.

First Carroll & Graf edition 1991

Carroll & Graf Publishers, Inc.
260 Fifth Avenue
New York, NY 10001

Library of Congress Cataloging-in-Publication Data
Gardner, Erle Stanley, 1889–1970.
    Honest money : and other short novels / by Erle Stanley
Gardner. — 1st Carroll & Graf ed.
    p. cm.
    Contents: Honest money — The top comes off — Close call
— Making the breaks — Devil's fire —Blackmail with lead.
    ISBN 0-88184-683-X : $18.95
    1. Detective and mystery stories, American. I. Title.
PS3513.A6322H64   1991
813'.52—dc20   91-12116
                                                          CIP

Manufactured in the United States of America

Argosy Communications wishes to extend its grateful appreciation to the following people who helped to make this volume possible:

Jean Gardner and Grace Naso
Lawrence Hughes
Betty Burke and Katharine Odgers
Kent Carroll and Herman Graf
Laura Langlie and Sheila Cavanagh
Robert Weinberg
and
Eva Zablodowsky

Contents

Honest Money

THE clock on the city hall was booming the hour of nine in the morning when Ken Corning pushed his way through the office door. On the frosted glass of that door appeared the words: *"Kenneth D. Corning, Attorney at Law—Enter."*

Ken Corning let his eye drift over the sign. It was gold leaf and untarnished. It was precisely thirty days since the sign painter had collected for the job, and the sign painter had collected as soon as his brush had finished the last letter of the last word of that sign.

The credit of young attorneys in York City wasn't of the best. This was particularly true of young lawyers who didn't seem to have an "in" with the administration.

Helen Vail was dusting her desk. She grinned at Ken.

He reached a hand to his inside pocket.

"Pay day," he said.

Her eyes glinted with a softness that held a touch of the maternal.

"Listen, Ken, let it go until you get started. I can hang on a while longer. . . ."

He took out a wallet, started spreading out ten-dollar bills. When he had counted out five of them, he pushed the pile over to her. There were two bills left in the wallet.

"Honest, Ken. . . ."

He pushed his way to the inside office. "Forget it," he said. "I told you we'd make it go. We haven't started to fight yet."

She followed him in, the money in her hand. Standing in the doorway, very erect, chin up, she waited for him to turn to meet her gaze.

The outer door of the entrance office made a noise.

She turned. Looking over her shoulder, Ken could see the big

9

man who stood on the threshold. He looked as though his clothes had been filled with apple jelly. He quivered and jiggled like a jellyfish on a board. Fat encased him in layers, an unsubstantial, soft fat that seemed to be hanging to his bones with a grip that was but temporary.

His voice was thin and falsetto.

"I want to see the lawyer," he shrilled.

Helen turned on her heel, called over her shoulder: "All right, Mr. Corning. I'll enter up this retainer." To the man she said: "You'll have to wait. Mr. Corning's preparing an important brief. He'll see you in a minute or two."

The pneumatic door check swung the door to.

Ken Corning turned in his swivel-chair and sent swift hands to his tie. From the outer office sounded the furious clack of a typewriter. Three minutes passed. The roller of the machine made sounds as the paper was ripped from it. The door of the private office banged open. Helen Vail pushed her way in, in an ecstasy of haste, crinkling a legal paper in her hands.

"All ready for your signature," she said.

The pneumatic door check was swinging the door closed as Ken reached for the paper. On it had been written with the monotony of mechanical repetition, over and over: "Now is the time for all good men to come to the aid of the party."

The door completed its closing. The latch clicked.

"Get his name?" asked Ken.

"Sam Parks. He's nervous. It's a criminal case. I'd have kept him waiting longer, but he won't stand for it. He's looking at his watch—twice in the last sixty seconds."

Ken patted her hand.

"Okey. Good girl. Shoot him in."

Helen walked to the door, opened it, smiled sweetly. "You may come in now, Mr. Parks."

She held the door open. Ken could see the big man heaving his bulk free of the chair. He saw him blot out the light in the doorway as the girl stepped aside. He was signing a paper as the big man entered the office and paused. Ken kept his eyes on the paper until the door catch clicked. Then he looked up with a smile.

"Mr. Parks, is it?" he asked.

The big man grunted, waddled over to the chair which was placed so close to the new desk as to invite easy intimacy. He sat down, then, apparently feeling that the chair was too far away, started hitching it closer and closer to the desk. His voice was almost a shrill whisper.

"My wife," he said, "has been arrested."

Ken laid down the pen, looked professional.

"What," he asked, "is the charge?"

The big man's shrill voice rattled off a string of swift words: "Well, you see it was this way. We had a place, a little restaurant, and the officers came busting in without a warrant . . . tell me, can they come into a place without a warrant, that way?"

Ken said crisply: "They did, didn't they?"

"Yes."

"Okey, then they can. They're not supposed to, but they did, they do and they can. What happened?"

"Well, that was about all. They claimed we were selling booze."

Ken's voice was sharp.

"Find any?"

"A little."

"How much?"

"Ten or fifteen gallons."

"Then they arrested you both?"

The fat man blinked glassy eyes.

"Just her. They didn't take me."

"Why?"

He fidgeted, and the layers of fat jiggled about.

"Well, we sort of outslicked 'em. There had been a guy eating at one of the tables. He got wise as soon as the first man walked in on the raiding party. He ducked out the back. I sat down at his table and finished up his food. The wife pretended she didn't know me, and asked the officers if she could collect my bill before they took her. They said she could. I paid her fifty cents for the food and gave her a ten-cent tip. Then they closed up the place, took the booze away with 'em, and put me out. The wife said she ran the place alone."

Ken Corning twisted a pencil in his fingers.

"I'll want a retainer of a hundred and fifty dollars," he said, "and then I'll see what I can do and report."

The glassy eyes squinted.

"You ain't in with the gang here?"

"I'm a newcomer."

The man opened his coat, disclosed a wrinkled vest and shirt, soggy with perspiration. He pulled a leather wallet from an inside pocket and pulled out a hundred dollar bill and a fifty. The wallet was crammed with money. He tossed the money carelessly on the desk.

"The first thing to do," he said, "is to see the wife. Tell her you're going to represent her, see? Let her know I'm on the job, and tell her to keep a stiff upper lip, and to keep quiet, see? Tell her to keep quiet, see?"

Ken Corning folded the money, got to his feet, stood there, signifying that the interview was over.

"Come back when I send for you. Leave your name and address and your wife's name with the girl in the outer office so I can get my records straight. Leave a telephone number where you can be reached."

The man turned on the threshold.

"You ain't in with the ring?" he asked, and there was a note of anxiety in his voice.

Ken Corning reached for a law book, shook his head.

The pneumatic door clicked shut.

Ken set down the law book and fingered the money. He turned it over and over in his fingers. He cocked his head on one side, listening. After a moment he heard the click of the outer door catch. Then Helen Vail was standing on the threshold of the inner office. Her eyes were starry.

Ken Corning waved the money.

"Start an account for that bird, and credit it with a hundred and fifty."

She was smiling at him when the door opened. Broad shoulders pushed their way across the outer office. From his desk, Ken could see the man as he crossed the outer office. Helen Vail barred the inner office door.

"Whom do you wish?" she asked.

The man laughed, pushed past her, walked directly to Ken Corning's desk. He flipped back a corner of his coat with a casual hand.

"Who," he asked, "was the guy that just left here, and what'd he want?"

Ken Corning pushed back the swivel-chair as he got to his feet.

"This," he said, "is my private office."

The broad shouldered man laughed. His face was coarse

skinned, but the gray eyes had little lights in them that might have meant humor, or might have meant a love of conflict.

"Keep your shirt on, keep your shirt on," he said. "I'm Perkins from the booze detail. There was a speak knocked over last night. The woman who was running it tried to slip a bribe, and she's booked on a felony. That big guy was sitting in there, eating chow. He claimed he was a customer. I happened to see him come in here. He looked phoney, so I tagged along. I want to know what he wanted."

Ken Corning's voice was hard.

"This," he said, "is a law office, not an information bureau."

The gray eyes became brittle hard. The jaw jutted forward. Perkins crowded to the desk.

"Listen, guy," he said, "you're new here. Whether you're going to get along or not depends on whether you play ball or not. I asked you who that guy was. I asked because I wanted to know. . . ."

Corning moved free of the swivel-chair.

"You getting out?" he asked.

The lips of the broad shouldered man twisted in a sneer.

"So that's your line of chatter?"

"That's my line of chatter."

The man turned on his heel, strode towards the door. He turned with his hand on the knob.

"Try and get some favors out of the liquor detail!" he said.

Ken's tone was rasping. He stood with his feet planted wide apart, eyes glinting.

"I don't want favors," he said, "from anybody!"

The broad shouldered man walked from the office, heels pounding the floor. Slowly the automatic door check swung the door shut.

KEN was ready to leave his office, seeking an interview with his client at the jail, when the door of his private office framed the white features of Helen Vail.

"It's Mr. Dwight," she said.

"What is?"

"The man who just came in. Carl Dwight. He's outside. He wants to see you."

Ken whistled. "Show him in," he said.

She motioned towards the desk.

"Shall I get you some papers?"

"Not with him. He's a wise bird. He knows. Shoot him in."

Helen stood to one side of the door and beckoned. Carl Dwight came in. He walked with a slight limp. His lips were smiling. He had pale eyes that seemed covered with a thin white film, like boiled milk. Those eyes didn't smile. His skin was swarthy and oily. There was a cut on his forehead, a slight bruise on his left cheek bone.

He wasn't large, and yet he radiated a suggestion of ominous power. He said, crisply: "I'm busy. You're busy. You know of me. I know of you. I've had my eye on you for the last week or two. You're a likely looking young man. I want to give you a retainer. Here's five hundred dollars. That'll be for this month. There'll be five hundred dollars more coming next month, and the month after that."

His gloved hand laid an envelope on the desk.

Ken picked up the envelope. It was unsealed. There were five one hundred-dollar bills in it.

"What," asked Ken cautiously, "am I supposed to do?"

The gloved hand waved in an airy gesture.

"Just use your head," said Dwight. "I've got rather extensive interests here. You've probably heard of me, know who I am."

Ken Corning chose his words carefully.

"You," he said, "are reputed to be the head of the political machine in this county. You are reputed to be the man who tells the mayor what to do."

The filmed eyes blinked. The swarthy skinned man made clucking noises in his throat.

"That, of course, is an exaggeration, Mr. Corning. But I have interests in the county, interests which are rather extensive. Now you can sort of look out for those interests. And, by the way, there's a criminal case, the matter of a woman who was running rather a disreputable joint, gambling, hooch and all that. Parks was the name, I believe.

"Do you know, I think it might be rather a good thing to have that case disposed of rather rapidly. A plea of guilty, let us say. I'm certain you'll agree that it's a dead open and shut case. She tried to bribe an officer. There were witnesses. She gave him fifty dollars. Having such things aired in front of a jury don't do any good."

He got to his feet. The swarthy skin crinkled in a smile, a

sallow, bilious smile. The filmed eyes regarded Ken Corning with the wisdom of a serpent.

"So now," he smirked, "we understand each other perfectly. I think you'll like it in York City, Corning."

Ken slowly got to his feet.

"Yes," he said, "I understand you perfectly. But you don't understand me, not by a long ways. Take back this damned money before I slap your face with it!"

Dwight teetered back and forth on his feet, made little clucking noises with his mouth.

"Like that, eh?" he said.

"Like that," agreed Corning.

Dwight sneered.

"You won't last long. You can't . . . ."

He didn't finish. Ken Corning reached out with the envelope which he held by a corner, and slapped it across Dwight's mouth. The filmed eyes blazed into light. The mouth twisted in a snarl. Dwight snatched at the envelope, crammed it in his pocket, whirled and started to the door. He paused on the threshold.

"Wait," he said, significantly.

And Ken Corning, standing by his desk, feet braced wide apart, jaw thrust forward, said: "You're damned tooting I'll wait. I'll be waiting long after you think you're finished with me!"

THE attorneys' room in the county jail was a dull, cheerless place. There was a long desk which ran down the center of the room. Above this desk was a heavy wire screen. The prisoner could sit on one side of the desk, the attorney on the other.

Esther Parks came into the room through the doorway which led to the cell corridor. Ken Corning watched her with interest. Her face was heavy, her walk plodding. She was a big woman, broad-hipped and big-shouldered. Her eyes were like oysters on a white plate.

She plowed her way forward.

The attendant who had charge of the room stood at the doorway, beyond earshot, but where he could see everything that went on in the room.

The woman sat down on the stool opposite Ken Corning. Her face was within three feet of his. Her big hands were folded upon the scarred wood of the long desk. The heavy screen separated them.

"Hello," she said.

Ken Corning kept his voice low pitched.

"Hello. I'm the attorney that your husband engaged to represent you. He thought you were just charged with unlawful possession of liquor. You're not. They've got you on the charge of offering a bribe to an officer. That's a felony."

He paused expectantly.

The woman said: "Uh-huh."

Ken stared into the oyster eyes.

"Well," he said, "I'm to do the best I can for you. Can we go to trial and beat the charge?"

The eyes didn't change expression. The heavy face rippled into dull speech.

"I was running a speak, me and Sam. We went in mostly for cheap food with drinks to sell to the right parties. I don't see why they had to pick on us. Everybody's doing it, that is, everybody anywhere round our neighborhood."

Ken frowned and shook his head.

"I'm telling you it isn't the liquor charge they've got you on. I could square that with a fine. It's the bribery charge. Can we beat that?"

The woman's voice was blurred in its accent, indifferent and stolid in tone.

"I don't know. I gave him the money. They all take the money. Twice before I've had men call on me and say they was the law. I've given 'em money. I gave this man money. Then he collared me. They didn't spot Sam. He sat down at a table and ate some grub."

Ken Corning made little drumming noises with the tips of his fingers. He regarded the woman through the wire mesh of the screen.

"Have they asked you for a statement?" he wanted to know.

A flicker of intelligence appeared in the pale, watery eyes.

"I ain't so dumb. I told 'em to wait until my lawyer showed up, then they could talk with him."

"Who was it?" asked Corning, "the one who wanted the statement?"

She moved her head in a gesture of slow negation.

"I dunno. Somebody from the Sheriff's office, or the District Attorney's office. He was a young fellow and he had a man with him that took down what I said in shorthand."

"What did you say?"

"Nothin'."

Corning squinted his eyes thoughtfully.

"How did it happen that they didn't spot Sam as your husband? Usually when they make these raids they've had a stoolie go in and make a purchase or two. They have all the dope on where the stuff is kept and who runs the place."

The woman's head turned again, slowly, from side to side.

"I dunno. They just didn't spot Sam, that was all. I was behind the counter at the cash register. They came walkin' in. I think I heard somebody say 'There she is,' or 'That's her, now,' or somethin' like that. I didn't pay so much attention. They made the pinch, and I tried to hand 'em the dough.

"It was their fault I slipped 'em the money, too. One of the men held up the jug that had the hooch in it, and said: 'Well, sister, what are you goin' to do about this?' I seen he had me, dead to rights, so I opened the cash register, an' asked him if he'd listen to reason. He said he would. I slipped him the cash, an' then they said something to each other and told me to come along with them.

"Sam had got wise to what was goin' on, an' he'd gone over to the table an' was boltin' down food. I asked the law if I could close up the joint, take the cash an' collect from the gent at the table. They said I could, an' I did, an' that's all I know about it. They took me here."

Ken Corning clamped his mouth into a thin line.

"Then we've got to plead guilty," he said.

She shrugged her shoulders.

"That's your job. I dunno. I'm tellin' you what happened. I figured Sam would get a mouthpiece an' spring me."

Corning continued to drum with his fingers.

"Look here," he said, "there's something funny about this case. I'm going to keep a close mouth for a while, and see if I can find out what's back of it. You seem to be on the outs with the ring that's running the town. Do you know why?"

The big head shook slowly.

"Well," said Corning, "sit tight for a while. Don't talk to anyone. If anyone asks you any questions, no matter who it is, tell them to see your lawyer, Mr. Corning. Can you remember to do that?"

"Uh-huh."

"I'll have you arraigned and get bail set. Can you raise bail?"

"How much?"

"Maybe three thousand dollars?"

"No."

"Two thousand?"

"Maybe."

"Any property you could put up as security with a bail bond company for the purpose of getting them to issue a bail bond?"

"No. Just cash. We had a lease on the joint. It paid fair money. Lately it ain't been payin'."

Ken Corning got to his feet.

"All right," he said. "Sit tight. Remember what I told you. Don't talk. I'm going to see what I can do."

The attendant moved forward.

"This way," he said to the woman, in a voice that was a mechanical monotone.

DON GRAVES, the Deputy District Attorney in charge of the case of the People vs. Esther Parks, was almost totally bald, despite the fact that he was in his early thirties. His face ran to nose. The eyes on either side were round and lidless. He had a peculiar peering appearance like that of a startled anteater.

He turned the nose directly towards Ken Corning, so that the twin eyes bored unblinkingly into those of the attorney, and said: "We won't reduce the charge. She bribed an officer. That's a serious offense."

Ken kept his temper.

"That's a hard charge to prove, and you know as well as I do that the officer kept angling to get her to give him money. You get a jury of twelve people together, and some of 'em are going to think it's a hell of a note to send a woman to the pen because she had some hooch and an officer kept sticking his palm out at her. It's only natural to slip a man something when he makes a stall like that. That isn't being criminal. That's just human nature."

The deputy licked his lips with the tip of a pale tongue that seemed, somehow, to be utterly cold.

"The penal code don't say so, brother."

Ken Corning frowned.

"The penal code says lots of things—so does the Constitution."

Don Graves said: "Yeah," and made as though he'd turn away.

Corning raised his voice.

"Well, listen, about bail. If you'll suggest to the magistrate that bail be reduced to a thousand dollars cash, I think she can raise it."

Graves turned back to Corning, stared lidlessly at him.

"You heard what the magistrate said: ten thousand bucks cash, or twenty thousand bond."

Corning's rage flared up.

"A hell of a bail that is. You'd think the woman was guilty of a murder or something. If you don't know that these cheap dicks are sticking their palms out right and left and shaking down the people that run the little speaks, you're just plain crazy! You keep riding me around, and I'll take this jane before a jury and see what twelve men in a box have to say about the way you're getting so damned virtuous in York City all of a sudden."

The lidless eyes remained hard and peering.

"Go ahead," said Graves.

"I will!" snapped Corning.

Graves spoke as Ken Corning was halfway to the door.

"Tell you what I *will* do, Corning."

Corning paused, turned.

"Take her into court right away, plead her guilty as charged, and I'll ask to have a minimum sentence imposed."

Corning asked: "Fine or imprisonment?"

"Imprisonment," said Graves. "To hell with a fine."

Corning's retort was emphatic. "To hell with *you!*" he said, and slammed the door.

HELEN VAIL had the afternoon papers for him when he walked into his office.

"News?" she asked.

He grinned at her, took the papers, touched her fingertips as he took them, and suddenly patted her hand.

"Good girl," he said.

"Why?"

"Oh, I don't know. You just are."

"How about the case?"

"I don't know. There's something funny. You'd think the woman had done a murder or something. And Graves, that billiard ball guy with the snake eyes, told me he'd let me cop a minimum sentence if I'd rush her through the mill and make a plea."

Helen Vail's eyes were sympathetic.

"You mean send the woman to the pen because she slipped one of these dicks a little dough?"

"Exactly."

"What'd you tell him?"

Corning grinned.

"That, precious, is something your little shell-like ears shouldn't hear."

And he walked into the inner office, taking the papers with him. He sat in his swivel-chair, put his feet on the desk, turned to the sporting page, browsed through the headlines, turned back to the front page.

The telephone rang.

He called out to Miss Vail: "I've got it, Helen," and scooped the receiver to his ear, holding the newspaper in one hand, the telephone in the other.

The shrill, piping voice of Sam Parks came over the wire.

"Listen, is this Corning, the lawyer?"

"Yes."

"Okey. This is Parks. I was in to see you this morning about my wife. Listen, I know why they're trying to give her the works. I can't tell you over the telephone. I'm coming over. You be there?"

"Come right away," said Corning.

"Yeah!" shrilled Parks excitedly, and banged the receiver into place. Ken Corning hung up, turned to the paper. There was a frown creasing his forehead. He looked at his watch. It was five minutes to four. Street noises came up through the open window. The afternoon was warm, the air laden with the scents of late summer.

Ken's eyes drifted unseeingly to the front page of the newspaper. Why should so much stir be made over the matter of a commonplace woman in a third-grade speakeasy giving some money to an officer who held out his hand for it? Why should a raid be made on a place where the officers hadn't collected enough information to know who was running the place, and had let the husband slip through their fingers?

He stared at the newspaper, let his forehead crinkle in thought, and tried to fit the ends of the puzzle together.

Minutes passed.

The clock on the city hall boomed the hour of four, and the big gilt hands crept around until the minute hand marked the quarter hour.

There was the sound of a truck backfiring in the street.

Something came trebling up through the window, the scream of a child, or of a very frightened woman. Then there was the sound of rubber tires, skidding into a turn on pavement, the shout of a man.

There was a second of silence, and then the noise made by many voices, the sound of feet running on cement. A siren wailed in the distance.

Ken Corning, lost in contemplation, did not interpret the significance of those sounds until the siren had become a scream, until the clanging bell of the ambulance sounded almost directly beneath his office window, and until the door of his private office opened and Helen Vail stared at him.

"There seems to have been a man hurt," she said.

Ken Corning put down the paper and went to the window. Helen put her hand on his shoulder as they leaned out. Corning was conscious of the touch of her hair against his cheek, the pressure of her hand on his shoulder. He slid his right arm out, around her waist.

They looked down upon the street.

There was no traffic. Such vehicles as were on the street were stalled. Men swarmed about like busy ants, moving in seething disorder. An ambulance was backing towards the curb. A uniformed officer was clearing a path for it. Stalled cars, their motors running, belched forth thin smoke films which made the air a light blue color.

A black circle of men were not moving. They were grouped about something which lay on the sidewalk. From that form there was a dark stain which had welled along the cement until it trickled in a thin, sluggish stream into the gutter.

The man was big and fat. He was lying on his back.

"Good heavens!" said the voice of Helen Vail, "it's the man who was in the office."

Ken Corning swung from the window. He reached the doorway of the private office in three strides, and gained the stairs. He went down them two at a time. He reached the sidewalk as the men were loading the stretcher. He pushed his way through the crowd. Men muttered comments, turned and stared at him, growled warnings to watch what he was doing. Corning paid no attention to them.

He reached the inner circle, saw the stretcher bearers heaving against the weight of the bulk that they strove to place in the ambulance.

Parks had been shot twice. To all appearances he was dead. The bullet holes welled a red trail which dripped from the stretcher. The eyes were half open and waxy. The skin was like discolored dough. The hands trailed limply at the ends of dangling arms.

One of the stretcher bearers spoke sharply.

"Give us a hand here, some of you guys!"

Ken Corning pushed through the circle as two of the spectators swirled forward. A uniformed officer also bent to give a lift. Corning asked a question: "Who saw it? How did it happen?"

Men stared at him with blank curiosity. He was hatless, wandering about asking how it had happened, and men regarded him as a part of the incident which had broken into the routine of their daily life. They watched him with that expression of impersonal curiosity with which fish in an aquarium stare at spectators who press against the glass tank.

On the fifth repetition of the question, a man gave an answer.

"I saw it. He drove up in an automobile and parked the car. He started walking along the street. The guy that shot him was in a roadster. He pulled right in to the curb, and he didn't drive away until he was sure the guy was dead. The first shot smacked him over. He shot again when the guy was on the cement. I seen him twitch when the second bullet struck!"

Corning led the man to one side.

"Drove up in a car, eh? Which car?"

He indicated the line of parked machines.

The witness shrugged his shoulders. "I ain't sure. I think it was the flivver over there. I remember that it was a car that had a smashed fender. You know, there wasn't no reason why I should notice him until . . ."

"Yes," said Corning, "I know. Now you want some advice?"

The man looked at him with curious eyes.

"Huh?" he asked.

"Get away from here and don't tell your story to a soul. Go to headquarters, get the homicide squad's office and ask for Sergeant Home. He's on the square. Tell your story to him, and ask that your name be withheld. Otherwise, if you got a good look at the man that did the shooting, you might find yourself parked on a marble slab. Killers don't like witnesses."

The man's face paled. "Gee," he said; then, after an interval: "Gee whiz!"

He spun on his heel, started walking rapidly away. From time to time he glanced over his shoulder.

His tip gave Ken Corning the chance to be the first man to examine the light car with the bent fender.

He looked at the registration certificate which was strapped about the steering post of the car. That showed the machine was registered in the name of Esther Parks, and the address which was given was the same address as that of the place which had been raided when the woman was arrested.

Ken felt of the seat. It was still warm.

He noticed an afternoon newspaper lying on the floorboards. He picked it up. There was nothing else on the inside of the car to give any inkling as to who had driven or owned it. Ken felt in the flap pocket of the right-hand door. His groping fingers encountered a lady's handkerchief, a pair of pliers, the cap from an inner tube, and a bit of pasteboard. He pulled out the pasteboard.

It was red, bearing the insignia of the police department. It was, he found when he deciphered the scrawled lines which were placed in the printed blanks, a ticket for parking within fifteen feet of a fire hydrant on Seventh Street, between Madison and Harkley. The time was checked at three-forty-five, of that day.

Ken pocketed the ticket and walked around to the front of the car, inspecting the dent in the fender. There was but little paint left upon the nondescript car which Parks had been driving. That little paint had been cracked and chipped where the fender had crumpled. And, on the tip of that crumpled fender, was a spot of bright red enamel, evidently taken from the car with which the flivver had collided.

Ken examined the front of the springs, the radiator, found further evidences of a collision, further bits of red paint. The accident had evidently been very recent.

Aside from those things, there was nothing to indicate anything whatever about the occupant of the car, or the errand upon which it had been driven.

Ken walked to the curb, looked at the crowd which was commencing to move along under orders of the uniformed police. The traffic was moving now, crawling past at a snail's pace, horns blaring. An officer, accompanied by a woman, moved along the parked lane of cars, inspecting them.

Corning felt that this woman had seen the fat man emerge from a machine, but couldn't identify the machine. Ken let himself drift away with the scattering spectators. He walked around the block, and back to his office. He climbed the stairs, smiled at Helen Vail's white face.

"Was it . . . ?"

He nodded, passed into the inner office. She came and stood in the doorway. Ken smoothed out the newspaper he had taken from the car Parks had driven. He spread it out.

A knife had cut away a section of the front page.

"Was it because he came here?" asked Helen, mustering her courage.

Ken Corning reached for the other afternoon newspaper he had been reading when the sound of the shots had interrupted him. He nodded absently as he spread the two front pages out on the desk, one over the other.

The paper from the death car showed the page of the other paper through the opening where the knife had cut. That which had been cut out was a picture with a small paragraph or two below it.

Ken looked at the picture.

It showed a man with a square-cut chin, shell glasses, a firm, thin mouth, high cheek bones and a high forehead. Below it appeared the words *Mayor Appoints Harry B. Dike as New Head of Water Department.*

Corning read the few paragraphs appearing below the headlines of the accompanying news article. Those paragraphs recited the enviable record Harry B. Dike had enjoyed in connection with his own business enterprises and such civic activities as had claimed his time. It also mentioned that Dike was firmly opposed to the granting of contracts and concessions to those who enjoyed political pull, and that, in the future, the water department would be conducted upon a basis of efficiency with all work thrown open to the lowest responsible bidders, although the department would reserve the right to let private contracts.

The article sounded very promising. It gave the location of

Dike's office in the Monadnock Building. The Monadnock Building was on Seventh Street, between Madison and Harkley.

Helen Vail watched Corning as he clamped his hat down on his forehead.

"Ken," she said, "you're going out . . . on this thing, into danger?"

Her face was a dead white. The eyes were starry and tender.

He laughed at her, saw the pale lips stiffen, quiver and tremble into the first sign of a sob, then lift into a half smile. He patted her shoulder, grinned at her.

"Listen, kid, I'm a newcomer here. I'm here to stay. Some of these chaps don't recognize that fact yet, that's all. It's time they did. I'm just going out and let a few of them know that when I hung out my shingle in this town I did it with my eyes open. I planted my feet here, and I'm staying here."

And he strode across the office, went through the outer door, made time to the street, caught a taxi. "Monadnock Building," he said, as he settled back against the cushions, "and make it snappy."

The cab lurched into motion.

"Man shot here a while back," said the communicative driver. "Raised hell with traffic."

Corning said: "Yeah," without interest and the conversation languished. The cab swung in to the curb at Seventh Street, Corning paid the meter, consulted the directory of the Monadnock Building, found that Dike's office was on the seventh floor, and took the elevator up.

There was no one in the reception office except a typist who was tapping frantically at the keys of a noiseless typewriter, and a rather stern-faced but pretty secretary who sat stiffly behind a desk in the corner of the room, three telephones in front of her.

Corning walked to her, smiled.

"I'm anxious to get in touch with a man who was to have met me here earlier this afternoon, but I had a puncture and was delayed. He's a great big man, fat, about forty-eight, wearing a gray suit that's in need of pressing . . ."

Her voice was crisply efficient.

"You mean Mr. Parks. He's been here and gone."

Corning made a gesture of disappointment, but his mouth clamped shut to keep from showing his elation.

"Mr. Dike's in?"

"Yes. He's busy. You haven't an appointment?"

"No. Can you answer the question? What kind of a car does he drive?"

"A Cadillac. It's a sedan. Then he has a roadster, a Buick."

"Thanks. I think I'm interested in the Cadillac. It's a bright red, isn't it?"

"It's red, yes."

"I'm afraid I've got to disturb Mr. Dike. Tell him it's Mr. Corning, and that I'm in a hurry."

She shook her head.

"He's not to be disturbed. You haven't an appointment, and . . ."

Corning gained the door to the inner office in a swift stride, without waiting for her to finish the sentence.

"And I'm in a hurry," he said, and opened the door.

Harry B. Dike was even more dignified in his frosty appearance than the newspaper photograph would have indicated to a casual observer. The light glinted from the bald reaches of his high forehead. His eyes were steel gray and bored steadily out from behind his shell spectacles. He looked up from a desk which contained a sheaf of papers, stared at Corning and said: "Get out! I'm busy."

His eyes went down to the papers.

Corning walked across the room.

Dike didn't look up again. He was moving the point of a pencil along the typewritten lines of a document. "Get out," he said, "or I'll call a cop and have you thrown in for disturbing the peace. I've canceled my appointments. I don't want any life insurance, any books or a new automobile."

Corning sat down.

Dike scowled at him, banged the pencil down on his desk and reached for the telephone.

"I'm Kenneth D. Corning, attorney for Sam Parks, the man who called on you a little while earlier this afternoon," he said.

Dike dropped the telephone. His eyes widened, darkened, then became fixedly steady in gaze and expression. He said coldly: "What's that to me?"

"It has to do with your acceptance of the position of Superintendent of the Water Department," said Corning. "I think it would be far better for you to refuse the appointment—particularly in view of the fact that Parks was murdered about twenty minutes ago."

The face did not change by so much as a line.

"You mean that you think I had something to do with the murder?" asked Dike coldly.

Corning's tone was equally cold.

"Yes," he said.

The two men stared at each other.

"Corning," said Dike, as though trying to place the name. "A newcomer here, eh? I presume you're crazy. But if you've got anything to say, I'll listen."

Corning spoke, his tone dispassionate.

"He made the mistake of coming to you first. I presume he wanted a shakedown. When things didn't go to suit him here he called me. It was Dwight's men who put him on the spot. You probably weren't directly connected with it. You notified Dwight, that's all. You weren't entirely surprised to hear of the murder, but you hadn't exactly expected it."

Dike got to his feet.

"All right. You've had your say. Now get out."

Corning held his ground.

"You accept that position of Superintendent of the Water Department," he said, slowly and forcefully, "and I'll have you before the grand jury for murder."

Dike laughed scornfully.

"A man calls at my office. Later on he's found murdered. I have been sitting here all the time. Simply because he came here you think that I should give up my career, eh?"

Corning played his bluff.

"Forget it," he said. "I know what I'm doing. Parks talked before he died. It was on the road to the hospital. I rode with him in the ambulance."

That statement shook Dike's self-control. The eyes wavered. The mouth twitched. Then he gripped himself and was as granite once more.

"I presume he said I ran alongside his flivver and stabbed him!" he snorted.

Corning grinned.

"So you know it was a flivver, eh? Well, I'll tell you what he said. He said that he and his wife were out driving and that they had an automobile accident. The car that they ran into was your

car. You were in it, and there was another man in it, Carl
Dwight, the head of the machine that's milking the city of mil-
lions in graft money. The people had been demanding a change in
the water department because of that very graft. The mayor
made them a gesture by putting you in charge. You were supposed to put an end to the graft on water contracts. Yet you were
out riding with Dwight, the man you were supposed to fight.

"You didn't get the man's name. But you found out about the
woman. She was driving the car. You learned she was running a
speakeasy. You thought it'd be a good plan to get her where her
testimony wouldn't count. So Dwight raided her place and
framed a felony rap on her. She didn't know the full significance
of what she'd seen. You thought it'd be a good plan to forestall
developments. The testimony of a convicted felon wouldn't go
very far in a court of law."

Corning ceased talking. His fists were clenched, his eyes cold
and steady.

Dike's gaze was equally steady.

"Corning," he said, "you are a very vigorous and impulsive
young man. You are also either drunk or crazy. Get out and stay
out."

Corning turned towards the door.

"I thought," he said, "that I would have the satisfaction of
telling you what I know, and showing you that you can't gain
anything by railroading this woman. Also you'll either resign
your post, or you'll be mixed up in murder."

Dike scooped up the telephone.

"When you go out," he said, "tell my secretary to put the
spring catch on the door. I don't want any more crazy guys
busting in here."

Corning grinned at him.

"I'll put the catch on the door myself," he said, and pushed the
thumb snap down, walked out and closed the door behind him.
The typist paused in her pounding of the keys to watch him. The
secretary stared with wide eyes. Corning walked to the corridor
and took the elevator.

He stepped into a drug store on the corner and called police
headquarters. He asked for the homicide squad, and got Sergeant
Home on the line.

"This," he said, "is a tip."

"What is?" gruffed the sergeant.

"What you're hearing. A man named Parks was killed this afternoon. He'd been driving a flivver that had collided with a red car. Harry B. Dike owns a red car that's been in a collision. Parks had been to call on Dike just before he got killed. Carl Dwight has been in some sort of a smash. There's a cut on his forehead, and he walks with a limp. Sam Parks has a wife, Esther. You've got her in jail right now on a felony charge."

Sergeant Home's voice betrayed his excitement.

"Tell me, who is this speaking? Where do you get that dope?"

Ken snapped his answer into the transmitter.

"Have a man you can trust at the *Columbino* at eight tonight. Have him wear a white carnation and sit near the front door. Look up the information I've given you in the meantime."

And Corning slammed the receiver back on the hook, waited a moment for a free line, and then called Harry Dike's office on the telephone. The line was busy. He called three times with the same result. The fourth time he got Dike on the line, after some argument with the secretary.

"Corning," he snapped crisply. "I'm giving you one last chance to get out of the tangle Dwight's got you in. I'll be at the *Columbino* tonight at eight. If you want to make a written statement and get out of the mess I won't put the screws down."

Dike's voice was smoothly suave.

"Kind of you, I'm sure, but I don't think I care to see you there. However . . . where are you now?"

Corning laughed into the transmitter.

"Wouldn't you like to know!" he said, and hung up.

He waited in front of the drug-store, keeping in the background, yet being where he could watch the entrance to Dike's office building.

Carl Dwight didn't show up. But a speeding automobile, slamming into the curb at the fire hydrant, disgorged Perkins, the detective. Half a dozen minutes later a taxicab paused to let out Fred Granger, who was Dwight's right-hand man.

Perkins came out, almost on the run, within fifteen minutes. Granger didn't come out for half an hour. Dike followed him. Ten minutes after that, a police car bearing a detective stopped in front of the office building.

Ken Corning terminated his vigil, stepped into a barber shop, had a shave, hot towels, massage, haircut and shampoo. He was careful not to go near any of his regular haunts, or leave a trail which could be picked up.

THE *Columbino* ran fairly wide open. Anyone could get in there who had the price. It went in somewhat for music, atmosphere and an aura of respectability. The liquor was very good.

It was early when Ken Corning walked into the place, exactly eight o'clock, and there were but few patrons, most of them eating. The dance floor would fill up later on, and by midnight the place would be going full blast.

A man in evening clothes, with a conspicuous white carnation in his buttonhole, had a table in the front of the place. Ken heaved a sigh as he saw that Home had investigated his tip, found out enough to go ahead on the lead.

Ken Corning ordered a full dinner with a cocktail at the start, a bottle of wine with the meal, a cordial afterwards. Momentarily he expected action, and the action did not come.

It was nine-fifteen when he reluctantly called for the waiter and paid the check. The man with the white carnation continued to sit by the door.

Evidently the powers that ruled the city had decided to ignore Ken Corning, and Ken was disquieted at the thought. Things were not turning out as he had anticipated.

The waiter was gone some little time. Ken waited for the change. The man in the dinner coat with white carnation looked at his watch, pursed his lips. Ken got the idea that this man had a definite time limit fixed. At nine-thirty, probably, he would leave.

The waiter returned.

"I beg your pardon," he said, "but the manager wants to see you in his office. There's a bit of trouble, sir."

Ken got to his feet, followed the waiter. He was walking lightly, his hands slightly away from his sides, his head carried alertly, eyes watchful.

The manager stared coldly from behind the desk.

The waiter turned to go. Ken thought that something brushed against his coat. He couldn't be sure. He glanced at the waiter's retreating back.

The manager said: "I'm sure it's a mistake, but it's something I'll have to investigate."

"What is?" asked Corning.

"This," said the manager, and placed on the desk in front of him the bill which Ken Corning had given the waiter. "It's counterfeit."

Ken laughed.

"Well," he said, "it happens that I can give a complete history of that bill. It was paid me this morning by way of retainer in a legal matter, in the presence of my secretary. What's more, I don't think it's counterfeit."

A door opened. A man stepped purposefully into the room.

The manager waved his hand.

"I'll let you discuss that with McGovern, of the Secret Service. You probably don't know it, but we've been flooded with clever counterfeits here the last week. McGovern has been waiting on call."

Ken turned to meet the man's eyes.

McGovern smiled, and the smile was frank.

"If you can tell me where you got it, that's all I need to know," he said. "One look at you's enough to convince me *you're* no counterfeiter."

Ken smiled in return, then let the smile fade.

"Look here," he said, "this bill came from a client. I have an idea certain interests would like to frame something else on that client and his wife. The man is dead. The wife isn't—yet. I don't want to play into any frame-up. . . ."

The other smiled, waved his hand.

"Just a formality, but you'll have to tell me. You're dealing with the Federal Secret Service now. You won't find any political frame-ups with us. As a matter of form, would you mind letting me see the rest of your money?"

Ken laughed, reached in his coat, took out his wallet.

That wallet felt strangely bulky. He stared at it. It wasn't his wallet. It was crammed with currency. He made a move as though to put it back in his pocket. The Federal man whipped down a swift arm.

"Here," he said, "none of that. Acting funny ain't going to help you."

He grabbed the wallet, opened it, whistled.

There was a moment of silence.

"That," said Ken, "is not my wallet. I demand that the waiter who brought me in here be called. I want to have him searched. He slipped this wallet into my pocket and took mine out. He's a professional dip, and this is a plant."

The lip of the Federal man curled.

"Yeah," he said. "How often I've heard that one! You've got to come along. Want to go quietly, or would you rather make a fuss?"

Ken stared at the wallet.

"I'll go quietly if you'll pick up that waiter and take him along, too," said Ken.

The Federal turned to the manager.

"Who was it?" he asked.

"Frank," said the manager.

"Get him," said the Federal. "In the meantime I'll take this guy along in a cab. Come on. You can tell your story where it'll be appreciated. They don't pay me to listen, only to do things."

Ken went out through the cabaret.

The man in the dinner coat, who wore the white carnation, was looking at his watch with an air of finality. Ken walked rapidly so that he was a step or two ahead of McGovern. There were couples standing on the floor. Many of the tables were vacant. The music stopped when Ken was some twenty feet from the table occupied by the man in the dinner coat who wore the white carnation. There was a perfunctory spatter of applause and then couples stood, waiting, staring at the orchestra expectantly.

Ken Corning raised his voice and called over his shoulder to McGovern: "This is just a frame-up, because I've got some evidence in that Parks murder case."

McGovern spoke in an even, ominous tone. "Shut up!" he said.

Ken flashed a glance to the man who wore the white carnation. He was signaling a waiter for his check. There was nothing on his face to indicate that he had heard what Ken had said; or hearing, was in anywise concerned with it. The orchestra struck up an encore. As the couples started to twine and twist to the strains of the dance, Ken flashed a glance at McGovern, then at the man who wore the white carnation. The man was handing the waiter a bill. The waiter was pushing an oblong of pink pasteboard at him from which had been figured the items of the check. The man pushed away the pasteboard, made a sweeping gesture with his hand as though to indicate that the waiter should keep the change. Staring at his face, it was impossible for Ken to tell whether the man had hurried his exit because Ken was leaving, or whether he had simply grown tired of waiting, and decided to knock off for the day.

* * *

BEHIND him, McGovern said: "Get your hat and coat and
don't try any funny business."

Ken moved up to the checking stand. A girl with a beautiful
face flashed him a smile that was meant to be dazzling, but was
only mechanical, took the square of pasteboard which he handed
her and pushed Ken's hat out over the counter.

The man who wore the white carnation in his dinner coat had
evidently found some people he knew. He was chatting with
them, a young man of about thirty, and a red-haired woman who
could not have been over twenty-three. As he chatted, he reached
up and plucked the white carnation from the dinner jacket,
dropped it to the floor and stepped on it.

Ken said to McGovern: "Can I talk with you? Will you listen
to reason?"

McGovern said: "Sure, I'll listen to any guy who wants to talk;
only remember that anything you say will be used against you."

Ken lured him over to the far corner of the checking counter
and said: "All right now, listen. I told you that this thing was a
frame-up because I was a witness in the Parks case. You don't
seem to be interested."

McGovern said: "Why should I be interested? That's a state
case, I'm a Federal. You tell me where you got this counterfeit
money from and where the plates are and I'll sit here and listen
to you until daylight. But if you've got anything to say on the
Parks case you can tell it to the state authorities—I'm not interested."

Ken fixed his eyes on McGovern and said: "Listen, suppose
that I could show you that this man Parks had something on the
administration and was going to keep Dike from accepting the
position of Superintendent of the Water Department? Suppose I
could show you that Carl Dwight is mixed up with Dike; that, in
place of being enemies, those two fellows are working hand in
glove regardless of all this newspaper talk about Dike wanting to
clean up the graft. . . ."

McGovern took his arm above the elbow and gave him a push.

"Listen, guy, I told you I wasn't interested in all that stuff. Are
you going to tell me where you got the plates or where you've got
the rest of this queer cached?"

Ken Corning's eyes narrowed.

"Okey," he said, "I tried to give you the breaks and you

wouldn't listen. Now I'll take a look at *your* credentials before I leave this place."

McGovern grinned easily and dropped his right hand to the side pocket.

"Gee," he said, "you sure are full of alibis and stalls. Come on and let's get going. This is all in the day's work with me and I want to get home and get my beauty sleep. You can stall all night, but you can't keep me from taking you to jail and booking you on a charge of possession of counterfeit money. If you want my authority, here it is."

Ken felt something hard prodding against his ribs. He glanced down to where the right hand of McGovern was holding the gun concealed by the right-hand side pocket of his coat. He said: "Oh, it's like that, is it?"

McGovern said: "Yes, guy, it's like that. You're going to take it and like it. Get started out of here. You've got counterfeit money in your possession and there are witnesses that you tried to pass it. You can either go quietly or you can get your insides blown out right here. Which is it going to be?"

Ken grinned and said: "Under the circumstances, I guess I'll go quietly."

McGovern said: "Now you're talking sense. You can't gain anything by talking any other way. I'm on the square and I'm going to take you in, but I ain't going to stand here all night and listen to a lot of hooey and I ain't going to have you pull any smart aleck stuff on me. Get started!"

Corning moved towards the door. He noticed that the man who had worn the white carnation was moving towards the door also and that the man who had been with the red-haired girl was walking with him. The red-haired girl moved off towards the left and went into the women's dressing room. The man who had worn the white carnation lit a cigarette. He seemed in no hurry. Ken Corning went out of the door painfully conscious of the pressure of the gun which was held against his ribs. The doorman looked at them and said: "Taxicab?"

McGovern shook his head and said: "No, I've got a car."

The big limousine which had been parked near the curb with motor running slid smoothly up to the front of the cabaret and stopped. The doorman started to open the door and McGovern spoke sharply: "That's all right," he said, "I'm a Federal dick and this man is a prisoner. He's desperate and may try to start something. Keep back, I'll handle this!"

He reached out and opened the door. His gun prodded Ken in the ribs. "Get in," he said.

Ken put his right foot on the running-board of the limousine. He could see two men seated in the back seat. They were grinning. Ken swung his body in a pivot, grabbing with his left hand at the gun which McGovern was holding against his ribs and pushing down with all his strength.

McGovern fired twice before Ken's fist connected with his jaw. Neither shot hit. Somebody shot from the interior of the limousine but the bullet hit the plate-glass window, shattered it into a thousand fragments and deflected. McGovern went down like a sack of cement. Ken swung himself on him and reached for the gun. Over his shoulder he could see the swirl of motion from the interior of the limousine. A man jumped to the running-board while Ken was still struggling for the possession of the gun. Ken heard him say: "All right, guy, take a load of this!"

Two shots roared out as though they had been one explosion. The man who had stood on the running-board of the limousine pitched forward and struck on his face. Ken jerked the gun from the pocket of McGovern and saw that the man in the dinner jacket was standing on the steps of the cabaret, an automatic in his hand. The man who had been with the red-haired girl was standing on the sidewalk a little bit to one side with a double-action revolver spouting fire. The doorman was running heavily, his gold-braided coat flapping grotesquely behind him. The limousine had lurched into motion. Somebody was rolling down the back window, which had not been shattered. Guns blazed over Ken's head. A bullet whistled past his cheek. The two men standing in the front of the cabaret answered the fire.

Ken got McGovern's gun in his hand and took a couple of shots at the limousine. He heard the bullets give forth a clinking sound as they struck against the metal of the body. The limousine swung far over to one side as it rounded the corner to the accompaniment of screaming tires.

The man in the dinner coat ran towards Ken as McGovern, recovering from the daze of Ken's blow, started to struggle to his feet.

Ken said: "Those men were trying to take me for a ride. This guy posed as a Federal agent . . ."

McGovern spoke up and said: "I am a Federal agent. This crook's been shoving the queer. He's got a wallet of phoney stuff on him right now."

The man in the dinner coat laughed and said: "Federal, hell! I know you, you're Jim Harper, and you've done time!"

A uniformed policeman, on beat, ran up. The man in the dinner coat spoke to him sharply: "All right, Bell. Get the crowd back. I'll handle what's left of this."

A curious crowd was commencing to form a ring around the men, and the uniformed policeman started to herd them back.

The man in the dinner coat said: "That's all right, buddy, I know this guy, he's a crook. You're a witness in the Parks case, huh?"

Ken Corning stared at him with round eyes and shook his head.

"No," he said, "I'm not a witness, I'm attorney for Mrs. Parks and I came here to meet a witness but he didn't show up."

The man in the dinner jacket stared at Ken Corning for a long five seconds. Then his right eyelid slowly closed in a solemn wink: "So," he said, *"that's* your story, eh?"

Ken Corning kept his face perfectly straight and his eyes perfectly steady. "That," he said, "is my story and I'm sticking to it. I'm not a witness, I'm a lawyer. I was to meet a witness here. These guys tried to keep me from meeting him, that's all."

The man in the dinner coat said: "Who were they? Would you recognize any of them if you saw them again?"

Ken Corning shook his head.

"No," he said, "the light wasn't good enough. I couldn't see them."

The man in the dinner coat turned to the fake Federal agent. Ken Corning slipped away. No one tried to stop him. There was the sound of a police siren, approaching fast, as he turned the corner.

KEN CORNING walked into his office.

The morning sun streamed in at the east window. Helen Vail stared at him with eyes that were dark with emotion, warm with pride.

"Got your name in the papers, didn't you?"

He grinned at her.

"How about our client?" she asked.

He spread his hands, palm up, made a sweeping gesture. "Gone. Case is closed, dismissed."

"And all we get then is the hundred and fifty dollar retainer?" Ken nodded.

"That's all. The woman was driving the car. Her husband wasn't with her. I figured that he must have been, but he wasn't. Dike and Dwight had been having a secret meeting. They'd been out in the country at a road-house where they were safe. Coming back they were riding in the same car. Dike was driving and he was a little bit 'lickered.' The woman was driving the flivver and they had a smash. She was a little bit belligerent and insisted on taking down the license number of the automobile. They paid her for her damage but she acted a little suspicious so Dwight got the license number of her automobile and found out who she was. They knew that she was running a speak, and figured that she was too dumb to know what it was all about, but they wanted her out of the way, just the same. With the deal Dike was planning to pull, it would have been fatal if somebody had uncovered this woman as a witness, so Dwight decided that he'd get her convicted of a felony. That would have discredited her testimony if she'd ever been called as a witness.

"She probably was suspicious, because she told her husband about it. Nobody knows just how much she told him or how much he knew, but it's a cinch that he knew enough to put two and two together when he saw Dike's picture in the paper with the blurb about his taking over the Water Department and eliminating graft."

Helen Vail watched him with wide eyes.

"Can we prove any of that?" she asked.

Ken Corning shook his head. "We can't prove anything," he said. "Wouldn't do us any good if we could. They've dismissed the case against the woman, released her from custody and she's gone. They probably made a deal with her, gave her some money and started her traveling."

"Why would they do that?" asked Helen Vail. "Her testimony is just as damaging now as it ever was."

Ken Corning smiled and motioned towards the morning paper.

"Read the news," he said, "and you'll notice that Dike has declined the appointment. He said that his private business was taking up too much of his time for him to make the sacrifice of accepting a public position."

Helen Vail blinked her eyes thoughtfully and said: "How about the people in the automobile—don't you know any of them?"

Ken Corning said: "You mean the ones who were trying to take me for a ride?"

She nodded her head.

Ken laughed and said: "Sure I do. Perkins was one of them. He was the detective who barged into the office here. He's a cheap heel who does dirty work for the Dwight machine."

"But," she said, "you told the officers that you couldn't recognize any of them."

Ken Corning laughed mirthlessly and said: "Of course I did. I'd never get anywhere trying to pin anything on Perkins. He'd produce an alibi and get acquitted. Then they'd turn around and prosecute me for perjury. I'm bucking a machine in this town, and the machine is well entrenched with a lot of money back of it. I'm not a fool!"

"How about the man who pretended to be a Federal officer?" she asked.

"He's got to take the rap. They've got the goods on him. They might have managed to make some sort of stall there, only I knew it was coming. I had worked the wallet that the waiter had planted on me out of my pocket. When they opened the door of the limousine I tossed the wallet in with my left hand before I grabbed at this guy's gun and socked him with my right."

She shuddered and said: "Oh, Ken, I don't like it."

He stood with his feet planted far apart, his jaw thrust forward, hands thrust into the pocket of his coat.

"I like it," he said, "and I'm going to make them like it. I'm going to bust this town wide open. They're going to stop me if they can. They'll try to frame me, try to take me for a ride, try to freeze me out. I'm going to stay! I'm going to be here after they're gone."

"But, Ken," she objected, "you've done all this work and risked your life and we only get a hundred and fifty dollars out of it."

Ken Corning nodded and laughed.

"A hundred and fifty dollars," he said, "and it's honest money."

Then he walked into his private office and the door clicked shut.

Helen Vail could hear him moving around in the inner office. He was whistling cheerfully as though he didn't have a care in the world.

She opened the drawer of her desk, took out a ledger which was innocent of entry, took a pen and wrote in a hand which trembled slightly: "People versus Parks—cash retainer $150.00."

The Top Comes Off

LAWYER KEN CORNING was reading a printed pamphlet which contained the advance decisions of the supreme court when his office door opened and Helen Vail, his secretary and only helper, came slipping into the room.

Corning looked up and frowned. Helen Vail's eyes were big.

"She's a beauty, Ken!"

"Who is?" he asked.

"The jane that's outside."

"What's her name?"

"I don't know. She won't give it."

Ken Corning's frown deepened. "Listen, kid," he said, "this is a law office, and we've got to run it like one. I'm just getting started here, but that isn't any reason we're going to let anybody ritz us. Go back and get her name."

Helen Vail stood with her back against the door, slim, straight and pretty. Her lips were pressed together. Her eyes showed concern.

"Listen, Ken, that's why I came in. I tried to get her name. I told her if I didn't get it she couldn't see you. She said that she couldn't see you then, and got up to go. I called her back and told her I'd see what I could do. She's pretty, and she's been crying."

"How old?" asked Corning.

"Her face says twenty-five, her hands say thirty. You know, the backs of her hands."

"Yes," said Corning, "I know. What else?"

"She's got trim ankles, a sport outfit that cost money, and there was a diamond ring on her engagement finger, but it's gone. You can see where she'd been wearing it."

"Maybe it was a wedding ring," said Corning.

41

"No. She's still got the wedding ring. She'd been wearing two. The diamond's gone."

Ken Corning put down the advance decision. "Okey," he said, "shoot her in. But don't leave that outer office no matter what happens. This may be a frame. After the way I dented the political ring that runs this burg, you can figure they'll frame me if they get half a chance."

Helen Vail nodded. Her eyes brightened.

"I'm glad you're going to see her," she said. "I like her, and I was afraid you were going to get obstinate and turn her away."

Ken Corning grinned.

"Be your age, kid! Do you think I'd turn away a good-looking woman who's been crying and who has just hocked a diamond ring? I'd be crazy. Send her in and I'll find out how much she got for the ring."

Helen Vail opened the door and said: "You may come in. Mr. Corning will see you now."

Ken Corning heard swift, nervous steps. Then Helen Vail stood to one side, and he found himself looking into a pair of steady dark eyes, an oval face with skin that might have given inspiration to an artist painting an ad for a facial cream.

Her teeth showed as the lips twisted into a mechanical smile, but the eyes did not smile. There was no sign which Corning could observe which indicated that the woman had been weeping; but Ken Corning knew women well enough to know that Helen Vail would have been right about it.

He indicated a chair. "Sit down," he said.

She sat down.

"You're Ken Corning, and I've heard about you," she observed.

He smiled.

"You've got a good ear for news, then. I haven't been here very long, and I haven't had very much business."

She nodded, a quick little jerk of the head that seemed swiftly decisive, exactly the sort of a gesture of crisp affirmation which one would have expected from her.

"You handled that Parks case. I don't suppose it was big business exactly, but you ran up against Boss Dwight, and you won out."

Corning said: "Who told you Carl Dwight was interested in that case?"

She answered promptly and in a voice which held more than a trace of mockery. "A little bird," she said.

Ken shrugged his shoulders. His face became a cold mask. "All right," he said. "What did you want to see me about?"

Her voice lost its mockery, her manner its assurance.

"About George Colton," she said.

Ken Corning stared at her, then gestured towards the folded morning newspaper which lay on the desk. "You mean the man . . ."

"Yes," she said. "I mean the man who's smeared all over the front page of the newspaper, the one who's accused of murdering Harry Ladue."

Ken Corning stiffened. His eyes became wary and watchful.

"What about him? What do you want me to do?"

"Defend him."

"Perhaps he'd prefer to pick his own lawyer," said Corning. "Are you authorized to act for him?"

Slowly, she shook her head.

"Then you can't retain me to act as his attorney."

"Could I retain you to act as my attorney, to . . . to do anything that you could for him?"

Ken Corning fastened his eyes upon hers. Then he said: "That would depend upon several things."

"What?" she asked.

"The size of the retainer, for one thing."

She opened her purse, took out thirteen fifty-dollar bills. The bills were crisp and new. She laid them down on the desk. As she laid them down, one at a time, her lips moved soundlessly, counting. When the last bill had been placed there she looked up at Ken Corning.

"That," she said, "is the retainer."

Ken Corning said: "It must have been a big diamond."

She gasped, stared at him, then clenched her left hand and dropped it below the desk. "I don't know what you're talking about," she said.

Ken Corning made no move to reach towards the money. He let it lie there on the desk, cool, crisp and green.

"The next thing I'd want to know," he said, "is who you are."

She seemed to have been prepared for that question. She smiled at him. "I," she said, "am a mysterious figure who wouldn't appear in the case at all. You could enter me on your books as Madam X. From the moment I walked out of this office you'd lose sight of me. You couldn't call me on the telephone, you couldn't reach me, no matter what the emergency. You could do just one thing, go ahead and see that George—Mr. Colton, got whatever breaks you could give him."

"And not let him know that you had retained me?"

"You could use your own judgment about letting him know that someone had retained you, but you wouldn't even describe me, or let him know that it had been a woman who called on you."

Ken Corning said, slowly: "Let's pass that for a minute. This is a sensational murder case. The newspapers are hinting at a something that's in the background and may develop at any minute. You want me to keep your identity secret because you'd be pilloried by the press if they could drag in a 'beautiful woman' angle. But there's something specific you want me to do. What is it?"

She said: "I want you to drag his wife into it."

Ken Corning raised his brows, said nothing.

She started to speak, rapidly: "He'll have another lawyer who will be handling the case for him. I don't know who that lawyer will be. But it'll be somebody who will do just as George . . . Mr. Colton says. It'll be somebody who will go before a jury with that story about someone else firing the shots from another room, and all that stuff that Mr. Colton told the newspapers.

"That's all hooey. He shot Harry Ladue because Ladue had been too friendly with his wife. The unwritten law is the defense he should make, and he'd be acquitted on it. But if he sticks with this yarn about some mysterious person standing in the darkness of another room, or in the corridor and firing the shots, he'll get the death penalty!"

Ken Corning's eyes narrowed.

"Have you any scintilla of evidence of what you're talking about?" he asked.

She nodded, reached in her purse, took out a sheet of stationery that bore the printed head of a cheap hotel. The stationery was covered with fine writing, in a feminine hand.

"Here," she said, "is a list of the places where Ladue stayed with George Colton's wife, and the names that they registered under. I want you to promise me that you'll drag them into the case, rip the facts wide open."

Corning said: "Through the newspapers?"

"I don't care," she said, "how you do it, just so it's done. I don't want Colton to think he's shielding the name of a woman and go to his death because of it."

Corning said: "So he's shielding the woman, eh? That's the reason he's pulling this line about someone standing in the corridor and doing the shooting as he walked into the office."

"Of course," she answered.

Corning took the sheet of paper and looked at the dates, names of hotels and names of persons.

"The handwriting would all be by Ladue," he said. "How could you prove who the woman was?"

"Get photographs of his wife, silly, and chase around through the bellboys. You can work up the case with that evidence. Just get the thing started and it'll work up itself. There's only one promise I want from you, and I want it made on all that you hold sacred. That is that I don't want you ever to tell a soul that I called on you. You've got to swear that."

"You mean," he asked, "that a woman called on me?"

"No. I mean that you'll never disclose my real identity."

"But I don't know it. You just mentioned that I'd never find it out."

"I've changed my mind about that. I . . . I think you'll find out who I am. You've got to promise."

He pursed his lips. Tears came to her eyes. She reached into her purse and took out a small handkerchief. As Corning followed the motion of her hands he saw that the handkerchief was soggy, saw, also, the glint of blued steel in the purse.

He spoke calmly.

"Is the gun new?" he asked.

She gave a little gasp and clutched at the purse. Ken Corning reached over, clamped his hand on her wrist, raised his eyes to hers, and said: "So you're Mrs. George Colton, eh?"

Had he struck her with his fist she would not have turned whiter. She stared at him with eyes that were dark with terror. "How—how did you know?"

He kept holding her wrist.

"And I'll take the gun, so that you won't get into any trouble with it," said Ken.

She let go her hold on the entire purse, and, as Ken freed her wrist, leaned forward and put her hands to her face. "It's horrible," she said. "He's trying to save my name. He doesn't love me.

But he'd take a death sentence rather than let the newspapers bandy my name about. I can't let him do it. I've got to force him to make the facts public, and then—"

She paused.

"And then?" asked Ken Corning.

She motioned towards the purse which held the gun.

"Then—" she said, and pitched forward to the floor.

HELEN VAIL sopped a wet towel on the woman's forehead and said: "What happened, Ken?"

He shook his head. "She kind of wobbled. Before I could catch her she'd gone into a nose dive. Her pulse is all weak and stringy. Guess she hasn't had much sleep. She seems to have been on a terrific strain. Where's that whiskey? Fine. Now hold her head while I see if we can get a little more down her."

He poured whiskey past the white lips. The woman's eyelids fluttered and she stared at them with fixed eyes that seemed glassy and unseeing, like the eyes of a cat that is just recovering from a fit.

"Feel better?" asked Ken Corning.

She didn't answer the question.

A knock sounded at the door of the private office. Ken Corning looked meaningly at Helen Vail. "Go out and see who it is. If it's anybody that's snooping around, hand 'em a stall."

Helen Vail went to the door, opened it, tried to block the entrance with her slender body. A man pushed her to one side. Ken Corning saw the glitter of light from the windows reflected from the lense of a camera. He saw a long arm hold up something above Helen Vail's head. Then there was a *"poom"* and the white glare of a flashlight exploded.

Ken Corning went forward, low to the ground like a football player charging the line. He went past Helen Vail like a charging bull. A man with a camera and a flashlight was running across the outer office. Ken Corning caught him at the door.

The man whirled as Ken's hands sought the camera. He made a swift pass at Ken. Corning dodged the blow, brought his foot sharply down on the man's instep, jerked at the camera. It came loose in his hand. Ken whirled it around his head, banged it down on the floor. He crossed his left, and, as the man staggered, got hold of his coat collar with one hand, jerked the door open with the other.

The man struck an ineffectual blow. Ken Corning leaned his weight against the struggling victim, pushed him down the hall, sped him on his way with the toe of a well-directed boot.

The man sprinted to the stairs, then whirled.

"You can't get away with that!" he yelled. "I'll have you in jail before night for assault and battery. My paper's got some prestige and you can't pull a stunt like that. I'll show you who's who in this man's town."

He was still talking as Ken snapped the door shut.

He walked into his reception-room, kicked the camera to fragments, jerked open the door of his private office, and said to Helen Vail: "Get her out of here, and keep her under cover!"

Helen Vail stared at him.

"Who is she?" she whispered.

"Don't ask me, and don't ask her," rasped Ken Corning. "Get her out of here. Take her down a floor and into the ladies' restroom. Keep her under cover until you can sneak her out. If she can make it, better make a try for a hotel right now."

The woman got to her feet, clutched at the edge of the desk for support. "I can make it," she said, smiling wanly. "Did—did the newspapermen follow me?"

"Some tabloid guy," said Ken Corning.

"Did he get a picture?"

"He did, but he can't use it. His camera's smashed."

The troubled eyes were filled with gratitude.

"The only thing for you to do now is to get under cover and stay there," said Corning. "Those babies are wise and they've been following you. Anyhow, they knew you were coming here, or knew it when you got here. Don't tell anyone what you told me. I'll bust into this fight as counsel that was hired by you. I'm going to try and work out some way of handling the situation."

The woman said: "The things I've told you have got to come out. When they do I can't face the world. I'm finished."

Ken Corning jutted his jaw at her.

"Shut up and get out of here," he said. "You talk like a damned fool. Get her out, Helen."

Helen Vail had moved with crisp efficiency while they were talking. She had on her hat and coat.

"I'll try the back way," she said. "I think we can make it. I'll telephone when I get located."

"Stay with her," said Corning, "every minute of the time,

night and day. Don't let her out of your sight. Here's some money for expenses."

He tossed her two of the fifty-dollar bills.

"But—" the woman started to protest.

Helen Vail's voice broke in, cool, efficient, determined.

"Can the chatter," she said, "and get started. Can't you see Mr. Corning has work to do?"

She pulled the woman out into the hall, let the door close. Ken Corning called, just as the door was closing: "Call me at the *Antlers Hotel,* ask for Mr. Mogart."

Helen's voice drifted through the open transom.

"Okey," she said.

Ken Corning grabbed a copy of the Penal Code, a volume on evidence, some blank forms which dealt with writs of *habeas corpus,* caught up his hat and lunged for the door.

HE didn't bother with the elevator, but took the stairs two at a time. Nor did he go out of the lobby of the office building to the street, but went, instead, through a back door which gave upon a storeroom, a musty corridor, and a barred door which opened on an alley. Ken Corning unbarred the door and emerged into the fresh air of the warm morning.

He took a taxicab to the depot, caught another there and went to the *Antlers Hotel,* where he secured a room under the name of E. C. Mogart of Kansas City.

The telephone rang while he was arranging his books on the dresser. He answered it and heard Helen Vail's voice.

"We're at the *Gladstone,"* she said. "We got a break getting away from the office. The guy you threw out was yammering at a cop in front of the place, and it was attracting a crowd. I picked this joint because it's close to the *Antlers.* What do I do next?"

"Just sit tight," he told her. "What name are you registered under?"

"Bess and Edna Seaton," she said. "The room's five-thirty-six."

"Which is Bess and which Edna?" asked Corning.

"Be your age!" she said, and hung up.

Ken Corning grinned, lit a cigarette and started pacing the floor.

He walked the floor like a caged animal, smoking cigarette

after cigarette, the smoke whipping back over his shoulder, his eyes squinted in thought.

There was a knock at his door. He opened it. Helen Vail grinned at him. "I came to tell you," she said, "that I'm going to be Bess. We tossed up for it."

"Anybody see you come up here?" he asked.

"No."

"Come on in."

She came in. He closed the door and locked it.

"How much do you know?" he asked.

"All of it," she said. "You didn't think she'd have someone to get weepy with without spilling all of the information, did you?"

Ken fell to pacing the floor again.

"I don't like it," he said.

"It's a mess," she agreed.

"How'd it happen?" he wanted to know.

She shrugged her shoulders. "She'd known Ladue before she got married—and she knew him afterwards."

"Wasn't she happy, Helen?"

"No."

"Why is she willing to ruin herself to save her husband, then?"

"Because that's her sense of loyalty. If she loved anybody, it was Ladue. I guess her husband's like all the rest of them. He didn't treat her with any particular consideration, and he was playing around with a blonde—a manicurist in a barber shop."

"Which shop?" he asked.

"Kelly's, down on Seventh Street."

"The wife knew about it?"

"Sure."

"Did she say anything to him about it?"

"Yes. They had it out."

"And then he accused her of being intimate with Ladue, I suppose, and she admitted that, and then he went out and shot Ladue."

Helen Vail shook her head.

"No. She didn't think that he knew anything about her and Ladue. If he did, he didn't mention it, and he should have mentioned it. They had some little scene. She didn't object to the blonde as long as he didn't flaunt her in the faces of their social set. But it had been getting pretty raw, and she wanted him to tame down."

"What'd he tell her?" asked Corning.

"What do husbands always tell their wives when the wives are in the right?" she asked.

Ken Corning shrugged his shoulders. "Never having been a husband, I'll pass. What'd he tell her?"

Helen Vail grinned. "Told her to go to hell," she said.

Ken Corning said: "And then he went out and shot Ladue, eh?"

"That seems to be about the size of it."

Ken Corning shook his head. "That doesn't make sense, Helen. I wonder if maybe it wasn't some sort of a frameup."

She sat on the edge of the bed, shrugged her shoulders, and said: "I'd take a cigarette if anybody'd offer me one."

He passed her the package. "Matches in the glass smoking stand," he told her. She pouted. "Don't I rate service?"

"No," he said, and started pacing the floor again. "I'm busy."

She lit the cigarette, and Ken Corning paused abruptly in his walking of the floor, strode to the telephone, scooped the receiver to his ear and gave a number to the operator.

"Who're you calling?" asked Helen Vail.

"District Attorney's office," he said.

"Hello," he said into the instrument when a feminine voice came over the wire, "who's handling the George Colton case?"

"Two or three," said the girl in the District Attorney's office. "Don Graves is going to sit in on the trial. Probably the D. A. himself will handle the prosecution."

"Let me talk with Graves," said Corning.

"Who is it?"

"Kenneth Corning, the lawyer."

"Oh, yeah. Just a minute."

There was a click of a connection, then Don Graves' voice came over the wire. It was a rasping, cold voice, bloodlessly efficient.

"Corning, eh?" he said. "Are you retained in the Colton case?"

"Yes."

"That's funny. Old Burnham of Burnham, Peabody & Burnham, has been employed by Colton."

"I'm retained by an intimate friend," said Ken.

"The wife, eh?" said Graves.

"I didn't say that," said Corning.

"I know," said Graves, "I said that. You didn't deny it."

"That's not the point," said Corning. "I want to talk with Colton."

"Yeah? Maybe he don't want to talk with you."

"Maybe," said Corning. "And then again, maybe he does. You going to pass me in to see him, or have I got to get rusty about it?"

"If he asks us to pass you in, we'll see that you get a pass as his lawyer," said Graves.

"But, if I can't see him," said Corning, "how the hell can I get him to make the request of you?"

"That," said Graves, chuckling, "is one of the problems that you've got in connection with the case. It's your hard luck. It ain't mine."

"Okey," said Ken. "As attorney for someone who is acting on his behalf I can file a writ of *habeas corpus* application and that'll bring him into court. I'll talk with him there if I can't talk with him any other way."

Graves spoke in icy tones.

"Going to get nasty, eh?"

"If I have to, yes."

"Okey," said Graves. "In that event you might be interested to learn that there's a warrant out for your arrest. Assault and battery on the person of one Edward Fosdick, reporter for the *Daily Despatch.* I believe I can add a count of malicious mischief in the breaking of one camera, too. Show up in court any time you want to, Corning, and the warrant will be served on you then."

Corning gripped the receiver.

"How long has that warrant been issued?" he asked.

Don Graves chuckled.

"It's on my desk for an okey on the complaint now," he said. "I wasn't certain that I was going to okey a warrant on it; but I'm doing it now. The more I think of it, the more it seems like an aggravated case. I wouldn't doubt if you got a jail sentence."

Ken Corning said: "Let me talk to the D.A. He won't stand for all these shyster tactics that you use, Graves, and you know it."

Graves said: "The D.A.'s busy. He won't talk over the phone. You know that as well as I do. Why don't you come to the office and make a squawk."

"Yeah," said Corning, "and have you get that warrant served on me, and me thrown in the can before I got a chance to see the

D.A. I wasn't born yesterday. You can just try and find me to serve that warrant, and you can just try to find out who my client is, and where."

Graves said: "We know who she is. That don't interest us any more. But there's another angle to this case that we want to investigate. We're interested in knowing *where* she is. And we're going to find out. You can't prepare to take part in this case and keep under cover at the same time."

"The hell I can't," said Ken Corning, and slammed the receiver on the hook.

Helen Vail said, blowing cigarette smoke out with the words: "You shouldn't lose your temper and cuss when you're talking with Don Graves, Ken. He's the kind that's always trying to make people lose their tempers."

Ken stared at her with his eyes cold as twin chunks of ice reflecting the glint of the Northern Lights.

"Before I get done with that bald-headed crook I'll show him something. He's hand in glove with Carl Dwight and the other crooked politicians that are running this town. The D. A., himself, wouldn't stand for the stuff they pull, if he knew about it. He just leaves things in the hands of his deputies, and they're a hot bunch of crooks! They're giving that reporter a warrant just because they know that Mrs. Colton came to my office, and they think I'm hiding her."

Helen Vail grinned.

"Well you are, aren't you?"

He nodded grimly, reached for his hat.

"You bet I am," he said, "and I'm going to keep on hiding her! That outfit up there is run by the newspapers. The reporters come in and yell for a fresh angle on the murder mystery, and the D.A.'s office has to dig it up for them. The more spectacular the better. Well, there's just one way to beat that game. I'm going to get one jump ahead of them, and keep there."

She watched him with speculative eyes.

"Be back?" she asked.

"Some time," he said. "You stick around the *Gladstone.* Thought I told you not to leave that woman alone for a minute."

She grinned. "That was because she was figuring on bumping herself off. She's over it now. She's going to cooperate. It's a wise steno that knows when it's safe to disobey orders."

He frowned down at her.

"You're a wise little rat," he said. "Some day that independence of yours is going to get you fired."

She grinned at him, and he slammed the door.

"Lock it when you go out and turn the key in at the desk," he called, and then went striding down the corridor. She could hear the pound of his heels on the carpet, all the way from the door of the room to the elevator shaft.

NELL BLAKE was plain, thirty-two and a man-hater. She did her hair back from her forehead in firm lines of rigid precision. She wore spectacles and made no attempt to disguise the fact. She scorned the use of cosmetics, and sat very erect. She was by far the most competent stenographer Harry Ladue had ever hired.

She sat at the lunch table and stared across at Ken Corning.

"So you followed me here to talk about the murder?" she asked.

Ken Corning nodded grimly.

"I don't know you, and I don't know anything about the murder," said Nell Blake in firm, precise tones. "I don't want to be annoyed, and unless you leave me I shall call an officer."

Ken Corning grinned at her.

"Listen," he said, "sooner or later you're going on the witness stand, maybe more than once. I'm going to be the attorney for the defense, and I'm going to cross-examine you. If you're willing to be fair with me, I won't hurt you much with a cross-examination. But you try to ritz me now, and I'll rip you wide open."

She blinked her eyes from behind the spectacles.

"Oh," she said, in a slightly altered voice, "you're the lawyer, are you? I thought you were another reporter, trying to force a sex angle into the case."

"I'm not. I'm trying to keep it out, if you want to know."

The mouth was a firm, thin line. The eyes behind the spectacles were cool and calculating.

"Precisely what," she asked, "was it that you wished to know? I have exactly one hour for lunch, and I don't propose to waste it listening to some man talk in circles. If you want to interview me, get to the point and keep there."

He leaned across the table.

"You were in the office at the time of the shooting?"

"Yes."

"Who else?"

"Adella Parks, the other stenographer; and Miss Althea Kent, his private secretary."

"All right. Now you and Miss Parks had desks on one side of the outer office, and Althea Kent had hers in a corner near the door to the private office. That right?"

"Yes."

"According to the newspaper accounts, George Colton came to call on Ladue. He gave his name to Miss Kent. She telephoned in to Ladue, and Ladue said to show him in. It was about nine o'clock at night. The office was working full blast trying to get out some letters in connection with a real estate campaign.

"Colton walked into the inside office and was heard to say: 'Hello, Harry,' then the door closed and there was silence for a few seconds, then the sound of two shots. When the door was opened, the inner office was in darkness, Ladue was lying on the floor, dead, and Colton was yelling that Ladue was shot.

"There was a gun on the floor. It was subsequently identified as having been Colton's gun. He admits that it was his, but swears that he didn't bring it with him. He says he was talking with Ladue when the lights went out and someone shot."

Corning quit speaking.

"Well?" asked Nell Blake, in a coolly superior tone of voice.

"I want to know if those facts are correct," said Corning.

"They are."

"Can you add to them?"

She hesitated, sipped her coffee, looked up at him and said: "No."

He kept his eyes on hers.

"Had there been someone else in the office that evening?"

"Which office?"

"The entrance office. Had anyone else gone in to see Ladue?"

"No."

"How about the other office? Had anyone else gone in there? There's a door that opens out to the corridor. It's used as an exit from the private office, but a person could have come in there."

"Not unless Ladue had let them in."

"Well, did he let anyone come in?"

She sipped her coffee again.

"I don't know," she said.

Ken Corning drummed with his fingers on the edge of the

table. His eyes dwelt upon the girl's face in calm appraisal. "You were all three in the outer office?"

"At the time of the shooting. Yes."

"Exactly who was in the private office at the time of the shooting, beside Ladue and Colton?" rasped Corning.

She said: "Why, I didn't know that anybody was. If anybody had been it's almost certain that Mr. Colton would have known it, isn't it?"

Ken Corning stared at her. She lowered her eyes and sipped the coffee again.

Corning said: "The newspapers say the lights were turned off at the switch. Why would Colton have turned off the lights?"

She set down the coffee cup and let her eyes stare into his.

"If," she said, "you're Mr. Colton's attorney, don't you think that would be a good question to ask him?"

Ken Corning pushed aside a sugar bowl and salt cellar so that he could lean his elbows on the table. He thrust his weight forward on those elbows, his forearms crossed, the fingers gripping the bend of the elbow.

"All right," he said, "if you feel that way about it, I want to know what there was about that inner office that you're concealing!"

She reached for the coffee cup again, then raised her eyes to his. They were cool, impersonal.

"Am I concealing something?" she asked.

He nodded grimly.

"Yes," he said. "Your answers ring true enough whenever I ask you about the outer office. But every time I mention that inner office you start reaching for that coffee cup. Now tell me what there is about that inner office that you're not sure about."

She locked her eyes with his, felt the full impact of those coldly questioning eyes of his, and lowered her own.

"Come on," said Ken Corning. "There's a human life at stake, you know."

She spoke more slowly now, and in a lower tone. She seemed less sure of herself.

"We have an extension telephone system," she said. "Miss Kent handles the incoming calls and puts through those that should go to Mr. Ladue, and weeds out the others. She stepped out of the office for a moment, and a call came in. I stepped over to her desk to put it through.

"It was a man by the name of Perkins. He'd been at the office before. I recognized his voice, and, in addition to that, he gave me his name. I think he was a detective. He asked for Mr. Ladue and I put the call through. I should have hung up then, but I wanted to make certain that I'd handled it all right, because Mr. Ladue was very particular about his calls, so I waited on the line.

"I heard Mr. Perkins call Mr. Ladue by his first name. He said, as nearly as I can remember: 'I've got some important information for you, Harry. I want to come right up.' And Mr. Ladue said for him to come along; that the time limit was about up.

"That was all I heard. I went back to my desk. Miss Kent came in, but Mr. Perkins didn't come in. At least he didn't come to the outer office. After a while Mr. Ladue rang for Miss Kent to come in and bring her book. She stepped into the office, and I thought there was just a bit of surprise in her manner as she opened the door to the inner office. It was just the way she would have acted if she'd expected to find Mr. Ladue alone, and had found someone else in there with him."

"That all?" asked Ken.

"That's all."

"I can't very well go before a jury with that as a defense," he told her.

She replied testily: "I didn't say you could. You're the lawyer, I'm not. You asked me for the facts, and I gave them to you. Incidentally, if you should mention that I told you this, as though I thought it was at all significant, I'd be out of a job—to say the least."

He looked at her with thought-squinted eyes.

"It's a corporation of some sort, isn't it?"

"Yes. It handles real estate."

"And Ladue was the head of it?"

"Yes."

"Didn't he handle the purchase for the city of a big tract? Wasn't there something about his getting options and selling them to the city?"

Her voice became utterly cold.

"If you wish to discuss the business affairs of my employers, you will have to ask your questions elsewhere. I am merely telling you what I know about the murder."

Ken Corning said: "Can you describe this man, Perkins?"

"Yes," she said. "He was at the office a few times. He's about forty-five with very broad shoulders and a short neck. He carries his head pretty well forward, and has a pair of shrewd gray eyes that seem to twinkle at times. He usually wears a tweed suit. . . ."

"I know him," said Corning. "His name's Charles C. Perkins. He works as a detective. I think he's on the force."

"I never did know," said Nell Blake, "exactly what he did. And now, if you'll pardon me, I'll be leaving."

"One question more. Have you asked Althea Kent about any of this?"

"Certainly not. You know what she told the newspaper reporters. I'm certainly not fool enough to go to her and insinuate that she was concealing any facts."

Ken Corning reached for the lunch check by Nell Blake's plate.

"Permit me," he said.

She drew herself up with dignity, taking the check and folding it in her fingers.

"I am perfectly capable of paying my own way," she said, coolly, turned on her heel and walked away.

KEN CORNING got the *Gladstone* on the telephone and asked for Miss Seaton in room five-thirty-six. After a few moments he heard Helen Vail's voice over the telephone.

"Where are you?" she asked.

"In a speak down on Madison," he said. "Know anything?"

"Lots," she told him. "I got to thinking about the mail, and wondering if there might not be something important in it. I wanted to get it. So I went down to a public telephone booth and called the assistant janitor of the building."

Ken Corning said: "You mean the one with the patent leather hair that's got such a case on you?"

She giggled.

"Well," he rasped, "go on. What was in the mail?"

She giggled again, and said: "A circular from a house that wanted to save you money on socks and neckties, and another circular advertising a privately printed book that was being sold to doctors and lawyers—and anybody else that had the price."

"That all?"

"That was all."

"Well, what the devil? What's so important?"

"It was what the assistant janitor told me," she said. "He said the wire had been tapped. They're fixed to listen in on your phone calls. He found it out by accident. He came into the office when they were working. They want . . . you know who . . . and they figure you're in touch with her. They're waiting for her to try and call up, or for you to call the office."

Ken Corning rasped out a curse.

"Naughty, naughty," she chided. "They'll take the phone out if you talk that way. Central might be listening in, and she's got tender ears."

Ken Corning said: "Okey. Never mind the comedy. You stick around there until I call you again. And don't disobey orders again. I'll tie a can to you one of these days for taking liberties with instructions."

"You've got to admit," she said, "that it always works out for the best."

He slammed the receiver back on its hook, left the telephone booth and had two rye whiskies, one right after the other. His eyes were cold and hard, and the black pupils seemed like bits of coal against lumps of ice.

THE apartment house corridor was redolent with the odors of cooking. There were odors of fresh meals which seeped through the cracks of doors and transoms, and there were the stale odors of long dead meals that clung tenaciously to wall paper and carpet to give a musty smell of human occupancy.

Apartment 13 B was near the end of the corridor. Ken Corning raised his hand and knocked.

After a moment there was the rustle of motion from the interior of the apartment. The door opened and afternoon sunlight streamed through the window and into the corridor.

Althea Kent was the exact antithesis of Nell Blake.

Her figure was distinctively feminine. Her complexion was well cared for. Her eyes held a deliberately provocative expression. The lips were full and shapely. There was a vague something about her, as elusive as the perfume of a flower and yet as persistently suggestive, which spoke of a knowledge of her attractiveness to men.

"What do *you* want?" she asked.

Ken Corning said: "I want to ask you a few questions."

"Come in," she invited.

As the outer door closed behind him, she asked: "Are you a reporter?"

"No. I'm investigating it from another angle. I want to find out one or two things that don't check up. The theory has been that Colton switched off the light and killed Ladue in the dark. Can you give me any reason why he should have done that?"

She shook her head. "Colton killed him. You'll have to ask him for his reasons," she said.

Corning nodded.

"The office was dark when you rushed in there?"

"Yes, except for the light that came from the outer office."

"The switch is near the entrance to the private office?"

"Yes."

"You turned it on when you went in?"

"Shortly afterwards."

"All right. Now think. Did the lights go on when you turned the switch on?"

"No," she said. "Not when I tried to turn it on the first time. I was excited. I didn't punch the button clear in, I guess. I remember snapping at it, and I heard a click, but the lights didn't go on. A little while later I tried it again and that time I snapped the switch on all right and the lights went on."

Ken Corning heaved a big sigh.

"Okey," he said. "Now tell me about Perkins. He was in the office when you went in there the first time, wasn't he?"

At his question she stiffened. She seemed to be holding her breath. When she spoke her voice had lost its cooing note of affectation, and her eyes were cold and hard.

"What are you talking about?" she asked.

"Perkins," said Ken Corning, without hesitation. "He was in the office when you looked in there to take some dictation a little while before Colton came. Was he there when Colton arrived?"

She said, in a cold monotone: "I don't know what you're talking about. And who are you? You haven't told me that yet."

"My name," he said, "is Corning. I'm a lawyer."

"Representing Colton, I suppose?"

"Yes."

She got to her feet.

"I've told all I know of the case to the authorities and to the newspapers. I haven't time to discuss it any more. I'm going out this evening and I want to get dressed. I'll have to ask you to excuse me."

She walked to the door. Gone was the suggestion of intimacy about her manner. She held the folds of the silken gown tightly about her. Her head was up, the eyes cold and distant. She turned the knob of the door and held it open.

"Did you know when Perkins went into the inner office?" asked Ken Corning.

Wordlessly, she held open the door.

"Can you tell me what the nature of the business was between Ladue and Perkins?"

She continued to stand at the door, holding it open, silent, distant, hostile. Ken Corning whirled on her.

"All right, young lady. I gave you the opportunity to save yourself a lot of trouble. This is a murder case. There's a life at stake, and if you think you can pull a line like that and make it stick you're sure going to be surprised."

She said two words, cold, crisp words.

"Get out!"

Ken Corning went into the corridor. The door slammed behind him. He heard the rasp of the key and the click of the lock.

He stood in the corridor, jaw protruding, eyes narrowed, lips clamped in a firm, straight line. Then he walked swiftly and purposefully towards the elevator.

THE police had finished with the office of Harry Ladue.

The man who made maps and diagrams had taken measurements. The police photographer had taken various and sundry photographs of the arrangement of the offices, the sprawled body, the exact location of the various articles of furniture at the time the crime had been committed.

The corporation of which Ladue had been the guiding head had appointed a man to fill the vacancy caused by death. There had been some attempt to make the business carry on. The new man had familiarized himself with the important matters which were pending; and now the offices were closed for the night.

Out on the streets there was still a little afterglow of light from the sky. In the building all was dark, except that night lights glowed in the corridors. Through the windows on the front of the offices came the colored lights of electric signs, one second glowing a deep red, then shifting to green, then vanishing.

Ken Corning moved down the corridor like some sinister shadow.

He was fighting the political powers that controlled the city. Already there was a warrant out for his arrest—a warrant that would never have been issued save for the fact that he was on the wrong side of the political fence.

If he slipped up he could count upon no mercy. The powers that were in the saddle would have railroaded him to the penitentiary without an instant's hesitation. The underworld which was dependent for its very existence upon a complacent toleration on the part of those political powers had already once tried to take Ken "for a ride."

And Ken Corning was carrying on.

He prowled about the corridor, looking for the fuse box which controlled the lights in the various offices. He found the box, a little recessed receptacle built into the wall, covered with a metal door which swung out on hinges.

Ken Corning tried the door of the office marked *Ladue Investment Corporation—Entrance.* The door was locked. He slipped a ring of keys from his pocket and tried them patiently, one after the other. On the third try he found a skeleton key which would operate the lock.

He went in and switched all the lights on in both offices. Then he went to the fuse box and experimented with the round fuses which were screwed into their places.

He found one which controlled a segment of the wiring.

He unscrewed it, and the lights went off in the private office. He screwed it in, and the lights went on. He smiled grimly, closed the door of the box and again entered the offices.

The desk of the secretary was in a corner by the door which led to the private office. That desk was locked, but the lock was of a pattern which yielded readily. Ken Corning went through the desk. He found a shorthand notebook. It was filled with pothooks and dashes which meant nothing to him. He found another one. There was a pencil thrust in between the leaves of this book. There was also a handkerchief between the same pages.

Ken Corning opened the book.

At the place where the handkerchief and pencil had been was the division point between that part of the book which had been filled with shorthand, and the blank pages. Ken Corning thrust this notebook into his pocket. He closed the desk, switched out the lights in the offices and departed as quietly as he had come.

WHEN he left the building, he removed the gloves which had been on his hands. He went at once to a telephone, called the *Gladstone Hotel* and was relieved to hear Helen Vail's voice over the wire.

"How's everything?" he asked.

"Fine as silk."

"Anybody spot you?"

"Nope."

"Can you slip over to the *Antlers* right away?"

"Give me ten minutes," she said. "I'm dressed formal."

"Dressed! I didn't know you took any clothes with you! You weren't foolish enough to go after a suitcase, were you?"

She giggled.

"You gave me expense money. I figured I'd be conspicuous if I didn't dress. You should see the gown. It's a darb, and cheap, too! It only cost——"

He groaned.

"Ten minutes then," he said, and hung up.

He caught a cab. Went to his room in the *Antlers,* and Helen Vail pushed open the door within three minutes of the time he had finished washing his hands.

She wore a low cut gown which accentuated the curves of her figure. Her eyes were laughing, radiant. She drifted over to him, whirled so that he could see the back, and wriggled her shoulders.

"Isn't it a darb? It only . . ."

"If you think that's a legitimate expense, you're crazy," he told her. "Snap out of it. This is a murder case, not a picnic."

She grinned.

"Murder case for you, picnic for me," she said. "I didn't have a darned thing to do all day except sprawl around and kick my toes at the ceiling."

Then, at the look on his face, she came close to him, put an arm on his shoulder.

"Don't be sore, Ken. I was kidding you about the gown. Mrs. Colton bought it for me. She has a charge account. She couldn't just sit around staring at the blank walls of a hotel room. She had to go down to dinner. You're a lawyer. You don't know women.

She'd have brooded over things and had hysterics if I'd left her in that room."

He pushed the girl away, held her at arm's length, stared into her eyes with his own eyes hot with wrath.

"You little fool, do you mean to tell me that you went to a department store, or wherever it was, and used Mrs. Colton's charge account with her written okey?"

She nodded.

"Why, they'll trace you from that. That'll give them the link they want. They're dragging the city for that woman. Someone's leaked. They're moving heaven and earth to drag her over to the D. A.'s office to question her on this Ladue business. Look at the evening papers!"

And he slammed an evening paper down on the bed so that the big headlines could be read as they streamed across the page.

"Sex Slant in Slaying!" read the headlines. Down below in smaller type were other headlines: *"Slayer's Spouse Seeks Lawyer! D. A. Awaits Wife as Witness!"*

She came close to him again.

"I'm sorry, Ken. But I'm not a fool. I fixed things so they'd never be able to trail me, and I engaged a private dining-room in the hotel, and I had a girl friend I could trust come in, and we had a nice little dinner, and Mrs. Colton's all pepped up again, and ready to see it through. She was getting weepy and had the suicide complex again this afternoon."

He patted her shoulder.

"I guess it's all right. It'd have been hell if your foot had slipped and they'd picked you up."

She grinned at him.

"But my foot didn't slip," she pointed out. "And, anyhow, all life's like that. It's fine if your foot don't slip. But there's always that chance of slipping, and that's what makes it so much fun."

She smiled up into his face. He pulled her suddenly towards him.

"Oh-oh!" she said. "You'll get powder on your coat if you do that!"

And, laughingly, she freed herself.

Ken Corning sighed, lit a cigarette, pulled the notebook out of his pocket.

"That your system of shorthand?" he asked.

She lost her bantering manner and instantly became serious.

She sat down on the bed, crossed her knees, put the notebook out on her lap, started studying the notes.

"I can read it," she said. "It's my system. She didn't write it any too legibly. Guess she could read her notes after they were cold. It'd take me a little while to get the sense of it. I can get words here and there."

"Okey," he said. "I'm guessing that nobody dictated to her today. Take that last bunch of shorthand that's there, and see if you can make it out."

The girl ran through the pages, found the last one, started frowning as she deciphered the words. Her lips moved soundlessly at first, and then made audible words.

". . . 'party of the second part, receipt of which is hereby acknowledged' . . . then there's something I can't make out . . . 'hereby bargains and sells, remises and forever quitclaims to the said party of the first part, all and singular, the lands, tenements and hereditaments.' . . . There's a lot of description. You don't want that, do you? It's surveyor's description. So many chains from a certain point, and then boundaries in feet and tenths of feet."

Ken Corning's eyes were narrowed to slits.

"Quitclaim deed, eh? Who's the party of the first part?"

She glanced back along the page.

"Some corporation. The Home Builders Realty Corporation."

Ken Corning's face showed keen disappointment. Helen Vail let her eyes travel down the shorthand notes. "That seems to be all that it is," she said, "a regular quitclaim."

Ken Corning said: "Why would they make a quitclaim if they had title to the property? You'd think they'd either have assigned a contract or else given a grant deed. Maybe it was a flaw in the title. . . . Wait a minute, Helen. Go back of that. What's the thing in the book that's just before that quitclaim?"

The girl thumbed back the page, let her eyes wander down the page. Suddenly she caught her breath in a quick gasp.

"Listen to this: 'Whereas the said undersigned, the said Charles C. Perkins, utilized the said confidential information to fraudulently and feloniously procure a transfer of title to The Home Builders Realty Corporation, a dummy corporation, organized, owned and controlled by the said Charles C. Perkins. . . .'"

Ken Corning made a dive, grabbed the notebook from her hand.

"That's enough. Get out of that damned dress. Get it off!"

She stared at him with wide eyes.

"Says which?" she asked.

He waved his hand towards the door.

"Get started. Back to your hotel. Get out of that bunch of glad rags."

He pushed her towards the door. "Get into your office clothes. When I give you a ring, you go to the office, open up the door and turn on the lights. If anyone asks you questions tell them I telephoned you to come to the office to take some dictation. Tell them you don't know where I telephoned from. And don't let on that you know the wire is tapped. I'll probably telephone you and start talking a bunch of stuff over the telephone. You follow my lead."

She nodded. He opened the door, pushed her into the corridor.

"And listen," he told her, "that's one bunch of instructions you're not to take liberties with. You disobey those, and I'll break your neck. Understand!"

She smiled at him, but her face showed a serious look as though she appreciated the gravity of the situation.

"Think I'm a fool?" she asked. "I know when I can cut corners, and when I can't. What'll I tell the jane over there?" And she jerked her thumb in the general direction of *The Gladstone.*

"Tell her nothing!" snapped Ken Corning. "She'll have to wait until we see how things turn out before she gets any information."

Helen Vail turned with a swish of the evening gown, a glimpse of shapely ankles.

"And that's an instruction I'll take liberties with," she called over her bare shoulder as she flounced the wrap off her arm, spread it. She grinned back at him as she covered her shoulders, and then tripped towards the elevator.

Ken Corning slammed the door shut, locked it, went to the telephone, called police headquarters. "Sergeant Home," he said, when the operator at headquarters answered.

Five seconds later he heard the deep bass voice of Sergeant Home, calmly reassuring, steady as a rock.

Ken Corning said:

"I'm a criminal. That is, there's a warrant out for my arrest.

It's a frame-up. I know you to be a square shooter. I want to surrender. But I want to do it on one condition. That is that you come after me alone and in person, that you promise you'll give me a chance to talk without interruption until I've stated my case."

Sergeant Home said: "I don't make promises to crooks. Who is this, and what's the warrant for?"

"This is Ken Corning," Ken told him. "I'm a lawyer. The warrant's on a charge of assault and battery for beating up a damned nosey reporter who busted into my private . . . ."

"Yeah," said the deep bass voice, "I know all about that. It ain't so serious. If you hadn't tried to conceal witnesses you might not have had any bail to put up. Why should I come after you personally?"

"Because I've got something that's so hot I don't dare to let it leak out around headquarters."

Home said: "Where'll I find you, Corning?"

Corning said: "I trust you enough to tell you where I am and let you come to me, but I don't trust the gang up there, and I'm not sure the line's clear. So you go to the corner of Seventh and Hattman Streets and stand there alone. Have a car parked at the curb with the motor running. I'll get to you."

"Right away?" asked Home.

"Right away," said Corning, and hung up.

KEN CORNING took a taxicab.

"Go to the corner of Seventh and Hattman, park near the curb and keep your motor running," he told the driver. "I'll be down out of sight until I see the coast's clear."

The driver said: "Listen, Buddy, I'm married and got a kid, so don't put me in no hot spots."

"If that's the case, you'll need the extra dollar tip all the more," said Corning, "and you won't be in any hot spots."

The cab lurched into motion. Ken Corning sat back on the seat until the cab was within two blocks of the place, then he dropped down on the floor of the cab. When it had pulled in to the curb he spoke to the driver.

"Okey," he said. "Tell me if you see a police car parked, with the motor running?"

"Yeah. There's one just ahead."

Ken Corning pushed up a cautious head. Sergeant Home was

standing on the sidewalk. He was alone. "Okey," said Ken.
"Drive up alongside it. Here's the meter and a buck extra. When
I open the door, you drive away."

The driver crept the cab forward. Corning got to the running-
board of the police car. The cab lurched away. Corning slid over
in the seat of the police car and pressed the horn button. Sergeant
Home gave a swift start at the sound of the horn, and his eyes
snapped to focus on Corning.

He walked over to the car, went around it, opened the door
and climbed in behind the wheel.

"Hell," he grunted. "How'd you get in here?"

"Little secret," Corning told him. "Drive slowly. I'm spilling
information. I've got to make a sale with you."

"On that murder case?" asked Home, slipping in the gears
with the careful clumsiness which characterizes a big man when
he is doing something which requires some deftness of touch.

"On the murder case."

"Shucks. There ain't a thing to that. Colton's a fool. It was a
fight over his wife. If he'd spill the truth he could probably make
out a case of self-defense. He wouldn't even have to use anything
else."

Ken Corning said: "Nix on that stuff. Listen here. You know
what's going on in this city as well as I do. There's a little ring
that's sold out to the underworld, only it ain't so little. The may-
or's a figurehead in some things. There's a power back of him
that has interests in various places, and those interests are pro-
tected. See?"

Home grunted.

"What's that got to do with murder?"

"Just this. Ladue was on the square. He made some money
buying property and selling it to the city, but he made it by
legitimate business guessing, and by using his head. Some of the
other crowd tried to horn in. They used a dummy, a detective by
the name of Perkins.

"Ladue found out about it and made Perkins disgorge. Otherwise he was going to blow the lid off the whole affair. Last night
was the last minute he'd given Perkins. There was to be a blow-
off if Perkins didn't disgorge. All right. What did Perkins do? He
framed it so Colton would be coming to the office while he was
there. He sneaked in the side entrance. He and Ladue had been
good friends. They called each other by their first names. Proba-

bly Ladue was deeply sympathetic with Perkins, the individual. It was the system that he was fighting.

"So he slipped Perkins in to his private office. Colton came. The girl announced him. Perkins said he'd duck out and come back when Colton had gone. Colton wasn't the sort Ladue could keep waiting.

"So Perkins stepped out in the corridor. He went to the fuse box and unscrewed the fuse which gave light to Ladue's office, the private office. Then he opened the corridor door. There was light enough for him to see what he was doing. It came from the little window over Ladue's desk. He fired twice. He's a dead shot. He tossed in the gun and went back to the fuse box. It was Colton's gun.

"In the meantime the office force had rushed into the room. Seeing it dark, they snapped the switch. That turned the lights in the room off. They were on already. Perkins had counted on that. He then screwed in the fuse plug. That left the lights ready to come on when someone punched the switch again."

Sergeant Home slowed the car almost to a crawl. His forehead was washboarded with thoughtful concentration.

"That's a wild alibi to make," he said. "Even a jury wouldn't believe that, but——"

He paused, and his voice trailed off into silence. The car continued to crawl along at a snail's pace.

"But," said Corning, "for some reason or other you think it may be so, eh?"

Sergeant Home spoke after the manner of one who is merely thinking out loud. "The tip on this unwritten law angle came from Perkins," he said. "He's the one that gave us all the dates and stuff."

Ken Corning said, slowly: "You've got that?"

"We've got Perkins' word for it," said Home. "The dead man can't talk, and we can't find his wife—Colton's wife."

Ken Corning said: "Well, how'd you like to prove the facts as I've given them to you? How'd you like to nail this case on Perkins with absolute proof?"

Sergeant Home shook his head. "Don't be foolish, Corning. It can't be done."

Corning countered with a question.

"You're on the square, Home, but your department's honeycombed to such an extent that Perkins would know any important development that broke, wouldn't he?"

Home frowned. "He would if it ever got to the department, and wasn't kept entirely under my own dome."

"Okey," said Corning, "this thing is going to be handled so it won't be kept under your own dome. But Perkins will never smell it for what it is. It's bait for a trap. Can we get a shorthand reporter who's a good one?"

"I guess so," said Home, staring meditatively and unseeingly at the road which was flowing past them at a slow pace as the car purred steadily along the deserted thoroughfare.

"Let's go, then," Corning told him, his face grim and purposeful.

KEN CORNING called his office from the public pay station. Helen Vail's voice answered. She sounded sleepy.

"Been waiting long?" asked Corning.

"So so. Thought you were going to come up and give me some dictation, Ken."

"I am. You wait right there until I get there. But I won't be there for a little while. There's been a matter come up that's most important."

He paused, wondering if she would give him a lead.

"You mean on that Colton murder case?" she asked eagerly.

"Yes," he said, lowering his voice as though thereby making the confidence more safe. "You see there's a key witness in that case who's really been overlooked by the police. She's Althea Kent, the secretary for Ladue. The murderer knows of her, but thinks he's got her under his thumb.

"I just talked with her, and I'm going to meet her again later on. She's gone out now, but she'll be back. She says she won't make any statement for publication in advance, but she will give me the facts in the form of an affidavit. I can call her as a surprise witness, and when I put her on the stand, she's going to tell the whole truth."

"Gee," said Helen Vail, "that'll be swell, Kenneth. You bust that murder case wide open, and the newspapers will give you all the publicity you can handle."

Ken Corning said: "Okey. Don't say anything to anyone. Wait there and be ready to go out and take that affidavit when I call you. Have your notarial seal ready. G'bye."

"G'bye," she said, and the receiver clicked in his ear.

Ken Corning hung up. Home said: "Good work. Your line's tapped. That conversation'll be at headquarters inside of five minutes, all typed out. Let's go."

They went, went in a police car, four of them; a shorthand reporter who was bored, a technical man who was anxious, Home who was grim, and Ken Corning who was jubilant.

They went to the apartment house where Althea Kent had her apartment, the place where Ken Corning had called on her earlier in the evening. They filed into an adjoining apartment which had been secured through the police influence of Sergeant Home, and equipped in record time under the supervision of the technical expert.

There was a table, a drop light with a green shade, giving to the surface of the table a white glare of illumination. The shorthand reporter sat down at the table. The technical expert busied himself with a last minute inspection of certain matters of wires and the arrangement of a disc-like contrivance.

A telephone rang.

Sergeant Home answered it, listened for a moment, said: "All right!" and hung up.

He turned to the tense group about the table, their faces showing drawn and white under the glare of the incandescent.

"She's coming in," he said.

After a few moments the disc-like contrivance gave forth little humming noises. The technical expert cocked his head to one side.

"She's telephoning from the other room," he said.

Another period of tense silence, then the telephone again. Once more Sergeant Home lifted the receiver, listened, said: "All right," and hung up.

"Perkins," he said, "is on his way. He was waiting."

The reporter tested his fountain pen, spread his elbows, gave his notebook a final adjustment. There was the faint sound of knocking, then the voice of Althea Kent, sounding metallic and flat, but perfectly distinct:

"You! What are you doing here? I thought you weren't to come near me!"

A man's deep voice growled a surly answer.

"You know damned well what I'm doing here, you two-timing little ——!"

"Say, are you cuckoo? What're you talking about?"

"You know. You saw that lawyer this evening, didn't you?"

"Sure I saw him. What about it? I thought he was another of those tabloid boys that wanted a leg picture for the front page. I got good legs, and I'm proud of them. He turned out to be a lawyer, so I played clam on him and showed him the door."

Perkins laughed, and the laugh was not pleasant.

"Played clam, eh? Like hell you did! You came to an understanding with him you'd spill the works when you got on the stand."

The girl's voice was shrill and hysterical.

"My ——!" she screamed, "you're crazy. Take your hands off of me!"

Then the deep voice, sounding vague and indistinct.

"You damned little —— I'll tear your tongue out by the roots if I thought you'd try that stuff. And you have. I've got the deadwood on you. He telephoned his office and spilled the beans. We had the wire tapped!"

There was the sound of confused noises coming through the disc. The shorthand reporter laid down his pen, looked expectantly at Sergeant Home. Home said: "Okey, boys," and barged towards the door.

They sent their shoulders against the door of the adjoining apartment. The door smashed inwards, shivering on its hinges, the lock torn loose from the wood. Perkins was choking the woman with one hand, beating her with his fist, cursing.

He was going about it with a grim intentness of purpose which made him temporarily oblivious of the sound of that crashing door. Then he looked up and saw them. His hand flashed towards his hip pocket. Sergeant Home stepped forward. His great broad shoulders swung in the perfect timing of a golf professional making a drive. His right shoulder sank a bit at the last, as his hand shot out in a wicked blow.

Perkins went back.

The light shone for a moment on his heels as the feet flung up from the floor. Then he hit with a jar that shivered the pictures on the wall and set glassware clattering.

The girl staggered to a chair. Her clothing was torn from her shoulders. Her lips were bleeding. One eye was closed. Hair was about her face in wild confusion, and there were livid marks on her throat.

"The dirty —— ——" she said. "Accuses me of squealing, does he? All right, damn him! If that's the way he feels about it I *will* get a load off my chest. I'll give this burg a blow-off it'll remember for a while."

Sergeant Home turned to the shorthand reporter.

"Get this, Bill," he said.

CORNING left headquarters at one o'clock in the morning.

His hat was on the back of his head, his hands were thrust deep in his side pockets. He was smoking a cigarette, and the corners of his mouth were twisted in a faint smile.

He called a cab, gave it the address of his rooms, yawned his way up the stairs, and flung himself into a chair. He looked at the clock, yawned, started to undress.

Suddenly his eyes widened. He stared at the clock again, blinked, reached for his shoes and trousers.

"Damn!" he said.

He had his clothes on and a cab at the door within five minutes. He gave the driver the address of his office. "And make time," he added. At the office he went up the stairs and let himself in with his key. The outer office was dark, but there was a ribbon of light coming from the underside of the door to the private office.

He pushed the door open.

Helen Vail was lying in his swivel-chair, tilted back, her feet up on the desk, legs crossed. Her eyes were closed and her mouth open. She was gently snoring. On the desk beside her was an ash tray with the ends of a score of cigarettes in it. The little flask of whiskey which he had taken from a drawer when he had tried to revive Mrs. Colton from her faint was on the desk beside her. It was empty.

Ken Corning stood in the doorway, took in the sight, and chuckled. Then he said: "Stand by for a time signal. When you hear the gong it will be precisely fourteen minutes past two o'clock in the morning!"

And then he made a deep, bonging noise in imitation of a gong.

Helen Vail stared at him, took her feet down from the desk, rubbed her eyes, and made little tasting noises with her tongue against the roof of her mouth.

"I presume," she said, "you think you're being funny. My
—— it *is* two o'clock, and after!"

He grinned at her.

"Gee, I'm sorry, kid. I busted that Colton case wide open, and
we're going to have notoriety of sorts. The ring has crawled in a
hole and pulled the hole in after it. And, incidentally, they're
laying for me. If they ever get me now—Good-night!"

The girl got to her feet, straightened her skirts, then ran careful fingers up the seams of her stockings. "In other words," she
said, her head down, eyes inspecting her hose, "you clean forgot
that I was waiting up here, in accordance with your iron-clad
instructions!"

He said: "Aw, Helen, have a heart! I . . . ."

She sighed and said: "Well, I had a hunch I should have done
exactly what you told me until that telephone call came in, and
then I had a hunch to go home. I should have followed that
hunch!"

He smiled, a little wistfully, and said: "You talk as though
good jobs grew on bushes. You can't go home now, anyway.
You've got to go find Mrs. Colton and break the news to her.
She'll be wild with suspense."

Helen shook her head.

"Not that baby," she said. "I got the bell hop to stake us to a
quart of liquor before I changed my clothes and came up here.
She'll be bye-bye."

Ken Corning sighed. "You sure do take liberties with my clients and my expense money. We've got to wake her up and tell
her, anyway. She'll be glad to know George Colton was framed
all the way through. But it's hell from my standpoint. Colton
doesn't even know I was representing him!"

And he grinned.

"Meaning you won't get any more fee?"

"Meaning I won't get any more fee," he told her.

"Cheer up. You'll get the fee for handling her divorce. She's all
washed up. She had been two or three years ago, but Colton
wouldn't let her break away. He's one of those obstinate men
who want to dominate everybody."

Ken Corning shook his head and said: "No. I won't handle her
divorce. There's been too much talk already. Perkins had a lot of
dope and the tabloids will be hounding her again as soon as

Perkins gets off the front page. She's got to go to Reno, and she's got to take the first train out."

Helen reached for a red-backed legal directory.

"Oh, well," she said, "we can at least look up some good attorney in Reno to send her to. Then we'll get a cut on the fee."

And she started thumbing over the pages, while, from the street outside, the calls of the early newsboys informed belated stragglers of the sensation which had broken in the Colton-Ladue case.

Close Call

KEN CORNING stood in his office, feet planted well apart, eyes very cold. They surveyed the officer in coal-black appraisal, steady, hard, hostile, and with obvious annoyance.

"I tell you," he said, "that I don't know where Mr. Dangerfield is."

"He's your client," said the officer.

"That doesn't mean I'm his keeper, does it?"

The detective, who had been standing back of the officer, thrust his way forward.

"Just so there won't be any misunderstanding about this, I want to state that we hold a warrant for the arrest of Amos Dangerfield. He's charged with the murder of Walter Copley. Apparently he's in hiding, and, apparently, he consulted you before he went into hiding."

Ken Corning said: "All right. Now that you've got that off your chest, I still don't know where he is."

The detective sneered.

"And I presume you mean to imply that, if you did know, you wouldn't tell us. Is that right?"

There was a knock at the door of the office.

"Come in," said Ken Corning.

The door opened. Helen Vail, his stenographer, thrust her hatted head through the opening.

"I was a little late," she said. "I heard voices, and wondered if you wanted anything."

Corning smiled affably at the officer and the detective. "Yes," he said, "I want you to come in here and be a witness. These *gentlemen* are trying to trap me into being an accessory after the fact. I wish you'd take a notebook and take notes of the conversation. And don't bother about taking your things off."

Helen Vail sized up the situation with alert, intelligent eyes.

She reached out through the opening in the door, snatched a notebook from her desk which was by the door, grabbed a pencil, dropped down into a chair, crossed her knees, opened the book on her knee, and said: "Go right ahead. I'm ready."

Ken Corning said: "Your question was, I believe, whether or not I would tell you where Mr. Dangerfield was, if I knew. Permit me to remind you again that, as I don't know, the question is beside the point."

The detective said: "All right. Now *you've* got that off *your* chest, you'll admit that we told you we had a warrant for his arrest?"

"Certainly," said Corning.

"You're a lawyer. You'd oughta know that it's a crime to shield anyone accused of murder."

Ken Corning smiled.

"This man came to you, charged with murder, and you advised him to skip out," charged the detective.

"I most certainly did nothing of the sort," replied Corning.

He was smiling now, a smile of cold scorn.

"You knew he was charged with murder."

"I did not."

"You knew he was going to be."

"I am not a mind reader, nor am I a prophet."

"You know it's a crime for a lawyer to listen to a man confess to murder, and then advise him to skip out before a warrant can be issued."

"Perhaps. How about if a man tells you he's innocent of a murder, but thinks he may be charged with it?"

"Is that what Dangerfield told you?" asked the detective.

Corning's voice was edged with scorn.

"Since you're quoting law," he said, "you might look up some more law and find that whatever a client tells his attorney is a confidential and privileged communication."

The officer said to the detective: "We ain't getting anywhere, Bill."

The detective nodded.

"Listen, guy," he said, "you're new to York City. You'll find out that you can't be so damned high and mighty and make it stick. This place ain't healthy for smart alecks like you."

Corning strode forward towards him. His eyes were cold, scornful and very hard.

"I've heard all from you that I want to hear. Get out. My secretary has taken down your threat. It will be available if anything should happen to me."

The detective laughed, a mirthless cackle of sound.

"Okey," he said to the officer, "let's go. Maybe when we come back we'll have a warrant for *this* guy."

Ken Corning stood in the center of the floor and watched them leave the office. When the door had clicked shut, Helen Vail dropped her notebook on the chair, thrust the pencil in her hair and took off her coat.

"What a sweet morning *I* picked to be late," she said.

Ken Corning grinned at her.

"It's okey, Helen. They didn't get anywhere. Just trying to run a cheap bluff."

"How long you been here, Chief?" she asked.

"Since two o'clock this morning."

"Since two o'clock! Good grief! Why didn't you call me?"

"No use. Nothing for you to do."

"Something broke?"

"I'll say. It'll be announced in the papers in an hour or two. The police suppressed the news until it was too late for the regular morning papers. They'll probably run an extra."

"What was it?" she asked.

"Walter Copley, editor of *The News,* was murdered."

She whistled.

"What's our connection with it?" she asked.

"We're retained by Amos Dangerfield. The police claim that it was his car that did the killing."

"GO on," she said. "What happened?"

"The News," he told her, "goes to bed around two-thirty or three o'clock. Copley was leaving the paper. There's an owl street car that makes a swing, and Copley had been in the habit of taking that car. He didn't see very well, and he was afraid to drive his own car. He was always prejudiced against a hired chauffeur.

"Anyhow, he got to the front of his apartment house, got out of the car. The car started on. An automobile swung around the corner, coming fast, and Copley hugged the safety zone. That car held him there, so he couldn't dodge.

"Another machine was running directly behind it, without lights. As the first machine flashed past, the second swerved out from the rear, cut directly across the safety zone and smashed Copley down. Both cars sped away."

"Kill him?" asked the girl.

"Deader'n a door nail."

"Was Dangerfield mixed up in it?"

"He says not. He got me here, said he knew that the crime was committed by certain political enemies, and that he'd been tipped off there was going to be an attempt made to involve him in it. He didn't have any particulars, just had an anonymous telephone call telling him he was to be put in a bad spot, and he'd better run for cover."

"He didn't know who called him?" she asked.

"No. It was a woman's voice."

"You told him to skip out?"

He grinned down at her.

"Gosh," he said, "you're worse than a detective. No. Of course not. I told him that *if* he were not apprehended before morning papers came out, he'd doubtless have an opportunity to learn something of the facts of the case that would be built up against him. And, of course, in the case of a frameup, the more one knows of what the evidence is going to be, the more one can tell what to do about it."

He reached in the inside pocket of his coat and took out a leather wallet. From the wallet he took two fifty-dollar bills, a twenty, three tens, and a check for nine hundred dollars.

"Retainer," he said. "Enter it up in the cash."

She turned the check over in her fingers. It was signed *Amos Dangerfield* in a hand that showed slight irregularities.

"Looks like he was sort of nervous when he signed that check," Helen Vail said.

"Try waking yourself up at two o'clock in the morning and finding that there's a murder charge hanging over your head, and see how *you* feel," he told her.

She grinned. Her mouth twisted in a little grimace. "No, thanks," she said. She moved towards the door, paused. "They got any motive?" she asked.

"Lord, yes! They've got motives to burn. Dangerfield was at swords' points with Copley. At one time Dangerfield had political ambitions. He started getting them again, lately. Copley should have been the one to support him. His paper's against the administration. Of late he's been getting a lot of stuff on graft. He was preparing to blow the lid off the town and expose the whole machine that's in power.

"If the campaign had been successful it would have swept the old bunch out of office and Copley could have written the slate. Dangerfield thought Copley should give him something nice. Copley had other plans."

Helen Vail's eyes narrowed.

"They won't dare to show that as a motive," she said. "And, at that, it isn't much of a motive. A man wouldn't go out and murder someone just because he couldn't get some political job."

"Sure," he told her. "But be your age. They'll use the quarrel the two men had, a bitter quarrel. Everyone in the office of the newspaper heard it. Dangerfield accused Copley of giving him a double-cross. He threatened to do everything from horsewhipping Copley to blowing up the paper and suing him for libel. You see, in the mess of stuff that Copley had collected to show graft and what-not, he uncovered a dump down on Birkel Street. It's rather a tough neighborhood. There was a sort of dance-hall running there. It was a place that paid protection money, and the sort of things went on there that you'd expect to run if you were paying protection money.

"Copley chased back in the records to find who owned the building, just on general principles. He found that the owner was Amos Dangerfield. Dangerfield didn't even know what sort of a place it was or what was happening down there. He turned the whole thing over to an agent, and the agent ran the place and collected the rents.

"But Copley was going to publish the story of this dance-hall as the opening gun in his campaign. He had a sob sister story on a couple of the dancers there, and a straight case of bribery, clean up to a sergeant.

"Naturally, it'd have put Dangerfield on a political spot. He could have made all the alibis he wanted about not knowing what was going on there, and all the rest of it, but he'd never have been elected even to the office of dog catcher on a reform ticket. Copley knew that and that's why he was throwing Dangerfield over.

If he'd teamed up with Dangerfield, he'd have had to throw away one of his best stories. He figured it'd be cheaper to get some other guy for office."

Helen Vail let her face squint up with thought.

"Gee," she said, "some of that stuff must have been hot— politically."

"Of course it was," he said. "It was dynamite."

"What happened to it?"

He shrugged his shoulders.

"Nobody knows. Probably nobody ever will know. The authorities took charge of everything. They claimed that they had to dig up evidence about the murder. They pawed through a lot of stuff. They claim they didn't find anything."

"You mean they had someone slip it out of the safe or wherever it was, and destroy it?"

He said:

"I don't mean anything except that they didn't find anything. The authorities who made the investigation were the same authorities who were to be put on the pan by the evidence that Copley had collected. You can draw your own conclusions."

"Well," she asked, "what do you think?"

He grinned at her.

"Try reading my mind. It's what a jury will be asked to do."

"You think the case will go to a jury?"

"Sure. They want to make Dangerfield the goat. They've got to. They thought they could rub Copley out without leaving any back trail. But, *if* they *did* leave a back trail, it was going to be one that led directly to the fall guy, and that's what Dangerfield is. Even if a jury acquits him, the people will think that he was guilty."

"What you figuring on, Chief?"

"I'm going to try to beat 'em to it and dig up some witnesses."

"Going to hire a detective to do the leg work?"

"No. I'm going to do it myself. I can't trust anybody on this thing. It's too delicate."

CORNING rang the doorbell. The woman who answered the ring was broad of shoulder and hip. Her arms were bare, and they were well muscled. Her eyes had an expression of stony hostility.

"Well," she said, "what do *you* want?"

Ken Corning grinned.

"I'm an attorney," he said. "I'm representing Amos Danger-field who lives next door."

"Oh," she said, "the one who murdered the newspaperman, eh?"

Corning grinned.

"No," he said, "he didn't murder the newspaperman."

The woman said, uncordially: "Well, come in and sit down. Don't try to get me mixed into the thing, though. I don't want to go on a witness stand and have a bunch of lawyers yelling questions at me."

"Certainly," he soothed. "I'm just trying to get the facts. Mr. Dangerfield lives next door to you. That's his flat, the one on this side, I believe?"

The woman nodded, led the way into a sitting-room. The windows opened out on a strip of lawn. Across that lawn was a driveway. At the end of the driveway were three garages, beyond the garages was a large rambling house.

"What did you think *I'd* know?" asked the woman.

"Something about what time the car was taken from the garage," he said.

"I only know I heard a lot of men out there this morning. It was early, just before daylight. Right around when it was getting gray dawn. They trampled things up and took flashlight pictures. They claim they found blood and hair on the bumper of the car, and that there was a place on the left front fender where . . ."

"Yes," he said, "I know all about that. How about prior to that time? Did you hear the garage door open, or anything like that?"

"No."

"How many people on this west side of the house?"

"Three."

"Can you give me their names and where I can find them? I presume they're working now."

"Two of them are. There's one that isn't. He's out of work now. I think he's leaving here on the first."

"What's his name?"

"Oscar Briggs. He was an accountant. He specialized in income tax work. There ain't any business in his line now. His clients haven't had any income."

"I wonder if I could run up and speak with him."

"I guess so. I'll take you up to his room."

They climbed stairs, went down a corridor to the back of the house. She knocked on a door. Windows looked down in the driveway, right at the very entrance of the garage.

Steps sounded from the inside of the room. A man opened the door, saw the broad shoulders of the woman on the threshold.

"I'm sorry, Mrs. Markle, but I can't let you have——"

She interrupted him.

"There's a gentleman wants to see you."

She stood to one side so that he could see Ken Corning.

The man was tall and slender. He carried himself with an air of dignity. But there was a subtle something in his manner which suggested that his poise was punctured. He seemed a man who had made something of an established position for himself, and had come to regard that position as being secure. Then he had found his values dissolving before his eyes, his very foundations crumbling. He kept the outward semblance of dignity and poise, but there was something in the back of his eyes, a suggestion of panic.

Ken Corning moved forward and held out his hand.

"My name's Corning, Mr. Briggs. I'd like to talk with you for a few minutes."

"Come in," said Briggs.

"You'll excuse me," said Mrs. Markle. "I've got work to do, and there's no way I can help you."

Corning said: "Certainly, and thank you, Mrs. Markle."

Briggs indicated a chair.

Corning sat down. The windows of the room looked down directly upon the doorways of the garages. There was a writing desk in the room and Briggs had evidently been half way through a letter.

"I'm representing Mr. Dangerfield," said Corning.

"A lawyer?"

"Yes."

"I see."

"You've read the papers?"

"Yes. Of course we knew something about it. The police came somewhere around daylight this morning. They wanted to examine the car, and they were trying to locate Dangerfield. He had skipped out. Seemed a mighty nice fellow, too. I understood he was doing some research work. Has the entire upper floor of the building across from us, I believe."

Corning said: "Yes," and waited.

Briggs moved uncomfortably.

"That all you know?" asked Ken Corning.

"Yes."

"You didn't hear the garage doors open or close during the night, didn't hear the car come in? Didn't, by any chance, see that Mr. Dangerfield was in his rooms last night at any particular time, or see him driving the machine, did you?"

Briggs fidgeted around in his chair.

"Look here," he said, "who told you to come to me?"

"No one. I'm representing a client who's charged with a very grave offense, and I want to see if I can find out something about the facts."

Briggs kept his eyes averted.

"Well," said Corning.

"No. I don't know anything else."

Ken Corning said, very solemnly: "It's a murder case, you know, Mr. Briggs."

"And I don't want to be put on the stand and have a lot of lawyers yell questions at me," said Briggs.

Corning smiled affably.

"Oh, it isn't as bad as that. You'll be subpenaed, of course, and you'll have to tell what you know. But people won't do any shouting."

"You mean I'll have to go to court?"

"Oh, yes. You'll be called. The fact that you didn't hear anything might be of some value. Negative testimony, you know, and all that."

"But I don't want to go to court."

"Unfortunately, you'll have to. It's one of those things that come up at times, like jury duty. And, of course, Mr. Briggs, if you *do* know anything, it would be far better to tell me now. You see, if you get on the stand and testify under oath and conceal any facts it would be a grave offense. On the other hand, if you should insist to me that you know nothing, and then tell a different story when you got on the witness stand, it would make you very uncomfortable, put you in a false light, you know."

Briggs sighed, suddenly raised his eyes to Corning's.

"All right," he said, "if you put it that way, I'll tell what I know. I hadn't intended to tell a soul. But I guess I'd have had to weaken before the case was over, particularly if it got to looking bad for Mr. Dangerfield. I don't think he drove the car at all."

"No?" asked Ken Corning, sitting very still in his chair.

"No. I think he was at home abed. You see, I can look across into his flat. There aren't any women on this side of the house, and Mr. Dangerfield is a bachelor, something of a recluse, I understand. As a result we don't draw the shades at night, none of us.

"I was up late last night. I saw Dangerfield padding around in his pajamas. He went to bed about midnight. I was sitting up, trying to figure some way out of my personal situation. My business is none too good at the present time.

"Well, about one o'clock, or a little earlier, I heard the sound of the garage door downstairs being opened, rather slowly. I had turned out the light in my room because my eyes hurt. In fact, I'd put on pajamas, and had tried to sleep, but couldn't.

"I looked out of the window.

"There were four men who were pushing a car out of Dangerfield's garage. They had another car parked at the curb with the motor running.

"Of course, I thought right away of car thieves. They were evidently running the car out of the garage by man power so that the motor wouldn't make a noise and alarm anyone.

"I started to give an alarm, but I didn't know what to do. There's no telephone here in this room, you see, and I'd have had to go downstairs and alarm the house in order to get the telephone. By the time I could have notified the police it'd have been too late. And I didn't want to put my head out of the window and start yelling. One reads so much about gangsters shooting, these days."

Corning nodded. His eyes were slitted in concentration.

"I know," he said. "Go on."

Briggs said: "Well, it was done so smoothly and so rapidly that I couldn't do a thing. Even while I was sitting there, debating what I was going to do, it was all over. They got the car to the curb. A man jumped in, just one man. He started the car and drove away. The other three got in the other car that was parked at the curb, and followed. I figured Mr. Dangerfield had just lost a car, but I also figured it was insured, and that perhaps he'd just as soon have the insurance as the car, so I decided to forget it.

"I didn't go back to bed. I sat there in a chair by the window.

About one-forty, I heard a noise. Two cars drove up and stopped at the curb. Then one of the cars was rolled up the driveway, just the way it had been rolled down. It looked like Dangerfield's car. They had switched off the lights and the motor, and they pushed the car up into the garage and closed the door."

Ken Corning spoke very slowly, sat very still in his chair.

"Did you," he asked, "see any of the men so that you could recognize them if you saw them again, or give a description?"

"I saw the one who drove Dangerfield's car. He crossed in front of the headlights of the other car, once. I had a glimpse."

"What did he look like?"

"He was a heavy-set man with a white hat. That is, it looked white in the glare of the headlights. It was probably just a light color. He had on a tweed suit and brown shoes. I caught a glimpse of the face, but looking down on it, it was hard to tell very much about it. I saw that there was a scar along one cheek. That was about all I could see."

Ken Corning said: "And you've told no one about this?"

"No."

"You'd better write it out. Make just a brief statement in your own words. Sign that statement and give it to me. I'll promise you that I won't call you as a witness unless I have to. It may be I can get the case dismissed without having to go to a trial."

Briggs moved towards the desk with alacrity.

"If you could only do that," he said, "it'd sure be a load off my mind. I didn't know what to do. When I read of the murder in the paper, and the fact that the police claimed Dangerfield's machine had done the job . . . Well, I've been in a stew ever since daylight."

He sat down at the desk and started to write.

Ken Corning lit a cigarette. He sat, thoughtfully smoking.

A KNOCK sounded at the door, a heavy, imperious knock.

Corning looked at Briggs. Briggs got up from the desk, strode to the door, opened it. A man pushed his way into the room, without greeting, glowered about him.

"Which one of you guys is Briggs, the guy that lives here?"

"I am," said Briggs.

"Then this other guy is the lawyer, eh?"

Ken Corning got to his feet, pinched out the cigarette.

"Who are you?" he asked.

"Harry Smoot, of the Detective Bureau. I'm here looking around. I heard you was out here. Your name's Corning, ain't it?"

"Yes," said Ken Corning.

Smoot walked over to a chair and sat down.

"You ain't told this lawyer anything, have you?" he asked of Briggs.

Briggs seemed a little nettled.

"When you interrupted me," he said, "I was in the middle of a statement concerning what I had seen and heard."

"Oh, ho," said the detective, "you know something then."

"Yes," said Briggs. "I had just finished telling Mr. Corning about it."

Smoot's heavy face settled into a portentous frown.

"Listen, guy, when there's been a murder committed, and you know something about it, the thing for you to do is to get in touch with the police, not go running around telling lawyers all you know. Do you get that?"

Briggs said: "I guess I have a right to talk with whom I wish, haven't I?"

Ken Corning strolled nonchalantly over to the desk. Briggs had covered two pages of stationery with his statement. It was, of course, as yet unsigned. Corning slipped the papers into his pocket while Smoot glowered at Briggs.

"I'm just telling you," said the detective, "for your own good. You don't want to get in no trouble, do you? Well, the thing to do is to get in touch with the police when you know anything. Now what is it you know?"

Briggs said: "I know that Dangerfield wasn't driving his car last night, that other men took out that car, and that they returned it. I know that their conduct was suspicious when they took the car out and also when they returned it. I believe this whole crime was framed on Amos Dangerfield."

The detective's face was dark.

"Now listen, guy, you're goin' too far and too fast. You can't know all this stuff without being mixed up in the thing some way. And what you know ain't right. See? We got the deadwood on this case. What you've done is to listen to this lawyer until he's got you all balled up about what you did see."

Ken Corning said: "Don't let this man browbeat you, Briggs."

Smoot whirled on Corning.

"I've half a mind to run you in," he said, "tampering with witnesses."

Ken Corning said in low, ominous tones: "Have you a warrant for me?"

"Not yet," said the detective. "That ain't saying I ain't going to have one."

"All right," Corning told him grimly, "when you do get one, you can serve it. Until you do get it, your talk don't mean a damned thing, except that if you keep on looking for trouble you're going to find it."

"Yeah? Well, guy, I'm going to report what I've found out here, your tampering with a state's witness."

Corning suddenly pushed forward.

"All right. Go ahead and report. Now get out of my way!"

The detective stood on one side.

"How about that statement?" he asked Briggs. "You didn't sign anything, did you?"

"No. I hadn't finished it, so I didn't sign it."

"Where is it?"

Corning, at the door, turned.

"I've got it in my pocket," he said. "It's my statement, made for me at my request."

Smoot strode towards him ominously.

"You can't get away with that," he said. "Give it up!"

Ken Corning planted his feet wide apart.

"That statement," he said, slowly, "is in my inside coat pocket. It's going to stay there. Do you think otherwise? If you do, just try to get it."

His eyes blazed into those of the detective.

For fifteen seconds they stood there, the big detective sullen and enraged, Corning flashing fire from his eyes, standing his ground, cool and deadly.

"You'll hear from this!" said Smoot.

"Bah!" said Ken. "Go hand your line to some kid who's afraid of you!"

He turned on his heel and walked down the stairs.

HELEN VAIL took the sheets of paper.

"Put them in a lock box somewhere," Corning told her. "Don't trust to the safe in the office."

"You think it'll bust the case?" she asked, looking down at the scrawled writing on the paper.

"Can't tell. It'll give the District Attorney something to worry about. I want to get hold of Dangerfield now and have him surrender. Then I can get a date set down for the preliminary hearing and have a subpena issued for this witness."

"Do you know where Dangerfield is? Wouldn't that be dangerous?"

He grinned at her.

"I told them I didn't know where he is, and I don't. But I wouldn't be such a fool as to let a client charged with murder get away without knowing how I could get in touch with him. I can't go to him, but I can get him to come to me.

"I just put an ad in the personal column in the *Clarion* that'll do the trick. Dangerfield's watching that column. He'll communicate with me as soon as he sees the ad."

Helen Vail said: "Did you see the late papers about the witness the state has got?"

"No," he said. "Who is it? What will he swear to?"

"Some fellow named Bob Durane. Claims he was driving a car along the boulevard, just after Copley was struck down. He says that a car went past him at terrific speed, running without lights, and that there was a lone man in the car, driving. He says that when the man went past him there was a street light where it shone on the man's face, and that he'll recognize him if he sees him again."

Ken Corning blinked rapidly.

"Who is this bird, and where is he?" he asked.

"The District Attorney's office has got him sewed up over in the *Palace Hotel*. The paper said 'a downtown hotel,' but the *Palace* was where they buried those other witnesses, and I suppose that's where they've got this baby planted."

Ken Corning paced the floor.

"A plant," he said. "Pulling this stuff through the newspapers is going to make things rough for Dangerfield."

She stared up at him and said: "Isn't there anything you can do about it?"

He nodded grimly.

"Sure. They come busting in on my witnesses and browbeat them for even talking with the lawyer for the defense. They get their own witnesses and put them under guard. They'd probably arrest anyone that even tried to talk with them. When I try to get a statement about what happened it's 'tampering with a witness.' When they want a statement, they bury their witness somewhere and put a guard around him."

"That ain't fair," she said.

"Of course it ain't fair, but the people don't know it. They just can't be bothered."

"Maybe there's some way we could make 'em know it, Chief. We might be able to let 'em know. . . ."

"Exactly what I'm going to do right now," he told her. "I'm going to bust over there and demand to interview the witness. There'll be some news-hungry reporters hanging around there. They'll have a guard on the room, and I'll let the guard throw me out. That'll make news. Then the people will think maybe there's something funny about it."

She nodded.

The outer office door clicked. A shadow hulked into the room, then a man pushed his way into the office. It was the same man who had been in earlier in the morning with the officer.

He held out a copy of a newspaper, damp from the presses.

"What's the meaning of this, Corning?" he demanded.

Ken Corning glanced significantly at the papers which Helen Vail held in her hand.

She abruptly thrust them down the front of her dress. The detective stared at her.

"Meaning of what?" asked Ken Corning.

"Meaning of this personal ad: '*A.D. Have uncovered evidence desired. Any time now is all right. Telephone first. Ken.*'"

"How should I know what it means?" said Corning.

The detective moved towards Helen Vail.

"Say," he said, "you were hiding something. You don't want to get mixed in this, baby! It's going to be a fight. What was it you had in your hand when I came in?"

She pushed towards the door.

The detective reached out a hand and hooked two fingers down the V-shaped opening in the front of her dress.

"Now listen, sister. . . ."

Ken Corning crossed to the detective in two swift strides.

"Take your hand away!" he snapped.

The detective caught the blazing fire of the eyes, whirled around, snarling.

"Say-y-y-y," he said, "if you . . ."

Helen Vail ducked under his arm, scurried across the outer office and into the corridor. The detective turned awkwardly, made a clutch at the empty atmosphere, glowered at Corning.

"You don't try to get along at all," he said. "You're just a smart Aleck that don't know what he can do and what he can't do. This is your first big case, youngster, and you're going to wind up by being in awful bad."

Ken Corning stood rigid, poised.

"This is my private office. I don't want a bunch of roughneck detectives barging in here without invitation. You've had too damned many privileges as it is. Now, damn you, get out of here, or I'll bust your face wide open."

"Yeah?" asked the detective.

"Yeah. You've busted in here once too often. And when you presume to lay your dirty paws on my secretary, you've clean overstepped every vestige of authority you ever had."

The detective fidgeted.

"I didn't touch her. I just wanted to ask her a question."

"The hell you didn't touch her! You started pawing her over. I saw you and she felt you. Now are you going to get out, or shall I put you out?"

The detective turned.

"Oh, all right! If you're figuring on framing me, go ahead. But remember that you're bucking something that's licked many another guy that thought he was going to make a big reputation for himself as a criminal lawyer. You can't buck the system. If you're going to get on in this game you gotta play ball."

Ken Corning sneered.

The detective stalked through the outer door.

Ken Corning stood, feet planted widely apart, watching the automatic door check bring the door to a close. Then he got his hat. He waited for a minute or two, then left the office, locking it behind him. He took a cab to the *Palace Hotel.*

There were newspaper men in the lobby.

Reed Nixon, of the *Star,* recognized him.

"Hello, Corning. Hear you're representing Dangerfield. How about an interview? How about telling us something?"

"Sure thing," said Corning.

Nixon hurriedly piloted him over to a corner of the lobby, where he was screened from the other reporters.

"Listen, guy, how about this? Give me something nice, a defiant statement, something with a fight in it. Say it's a dirty political frame-up."

"It's a dirty political frame-up," said Corning.

"That's fine. Where's Dangerfield?"

"Dangerfield was called away hurriedly upon a business trip. As soon as he reads that he is wanted, however, he will surrender himself. You can say that I promise to have Dangerfield in the hands of the authorities within another twenty-four hours."

"Attaboy!" said Nixon.

"Where have they got this witness parked, Nixon?"

"Up on the third floor, 324. You can't see him. They got a couple of muscle men on guard. You've got to have a pass from the D. A. to get in."

"That's not right," said Corning. "A man should be given some opportunity to know what he's charged with. The lawyer of one side should be entitled to no advantage that the lawyer of the other side isn't given."

Nixon laughed.

"Gee," he said, "that's a fine lot of hooey, but I'd like to hear you tell the D. A. that."

"I'm going to," said Corning.

Nixon nodded.

"That's the old spirit. Let me in on the ground floor. Give me something else that's got a wallop in it."

"You got a photographer here?" asked Corning.

"I can get one pretty quick. Why?"

"Nothing, but if I should try to interview that witness, and should get treated rather roughly, and if you should have a photographer get a flashlight of me being thrown out on my ear, it would make a good action story, wouldn't it?"

"I'll say!"

Then, as the reporter thought a minute, he added: "It would maybe make the D. A. sore, though."

"Why?"

"Oh, some of the people might get to figuring there was something funny about a witness that the D. A. had to keep all buttoned up that way. When it came to trial you might be able to catch someone on the jury with the argument that the thing was a political frame-up."

"A *dirty* political frame-up," corrected Corning. "Don't forget the adjective."

"Okey then, a dirty political frame-up."

"Going to get the photographer?" asked Corning.

Nixon squinted his eyes.

"Stick around," he said. "I'll phone. Don't get chummy with the other boys. The boss might risk rubbing the D. A. the wrong way, if we got an exclusive."

Corning nodded, sat down and lit a cigarette.

INATTENTIVELY his eyes, watching the crowds on the street, strayed aimlessly. The big, overstuffed chair was placed in front of the plate-glass window, and he could see the people hurrying to and fro.

His eyes rested on a roadster in which two men sat. They seemed interested in the front of the hotel. Corning remembered that they had passed the taxicab in which he had been riding. He watched them.

The car was a police car. The two men were plain-clothes officers. Corning could not remember having seen either of them before, but the manner in which they wore their clothes, held their heads, stared at the entrance of the hotel, labeled them for what they were.

Ken Corning smoked up his cigarette. Reed Nixon came back to him.

"I've got the photographer," he said, "all planted with a flashlight and a camera that won't attract attention. He'll follow you down the corridor. Go up to the third floor and turn to the left when you leave the elevator."

Ken Corning got to his feet, grinned, and walked to the elevator.

Reed Nixon strolled to the stairways, vanished from sight.

Ken Corning left the elevator at the third floor, turned left and walked down the corridor. He checked the numbers on the doors as he went past them.

When he had passed 318 and was approaching 320 a man who had been standing in the corridor came towards him.

"What you looking for, buddy?"

"Three twenty-four."

"Got a pass from the D. A.?"

"No," said Corning gravely. "I'm Corning, the lawyer who is

representing Mr. Dangerfield. I understand that there's a witness here who knows something about what happened. I want to talk with him."

The man grinned.

"Well," he said, "he don't want to talk with you."

Corning's face was baby-faced in its utter innocence.

"Well," he said, "if he'd tell me that, it would be all I'd want. That would show that he was biased in favor of one side of the case, you see; and I could spring it on him when I cross-examined him."

The man frowned, stared fixedly at Ken Corning.

"Say, listen, what you doing? Taking me for a goof?"

Ken said: "Are you?"

"Am I what?"

"A goof."

The man pushed his way forward.

"Okey. That's enough out of you. On your way. I don't want any more of your lip, buddy."

Ken Corning stood his ground.

"I wish to see Mr. Robert Durane," he said.

"On your way, guy. Beat it!"

The man pushed out a big hand. Ken Corning pivoted from the hip, just the fraction of a deft turn, but it served to take his shoulder out of the path of the pushing hand. The big man lost his balance as he came forward. Ken Corning's foot moved slightly. As the man took a swift step forward to catch his balance, his foot tangled with Corning's. He sprawled flat on his face.

Corning moved forward, twisted the knob of room 324.

He heard a roar of rage behind him.

The door opened.

Ken Corning saw a man seated in a chair in front of a table, playing solitaire. He was smoking a cigar. He looked up as the door opened, and Ken saw that there was a livid scar down the right-hand side of his face, that the man had hulking shoulders, a thick neck. . . .

Another man who had been seated on the bed, reading, jumped forward. His form bulked in the doorway and blotted out Corning's gaze of the interior of the room.

"Got a pass?" he asked.

An avalanche of human indignation descended upon Ken

Corning from the rear. He felt powerful hands grasp his shoulder, felt himself spun around. A fist lashed out and caught him on the side of the face.

At that moment something went *"Pouff!"*

The corridor lighted up with the powerful glare of a flash gun.

Ken Corning dodged the next blow. The man from the interior of the room rushed him. Hands gripped his coat. He was pushed down the corridor. A foot impacted the small of his back, and he gave a swift leap to take him out of the way of another foot that sent a vicious kick.

Corning flashed a glance over his shoulder, then buckled down to the business of running, making time down the corridor. He hurled himself around the corner of the stairs. The bigger men made slow work of negotiating the turn.

Ken Corning distanced them on the stairs. They were slow and clumsy in their footwork. They followed him down the first flight, and part of the way down the second flight. When they found that pursuit was fruitless, they raised voices in maledictions.

Ken Corning kept right on going.

He paused to adjust coat and necktie on the mezzanine. A mirror showed him that one eye was swelling badly. The side of his face felt sore to the exploring touch of his fingertips.

He grinned. After a few minutes he walked down to the lobby, strolling through it casually.

He met Reed Nixon near the doorway.

The reporter said, under his breath:

"Gee, guy, you gave us a break!"

"You get the picture?" asked Corning.

"And how! He caught a picture just when the guy was socking you with a right. But when they both started chasing you, it was a break we'd been looking for. Our photographer stuck in another plate, dashed down the corridor, stuck his camera in the room and set off another flash.

"We're rushing 'em over to develop 'em. We think we got a peach of the mystery witness that they're trying to keep under cover. If we did, we'll play it up strong. It'll mean the D. A. will be sore, so we might as well go the whole hog. If I can sell the Chief on it, I'm going to give you a big play."

"Okey, thanks," said Corning, and walked out.

He was careful not to look directly at the automobile with the two officers, but was equally careful to observe, out of the corner of his eye, that the machine crawled into motion.

He walked to a drug-store on the corner and called his office.

"Anything?" he asked Helen Vail when he heard her voice on the line.

"I'll say. You got an answer to your ad."

"Fine. What was it?"

"Telephone call to meet the party at the *Fleming Hotel.* He said you knew the name he'd be registered under. He's in Room 526."

"Okey," said Corning. "If he calls in again, tell him that I'm on my way out there, but that a couple of dicks are trailing me in the hope that I'll lead them to him, so I'll have to take it a little easy."

"You going to ditch them?" she asked.

"No," he said, "this is my day for taking the police department for a ride. I'm going to kid 'em along strong."

He hung up, walked out and caught a cab.

He noticed that the police car fell in behind.

"Fleming Hotel," he said.

The cab made good time. The police car clung doggedly. Ken Corning sat back on the cushions and apparently was lost in thought. His right eye was swelling rapidly, and the soreness in the side of his face was increasing.

The cab swung in to the curb in front of the hotel. Corning paid the driver. The uniformed doorman made something of a ceremony out of opening the door of the cab.

Corning walked into the hotel.

He paused at the desk. One of the plain-clothes officers was walking in the lobby as Corning leaned over and asked the clerk: "Who's in 528?"

The clerk stared at him a moment, then consulted a card.

"Mr. Carl Grant, of Detroit," he said.

"That's the party," said Corning. "I'd forgotten the name. Will you give him a ring and tell him that Mr. Ken Corning, the lawyer, is on his way up? Tell him it'll only take a minute."

And he walked towards the elevators.

As the door of the cage clanged shut, he saw the plain-clothes officer who had followed him in, pausing to confer with the clerk at the desk.

Ken Corning left the elevator on the fifth floor, walked along the corridor, knocked on the door of 528.

The door opened.

A portly figure in a silk dressing gown stared at him belligerently.

"I don't know you!" he said.

Ken Corning heard the door of the elevator clang open and shut, heard steps in the hall.

He raised his voice.

"Okey, Amos, get dressed and we'll go and get it over with."

The man stared at him with bulging eyes.

"Say," he began, "I never . . ."

He didn't finish. Ken Corning heard the banging of heavy steps behind him, caught the glimpse of a heavy body rushing forward. Then he was pushed to one side as though he had been a floating cork in the path of a battleship. Reaching hands darted forward, came down on the shoulder of the man in the doorway.

"Mr. Amos Dangerfield," boomed the voice, "I arrest you in the name of the law for the murder of Walter Copley, and I warn you that anything you may say will be used against you."

The man sputtered.

"But I'm not Dangerfield. I don't know anything about the case except what I read in the paper! I'm Carl Grant of Detroit. . . ."

The officer pushed his way into the room.

"May I have a word with this man?" asked Ken Corning, making as if to push his way past the door.

The officer grinned.

"At the jail," he said, and kicked the door shut in Ken Corning's face.

Corning whirled, moving with the swift rapidity of a hunted animal. He stepped to the adjoining room, twisted the knob of the door, and walked into the room.

He slammed the door and twisted the bolt.

"All right, Dangerfield," he said. "They haven't got pictures and descriptions out yet. They shadowed me here, but the officers were going blind. I ditched them on to the party next door. The car's waiting down the street. Stick around until we see them drive away."

Corning walked over to the window, drew up a chair and looked down on the street. He could see the top of the parked police car, pushed against the curb in front of the space reserved for taxicabs.

Amos Dangerfield was a fleshy man much given to excitement. His voice was shrill and quavering. He came and stood by Ken Corning and asked innumerable questions.

Ken Corning didn't raise his eyes from the street, nor did he answer the questions. He waited a few seconds, then interrupted the flow of language.

"Never mind all that. Get ready to leave and keep quiet. I've got to get you in to headquarters before they grab you. Otherwise they'd make a point of your flight. They spotted the ad in the personal column, and figured I was going to meet you somewhere, so they put a tail on me. . . . Tell me, do you know a heavy-set man in the early forties with a scar down the right side of his face? Guy with black hair and gray eyes?"

"No," said Dangerfield, slowly.

"All right then," Ken Corning told him. "Shut up! I want to think, and the racket bothers me."

He sat and watched. Five minutes became ten. Then he saw the plain-clothes officer escort a man across the strip of sidewalk to the waiting automobile.

The pair stood at the door of the car.

"Okey," said Corning. "They'll probably split and leave a shadow here. On our way. Make it snappy!"

He led the way out into the corridor, down the back stairs.

Amos Dangerfield wheezed and sputtered his way down the five flights of stairs. The descent took all his wind, and he made no comments, asked no questions.

Ken Corning found a stairway to the baggage-room, went to it, tipped the porter, walked out the side entrance to the alley, went down the alley, caught a cab.

Amos Dangerfield tugged at the cab and lifted his bulk into the vehicle.

"Police headquarters," said Ken Corning.

MRS. MARKLE stood in the doorway of her boarding house. Her ample form was covered with a dress of silk which gave her a stiffly starched, dressed-up appearance. Her eyes surveyed Ken Corning without the hostility they had shown earlier in the day, but with a certain curiosity.

"He's gone," she said.

"When will he be back?" asked Corning.

"He won't be back. He's gone. Got a job, took a plane some-where."

"How about his mail? He must have left you with a forwarding address."

She rotated her head in a decided negative.

"No, he didn't. And, if you ask me, there was something fishy about the whole business. He left in less than an hour after you did. When you called on him he didn't have any more job than a tramp, and he owed me for two months' room and board. I wouldn't have let him get that deep into me, only he'd been a steady boarder for more than a year, and he'd always paid up regular when he had it.

"But after you left, the man that went up there left, and then another man came, a fish-faced little brat that was all smiles and smirks. He went up and talked with Briggs for fifteen or twenty minutes, and then Briggs came down all in a flutter, yelling for transfer men, and acting as though he was running to put out a fire.

"He paid me everything he owed me that was in arrears, and paid me for a week in advance. I saw his wallet when he took it out. It was just bursting with money. He said he had a job offered him, and he'd got to take a plane to get there. He didn't say where the job was. I asked him about his mail, and he said to forget it, that if any mail came it'd be a bill probably.

"He never used to be like that. Always was a quiet, self-re-specting, respectable chap. Now he's rushing around scattering money to the winds and taking aeroplanes. I don't like it. I'm as glad he's gone."

Ken Corning's face remained impassive.

"Thank you, very much, Mrs. Markle," he said.

"Can I let you know if I hear from him—where he is?"

He raised his hat politely.

"No," he said. "Thank you, but you won't hear."

And he turned down the steps.

He drove back to his office. Helen Vail stared at him and broke into laughter.

"What is it?" he asked.

"The eye," she said. "What a beautiful shiner!"

He grinned.

She indicated the paper which lay on the desk in front of her.

"Like to see yourself as others see you? Here's a photo of you on the receiving end of the wallop. It must have been a beaut!"

He touched his sore cheek bone.

"It was," he told her.

She said, "Well, the *Star* is giving you some swell publicity. I bet the D. A. is gritting his teeth. Notice that they don't say you tried to bust into the room, but that the guards of the D. A.'s office assaulted you when you made inquiries about the witness."

"That's what happened," he said, grinning. "I just acted dumb until the guy started to shove me around, and then I let him fall over himself. That made him mad, and he lost control of himself."

Helen Vail indicated another photograph.

"Look at this. Exclusive photograph of the mystery witness who claims that he saw Dangerfield driving the car. He looks tough, sitting there playing solitaire."

Ken Corning studied the picture.

"They give you an awful good play up," said Helen.

"They should," he told her. "Look at the story I got for them, and the pictures they had a chance to take. It makes good front page stuff. It gave them a chance to run out an extra."

She looked at him appraisingly.

"Well," she said, "it'll be good publicity for your side of the case. Makes it look as though the district attorney had something he was trying to cover up, eh?"

"That's right. That's the way I played it."

"Fine. Where you been all afternoon?"

"Going around, leg work. They got to my witness and bought him off."

She stared at him.

"The police?"

"Oh, no. Of course not. The police were all regular, just sore because any witness told anyone what he knew before he'd talked with the police. According to them, a witness is either a witness for the state, or else he's a liar."

Her eyes were wide and alarmed.

"But, Ken, what happened? Who did it?"

"Same old stunt," he said. "There's a leak around the detective bureau. And when the cops get a case worked up they figure that all evidence that conforms to their theory of the case is the truth; that all evidence that doesn't is framed.

"Anyhow, the detectives reported to the D. A., and there was a leak. The guys that are mixed up in the political exposé that Copley was figuring on decided that they couldn't afford to have this chap, Briggs, give his testimony. So they sent a fixer out there with a wad of dough and a fake job at the ends of the earth some place.

"Naturally, Briggs didn't want to testify anyway. The fixer persuaded him that his testimony wouldn't amount to anything one way or the other, held out the bait of a job and a cash advance, and Briggs just simply faded from the picture. You can't blame him."

She stared at him with stricken eyes.

"But, Ken," she said, "that was your whole case."

"I know it," he told her, his face a mask.

"But what can you do? You got Dangerfield to surrender on the strength of that witness. Now you've lost him—and Amos Dangerfield is in jail."

He shrugged his shoulders.

"The fortunes of war," he said.

But his voice contained something which had been kept from the expression of his face, a cold, hard something.

"What can you do?" she asked.

"I can fight the devil with fire," he told her. "I started out to play a decent ethical game. They come along and pull this stunt. It's crooked. All right. Now let them watch out. I'll pull some fast ones myself."

She shook her head.

"I don't like that, Ken. You know they're laying for you. If they can get you suborning perjury or fixing a jury or anything like that, they'll railroad you right over the road."

"Yes," he said, tonelessly, "*if* they can, they will."

She stared at him.

"I found another witness," he went on in that same dispassionate tone of voice. "They won't get *him.* I've got him buried."

"Witness to what?" she asked, and her voice lacked enthusiasm. It was as though she doubted the testimony of this witness, even before hearing what it would be.

"Do you know," he said musingly, "that this mystery witness of theirs, this Bob Durane, must be the man that drove the death car. They're using him both as the man to pull the murder, and as the star witness for the prosecution."

"You mean the D. A. is?" she asked.

"Of course not. Don't be silly. The D. A. isn't in the thing. But he's got a political office, and he knows the side of the bread that has the butter. D. A.'s are human just the same as anybody else is human."

"Well," she said, "what you talking about then?"

"I'm talking about the gang that did this and want to make Dangerfield the fall guy. Briggs got a look at the face of one of the men who wheeled the car out. It had a scar on the cheek, and the man answers the description of this guy, Durane, who is the star witness for the prosecution."

"How you going to prove it with Briggs gone?" she asked.

He walked wearily across to his desk, picked up the receiver, and gave a number. After a moment he said: "Is Reed Nixon there? . . . Put him on, please. . . . Hello, Nixon? This is Corning. . . . Yeah. . . . Fine stuff. You've given me the breaks, now I'm going to give you one. . . . Yeah, I've got another witness. . . . Yeah. This one saw the whole thing. It's a fact. He's a taxicab driver. He was parked in a cab that was at the curb. He was sitting there with the lights out, waiting for the owl street car to come along. He figured he'd pick up the street car and trail it, hoping that one of the passengers who got off somewhere would give him a short run instead of walking for a few blocks in the dark.

"Well, he saw the car come, and then he saw the two machines, and he saw Copley get off the car, and saw the murder. But as the death car went by, the lights of the street lamps flashed in it for a second, and he saw the face of the man who was driving. He swears that he can identify that man if he sees him again. The man had on a light hat and a tweed suit, and there were other things about him that can be identified.

"You can spill that yarn all over the front page of your paper if you want. I've got this witness buried where he can't be found until I'm ready to produce him. I don't like the way the D. A.'s office messes around with my witnesses. I'm going to let him tell his story from the witness stand."

Ken Corning sat silent, grinning wearily into the transmitter, while the receiver made rasping metallic noises.

"Sure," he said at length, "use it as a rumor if you want to. I'd rather you made it seem it hadn't come directly from me. You

can label it as coming from 'a source close to the defendant.'
Yeah, that's the line. Okey. G'bye."

He slid the receiver back on the hook.

Helen Vail looked at him with hurt eyes.

"If you suborn perjury," she said, "and they can catch the
witness before he testifies and break him down, they can still
hook you for conspiracy or something, can't they, Ken?"

He said, his voice flat and weary, "Are you asking me for legal
advice, or just talking?"

"Neither," she snapped. "I'm trying to tell you something."

He shook his head.

"Go on home, kid. It's way after five o'clock. There's nothing
to stick around here for any more."

She put on her hat.

"Okey," she said. "I'm going to find where Briggs went and
make him come back."

He shook his head listlessly.

"Not a chance, kid; they're too slick for that. You won't find
even the ghost of a trail to follow."

She said: "I won't know until I try, will I?"

"Not if you won't listen to me," he said.

She started for the door, turned, walked back to the desk,
stood by him for a moment, and then patted his cheek.

" 'Night, Ken," she said tenderly.

" 'Night, kid."

She walked swiftly across the two offices, let herself out of the
outer door, and threw on the night latch.

Ken Corning sat at the desk, his eyes heavy, his chin resting on
his hand, elbow propped on the desk.

ROBERT DURANE was going out.

The two guards flanked him on either side. A uniformed police
officer stood at the door of the elevator. There was another one in
the lobby. At the doorway of the hotel a police car was parked at
the curb, four officers strung out between the car and the hotel
entrance.

The preparations would have indicated that a shipment of gold
was being moved from a bank.

A little crowd collected. The crowd became more congested.
The police started detouring the people out into the street, keeping them moving.

The door of the hotel swung open.

Robert Durane stepped out into the light of day. Cameras clicked as newshawks snapped pictures. The D. A.'s office had yielded to the pressure of the disgruntled ones who had been scooped by the *Star.*

Bob Durane looked worried. His head moved about, nervously. Plainly the crowd worried him. His eyes were cold and hard, but shifty. The scar on his cheek glowed lividly. The cheek seemed pale.

He looked towards the police car.

Two men sat in a roadster that had been parked at the curb just behind the police car. The top of the roadster was down, but the men had been apparently engrossed in their own affairs, and had attracted but little attention.

One of the men put on a cap.

It was the familiar cap of a taxicab operator. Now that the cap was on, it was apparent that his coat was also labeled with the insignia of the cab company.

Bob Durane moved across the stretch of sidewalk.

The motor in the roadster was purring steadily.

The man in the uniform of a taxi driver jumped to the seat of the roadster. He extended a long arm with a rigid, pointing finger. His voice sounded high above the noises of the street.

"That's him! That's the guy that drove the car!"

People stared. Bob Durane stopped abruptly. Two policemen pushed towards the roadster.

Ken Corning, seated in the driver's seat of the roadster, yelled: "Sit down and hang on!"

The spectators saw, then, that the roadster was one of those cars with a small wheelbase which can be handled swiftly in traffic. They also saw that it had been skilfully parked with the front wheels warped so that the car could make a fast getaway.

The motor roared into sudden life. The rear wheels spun for half a revolution, and then the car shot out from the curb. One of the officers blew his whistle.

Bob Durane turned back towards the hotel, then hesitated.

The police car lurched forward. One of the officers yelled something. Bob Durane was pushed forward. The door of the police machine opened. Bob Durane was shot inside. One of the officers jumped in after him. The door slammed. Another officer caught the running-board of the police car. The siren screamed as the car roared into motion.

Metal crashed into crumpled wreckage. The crash was slight, but it was followed with a grinding noise. A light roadster, un-painted, with rusty fenders and battered body, had swung in so that the front wheels of the police car had smashed into it.

Traffic was blocked.

The car with the cab driver gained the corner and turned with swaying springs.

The woman who had been driving the roadster climbed out, her face ghastly white, eyes wide. She screamed hysterically.

A frantic police officer tugged at her car. The driver of the police car threw his gears into reverse.

"What the hell you trying to do?" he bellowed.

Helen Vail, her face made pale with white powder, stared at him with feverishly bright eyes.

"You started the siren!" she said. "That means get over to the curb. I tried to get over and you smashed into me!"

The officer swore some more. The police car banged forward. More metal rasped and crumpled. The car was free. "All clear!" yelled the officer. The police car roared into motion. A crowd collected about the battered roadster.

"Oh, dear," said Helen Vail. "I must telephone!"

Officers pushed forward. The crowd opened to let Helen Vail slip through. The crowd closed in behind her, around the bat-tered car. Officers started taking charge.

"Where's the woman that was driving?" asked one.

"She went to telephone," said someone in the crowd.

The officers waited.

Helen Vail did not return.

After a while they moved the roadster. The police car that did the moving threw a tow rope on the machine and dragged it to the police garage.

Exactly fifty-nine minutes later, newsboys cried through the streets. The *Star* was running an "extra." "Read about it!" yelled the newsboys. *"State's star witness identified as driver of the mur-der car by taxi driver!"*

KEN CORNING sat in his office and grinned at Helen Vail.

"Good work, kid," he said.

She sighed.

"About one more narrow squeak like that and I'll be in the bug house."

"I told you," he said, "just to sort of get in the way and give me a chance to get to the corner. I didn't want you to try and stall the thing up for a week."

She grinned.

"That's just my way of doing things," she said. "I do 'em up brown. I figured that I could lock a bumper with them and make it take long enough for them to get loose to give you all the time you wanted. Did you have it?"

"Yes. I never even heard their car from the time I rounded the corner. It was a cinch."

"What happened?" she asked.

He shrugged his shoulders.

"It hasn't happened yet, unless . . ."

He broke off as the telephone rang. He scooped the receiver to his ear. He said: "Hello," and the receiver started in making metallic squawks.

Ken Corning listened. As he listened, a grin spread over his face.

"Okey," he said, "thanks for the buggy ride. . . . Hell's bells, you reporters want to know everything. . . . Well, son, that's a little secret. You can state from me that the witness doesn't want the notoriety, and he's just a little afraid something might happen to him. When he goes for a ride he wants to be sitting at the wheel. Yeah. . . . G'bye."

He hung up the receiver, turned to Helen Vail.

"Nixon, of the *Star,*" he said. "Just called me to tell me that the case against Dangerfield had blown up. The star witness for the prosecution, Bob Durane, skipped out. They can't find him anywhere. He gave his bodyguard the slip, and has utterly vanished. The D. A. announces that, under the circumstances, he won't go farther with the case until additional evidence is uncovered."

"What evidence?" she asked.

"Nixon wants me to produce my mystery witness and insists on an indictment for Durane."

She looked at him fixedly.

"You going to do it?"

He grinned.

"Do I look crazy? It ain't any crime to have a guy stand up in a roadster and yell: 'That's him!' but when he walks in front of a grand jury and takes an oath and says the same thing, it's likely to be something pretty serious."

She said: "Is that why . . . ?"

He nodded.

"That's why I didn't dare to let them catch up with us. I said I was going to pull a fast one, and I had to do it fast. It was a close call—but we made it."

She said: "Will they ever try Durane for the murder?"

He grinned at her.

"Don't be silly," he said. "That's one position the District Attorney could never afford to get trapped in."

"Was that fellow really a taxi driver?" she asked him.

He lit a cigarette.

"You're getting worse than the reporters," he said.

Making the Breaks

THE desk was piled high with law books. On a space which had been cleared in one corner was an electric coffee percolator bubbling steadily. An electric clock on a bookcase showed the time as two o'clock in the morning.

Ken Corning sipped black coffee from a cup which he held in his left hand. His eyes moved steadily down the printed text of a volume of the *Atlantic Reporter*. From time to time he made notes with a pencil.

The outer door gave forth rasping noises as a key was inserted into the lock. Then the door swung inward, and Helen Vail, Ken Corning's secretary, walked across the outer office, stood in the doorway of the inner office, and surveyed the man at the desk with anxious, sympathetic eyes.

After a moment Ken Corning felt her presence, and looked up, scowling impatiently. The scowl changed to a tired smile. His eyes went swiftly to the windows, then back to the face of the clock.

"Thought it must be morning," he said, "and you were coming to work."

"No, it's two o'clock. I was out at a cabaret, and ditched the party."

"Why did you do that?" he asked.

Something in her face showed him that her visit was not at all casual, and that her eyes were anxious.

"Go ahead," he said. "What is it?"

Helen Vail crossed the room to the side of his desk, pushed back a stacked pile of leather-bound law books, and rested one hip against the side of the desk, swinging one foot, the other foot braced on the floor.

"I don't know, chief," she said, "what it is."

107

He looked at her, frowning. She slowly opened her purse and took out two one-hundred-dollar bills, which she placed on the desk in front of him.

He looked at them curiously.

"Been robbing a bank?" he asked.

She shook her head. "They were in my purse," she told him.

"So I saw."

"But," she said, "I don't know how they got there."

"Don't know what?"

"Don't know how they got there."

"What do you mean?"

"Just what I say. I was down at the cabaret, and a purse snatcher tried to grab my purse. One of the men in the party hit him on the jaw and knocked him down. A special detective ran up and there was quite a commotion. An officer came in, and there was a plainclothesman there in the cabaret. They recognized the purse snatcher as an old hand at the game, and arrested him. They wanted me to look in my purse and see if he'd taken anything. I told them it was impossible because he hadn't even had the purse in his hands. He'd simply made a grab at it, but I kept hold of the purse."

Ken Corning's eyes were level-lidded with intense thought. His pupils were contracted until they seemed mere black needle points in the midst of a cold background.

"Go on," he said.

"They looked in the purse."

"Then what?"

"Nothing, except these hundred-dollar-bills were in there."

"Did you say anything?" he inquired.

"No. Naturally I didn't speak up and tell them that I didn't know where this money came from."

"Why?"

"It was none of their business."

"When did you look in your purse last?"

"You mean before the purse snatcher?"

"Yes."

"I don't know. I got out my compact some time during the first part of the evening and put my mouth on straight. I don't know just when it was."

"Were the bills there then?" asked Ken Corning.

"I don't think so, chief. They might have been there, and I didn't notice them. But I don't think so."

Ken Corning picked up the bills again and studied them carefully. He pushed back his swivel-chair, got to his feet, and stood for a moment, staring down at the desk. Then he swung about and started to pace the floor restlessly.

Helen Vail looked at the money, then at him.

"Is it serious?" she asked. "Does it mean anything?"

"I think so," he told her.

Suddenly he whirled, strode to the desk, picked up the bills, looked at them once more, and then threw them down on the blotter.

"All right, kid," he said quietly, "we're framed."

"What do you mean, chief?"

THERE was a peremptory pounding on the outer door of the office. Helen Vail reached hastily for the two one-hundred-dollar bills.

"That's all right," said Corning. "Leave them there. Sit where you are."

He strode across the office, to the outer door, and jerked it open. Three men stood on the threshold. The tallest of the three pushed his way forward, grinning.

"Hello, Corning," he said.

"Hello, Malone," Corning replied. "What do you want?"

"Is your secretary here?" asked Malone.

Corning nodded. "She just came in," he said.

"We want to see her," said Malone.

Corning nodded.

"Come in," he said. "I want to see you. There's something funny here."

"What's funny?"

"A purse snatcher made a grab at her purse down in a cabaret."

"We know that," Malone said.

"He didn't take anything out," said Ken Corning. "He put something in."

"What do you mean?"

"He put some money in—two one-hundred-dollar bills."

Malone laughed mirthlessly.

"Show me," he said.

Ken Corning led the way to the inner office. Malone nodded curtly to Helen Vail, then walked over to the desk and stood staring down at the two one-hundred-dollar bills.

"This the stuff?" he asked.

Ken Corning nodded.

Malone reached forward and picked up the bills, then looked shrewdly at Helen Vail.

"Where did you get these?" he asked.

"I don't know," she said.

Once more Malone laughed, that mirthless laugh of his.

"Look around, boys," he told them.

"What the hell do you mean, look around?" Ken Corning demanded.

"Just what I say," said Frank Malone. "We're going to search the office."

"Got a warrant?" asked Corning ominously.

"Certainly not. Do we need one?"

"You need one," said Ken Corning.

Malone turned to grin at the two men who stood back of him.

"Okey, boys," he said, "we won't search. We need a warrant."

"Wait a minute," Corning told him, "I think I'll change my mind on that."

"Too late now," Malone told him.

"What kind of deal is this?" Corning demanded.

"Suppose you tell me," Malone replied.

"What are you driving at?"

"You know what I'm driving at. Those two one-hundred-dollar bills were taken from Samuel Grosbeck."

"You're crazy!" Corning said.

"No, we're not crazy. We've got the numbers of the bills. You should know that."

"I tell you," said Corning, "the bills were planted in the young lady's purse."

"Sure," said Malone, soothingly, "you told me that before, Corning."

Malone leaned forward, and copied the numbers on the bills into a leather-backed notebook. He took a fountain pen from his pocket and wrote his initials in small letters on the corners of the currency.

"All right," he said, "that's all we can do here. He won't let us search the office without a warrant."

"I said you could search," Corning replied.

"We didn't hear you except the first time," said Malone. "You've had a chance to ditch any of the stuff now anyway. Come on, boys, let's go."

Ken Corning strode rapidly across the room, and stood between Malone and the door.

"Malone," he said, "you can't get by with this."

Malone pushed forward and past Corning.

"I'm not getting by with anything," he said. "Because I'm not trying anything. Don't lose those bills. They're evidence."

The three men walked wordlessly across the outer office, pushed open the door, and went out into the corridor. The door swung shut, and a latch clicked mechanically.

HELEN VAIL left her position on the desk, where she had remained during the interview, and crossed to Ken Corning. She put her hand on his arm and stared up at him with wide frightened eyes.

"What is it, chief?" she asked.

"A frame-up," he told her. "A dirty frame-up!"

"But what?"

Ken Corning walked back to the desk, sat down in the swivel-chair, stared at the bills, then looked moodily at her.

"Samuel Grosbeck," he said, "had something like fifteen hundred dollars on him in one-hundred-dollar bills when he was murdered. He'd received the bills from his bank. They were new bills, and the bank happens to have the number sequence."

"But why should they plant them on me?" asked Helen Vail.

"Because you're working for me, and because I'm defending Fred Parkett."

"I don't understand."

"It's simple," he told her. "Grosbeck and a chap named Stanwood were sitting in a car parked near the curb. A hold-up man who limped, carried a cane, wore an overcoat and a cap, told them to throw up their hands. Stanwood put up his hands. Grosbeck didn't, or was slow about it, and got the contents of an automatic emptied into his vest. He died right then.

"The hold-up man went through his clothes and took a wallet; also a brown manila envelope. We don't know what was in the manila envelope. There was fifteen hundred dollars in cash in the wallet. The hold-up man ran as fast as he could with his game

leg, and turned at the corner. Stanwood found Grosbeck was
dead, managed to get to a telephone, and notified the police. The
police broadcast the call over the shortwave radio to all cars, and
Dick Carr, the detective, was the first on the spot. He cruised
around and picked up Fred Parkett.

"Parkett wore an overcoat, a cap, carried a cane, and limped.
He's a crook with a criminal record a yard long. He didn't have a
gun; he didn't have any money on him, and he claimed he hadn't
been near the car in which Grosbeck was killed. He was picked
up within six blocks of the place, however, and Stanwood identified him as being the murderer. Two other fellows, Arthur
Longwell and Jim Monteith, positively identified him as the man
they saw running within a block of the scene of the murder.

"I'm defending Parkett. It looks as though he might beat the
case if we can break down the identification. The District Attorney knows I'm planning a big fight. He doesn't know just what
kind of fight it is."

Helen Vail nodded her head impatiently.

"Of course," she said, "I know all about that. But . . ."

She broke off, gasped and stared at Ken Corning with eyes that
were dark with alarm.

"Do you mean that the District Attorney's office is going to
claim that Parkett paid you a retainer in money that he had
taken from the murdered man, and that you gave me a cut out of
it?"

"Exactly," he told her.

"Then the bills were planted earlier in the evening."

He nodded.

"But," she said, "where would they get the bills to plant? The
man who planted them must have been the murderer."

"He must have known the murderer," Corning told her. "It
looks like a frame-up and a tip-off. Somebody who was anxious
to have Parkett convicted planted the evidence and then tipped
off the police that they'd find it."

"And that's the reason the purse snatcher tried to grab my
purse?"

"Yes. You can see how they worked it," Corning said. "The
purse snatcher planted the money in your purse earlier in the
evening. Then he made a grab at the purse, and did it so clumsily
that he was caught and knocked down. The plainclothesman
may, or may not, have been a plant. He wanted to look into your

purse. You looked in and saw the two one-hundred-dollar bills. They figured you wouldn't say anything about them, but would come to me. They tipped off Malone to come up here and look in your purse."

"Why did he pull that stuff about a search warrant?" she asked.

"I walked into that," he told her. "The fact that I wouldn't let them search the office without a warrant suggests that I had something to conceal. It's simply one more thing to explain."

"What are you going to do?"

He stared down at the two one-hundred-dollar bills on the blotter.

"Did you hear the name of the purse snatcher who was arrested?" he asked.

"Yes. It was Oscar Lane."

"All right," he told her. "I'll take care of that. Leave the money here. Now here's something I want you to do. This murder was committed on December ninth, at 10:15 p.m. I think Stanwood is on the square. He identifies Parkett simply because Parkett wore an overcoat and a cap, had a limp, and carried a cane. I don't think he ever saw the face of the man who fired the shot; not clearly, anyway. But he's been over it so many times with the detectives and the District Attorney's staff that he thinks he remembers the man's face."

"How about these two men, Longwell and Monteith, who identify Parkett so positively?" she asked.

"I'm coming to those two," he said. "I think they're professional witnesses."

"How do you mean?"

"I think they were planted. I don't think they were within a mile of the place at that time."

"You mean the police planted them?"

"I mean," he said, "that somebody planted them. They are simply in the case to convict Parkett. I don't know why, or who's back of them, but I do know this: they've got girl friends. I've had detectives look that up. There's a girl named Mabel Fosdick, and one named Edith Laverne.

"They live in the same apartment house, the *Monadnock,* and they work in the same office—the Streeter Finance Corporation. I want you to go to the *Monadnock Apartments,* take an apartment there, and get acquainted with those two girls. You'll have to work fast. I want you to find out if they were out with Longwell and Monteith on the night of December ninth. There's a chance that they were together as a foursome, or a chance that one of the men may have been with one of the women."

"And this case comes up tomorrow?" she asked.

He looked at the clock and grinned. "Today," he told her.

"Aren't you going to get some sleep?" she inquired solicitously.

He shook his head and motioned towards the door. He was drawing a fresh cup of coffee from the percolator as she stood in the doorway, raised her hand in a mock military salute, and vanished.

IT was late in the afternoon when Ken Corning came in from court, carrying his brief case and two books under his arm.

"I haven't heard anything," she said, "about the money."

"You won't," Corning told her. "They'll save that for the last."

"Then they'll call you as a witness?" she inquired.

He shook his head, smiling. "No," he told her, "they'll let the story leak out to the newspapers."

"I thought the jurors weren't supposed to read the newspapers."

He looked at her and grinned, but said nothing. After a moment, he set the brief case and law books on her desk, and lowered his voice.

"Get anything on the two women?" he asked.

"I've moved out there and talked with one of them a little while this morning, just casually. How much time have I got, chief?"

"The case will last about a week."

"How does it look?"

"Bad," he told her. "And yet I think Parkett's innocent. His story sounds like it. Usually a guilty man tries to conceal something. This man doesn't. He says that he was walking along the sidewalk when the officers picked him up. That he'd been moving right along. He admits that he was on the prowl, but he says he didn't have a rod with him."

"What do the officers say?"

"They didn't find a gun. They didn't find anything else."

"How did they know he was there?"

"They just picked him up. But Parkett says that Dick Carr, the detective, cruised past him in a radio car but didn't see him. After he had gone, Parkett kept on his prowl, looking for something easy. About twenty minutes afterwards the police closed up the district, and Carr picked him up."

"You think it's a frame-up?" she inquired.

"He's either guilty," he told her slowly, "or else it's a deliberate frame-up."

They were silent for a moment. Helen Vail knew the political background of York City well enough to realize that it was readily possible to frame a man for murder. Ken Corning had been there for less than a year. During that time he had fought the crooked politicians who controlled the municipal affairs. Gradually he had made a name for himself, and his reputation had brought him business. That reputation had been founded upon but one thing—his ability as a fighter. He asked for no quarter and gave none.

The door of the outer office opened, and a man of about fifty-five, with keen, wary eyes and tight lips, walked into the room. He looked at Ken Corning, then at Helen Vail, then back at Ken Corning.

"Mr. Corning," he asked, "the lawyer?"

Ken Corning nodded, stood to one side, and indicated the door to his private office. The man walked with quick, purposeful strides across the room.

"What name?" asked Helen Vail.

The man flashed her a single swift glance and said: "B. W. Flint."

Helen Vail made a note with her pencil in the day book in which she listed the people who called.

Ken Corning followed his visitor into the private office, and closed the door.

Flint turned on him.

"You're the attorney representing Fred Parkett."

The man's restless eyes flashed swiftly over Ken Corning in shrewd appraisal.

"I came," he said, "to help you and your client."

Corning nodded, indicated a chair, walked to the swivel-chair back of his desk and sat down. Then Flint leaned forward and lowered his voice.

"When Parkett went through Grosbeck's clothes," he said, "he found some money, and he found a brown manila envelope that was sealed."

Ken Corning shook his head patiently. "The trouble with that is," he said, "that Parkett wasn't there at all."

"It might make it better for him if he *was* there," Flint said quietly.

"Now what does that mean?" Corning wanted to know.

"It means simply," said Flint, "that if you could get your client to tell you just what he did with that manila envelope that was taken from Grosbeck's pocket, and could produce that manila envelope and turn it over to me, your client might get immunity."

"If Parkett shows up with that envelope, it would be pretty good evidence that he committed the murder."

Flint made an impatient gesture. "Let's put it this way," he said. "If Parkett committed that murder, it's a cinch he's got the envelope."

"All right," Corning remarked. "It's the same in either event. When he surrenders the envelope, it means that he's convicted himself of murder. And yet you say he can get immunity. I'm just mentioning this thing so you can see how foolish your proposition is, and what a sucker I'd be even to listen to it."

Flint got to his feet and stared intently at the lawyer.

"I think we understand each other all right, Mr. Corning," he said.

"Where can I meet you, say, some time tonight, about nine o'clock?"

"I could come to your office."

"Not quite so hot," said Ken Corning. "Pick out some place where I can meet you."

"*The Columbino* is a good place," Flint told him. "I'll be there, dining. You can meet me there."

"You'll be alone?" asked Corning.

"Of course."

"Do you know what was in the envelope?" asked Corning.

Flint hesitated a moment, then shook his head.

"No," he said, "I don't. The people who are working with me do."

"And who are those people?" Corning asked in a tone of voice which showed he hardly expected a reply, but was asking the question mechanically.

Flint smiled. "Those people," he said carefully, "are big enough to get immunity for Fred Parkett."

"Well," Corning said, "that sounds reasonable."

Flint smiled. "You mean," he said, "it sounds hopeful."

"Nine o'clock tonight," said Corning, pushing back his chair.

Flint nodded, hesitated for a moment, half extended his hand, then turned and walked out of the door.

"At *The Columbino*," he called over his shoulder, and closed the door behind him.

Ken Corning heard his quick steps as he crossed the outer office, then the click of the outer door opening and closing.

Corning walked swiftly to his outer office.

"Whom do I charge that call to, and how much is the charge?" asked Helen Vail, indicating the name of B. W. Flint, which she had written in her day book.

"I think we'll charge it to experience," said Corning. "Could you write a good love letter?"

"How do you mean?"

"I mean a nice love letter. Spread it on pretty thick."

"Whom do I write to?"

"To Samuel Grosbeck," he said. "You can start it: 'My dearest, dearest Sammy,' and go on from there."

"What do you want to do with it?"

"I want to put it in a brown manila envelope, seal it up, and hand it to the man who was just in here. I want to see if he knows enough about the stuff he wants, to know that the love letter isn't it."

"What will he do when he gets it?" she asked.

"That," Corning told her, "is one of the things I want to find out. Make it fairly long. I want the envelope to be pretty bulky. You can sign it any name you want."

STEPPING purposefully from his car, Ken Corning strode up the cement walk, climbed the four steps to the porch and jabbed his finger against the doorbell.

Steps sounded on the inside of the house, and a sad-faced woman opened the door and looked at him lugubriously.

"Is Mr. Jason home?" asked Corning.

"What do you want?" she inquired, without answering his question.

"My name is Corning," he told her, "and I want to see Mr. Jason on a matter of business."

"He's eating his dinner now."

"I'll wait until he finishes."

She stood staring at him for a moment, then moved silently to one side.

"Come in," she invited.

Corning walked into the hallway, and the woman marched flat-footedly into a room which opened on the left. She indicated a chair. "Sit down," she said.

Ken Corning dropped into the chair and waited. The house was not large, and the odor of cooked food penetrated to the room where he sat. The dining-room was evidently next to it. Corning heard a chair scrape back. He got to his feet as a tall, slender man with a bald head came into the room.

"Jason?" he asked.

The man nodded.

"I'm Corning, attorney for Fred Parkett."

The man's face suddenly lit up with some swift flicker of expression which was instantly subdued. He nodded.

"I've read about the case in the papers," he said.

"You were foreman of the Grand Jury which indicted Parkett, I believe," said Corning.

"I read about the case in the papers," Jason repeated.

"I suppose that means you're not going to talk about the Grand Jury business."

"Not necessarily," said Jason. "There's no reason why I shouldn't, and," he added after a moment's pause, "there's no particular reason why I should."

"The shooting," said Corning, "took place right across the street. If you'd been home, you'd probably have been a witness."

"But," said Jason, "I wasn't home."

"Rather a peculiar thing," Corning told him, "that the shooting should have been in this neighborhood, and you should have been foreman of the Grand Jury which indicted a man for murder."

"Murders," Jason said, "have been committed in all parts of the city. I don't know that there's any reason a man can't be held up in this neighborhood simply because I happen to be on the Grand Jury."

"The evidence," persisted Corning, "shows that Grosbeck and

Harry Stanwood were driving in an automobile. Stanwood is a little bit hazy as to just why they happened to stop here. They had been sitting in the car for some fifteen or twenty minutes before the holdup, and, as I have said, the car was directly across the street from this house."

"As I remember the evidence that was introduced before the Grand Jury," Jason said, "that's an accurate statement."

"Has it ever occurred to you," asked Corning, "that there might have been a reason that the killing took place in this neighborhood?"

"How do you mean?"

"I mean has it ever occurred to you that the murder might have been committed here *because* you were foreman of the Grand Jury?"

"What would that have to do with it?"

"It may have been that Grosbeck wanted to see you, and was waiting across the street for you to come home so that he could see you as soon as you arrived."

"What makes you think that?" Jason inquired with mild curiosity.

"Because it is very possible it was so. Have you any reason to believe that Grosbeck was waiting in this neighborhood to see you?"

"No."

"Do you know why Grosbeck was there?"

"No."

"Do you know anything about Grosbeck?"

"No."

"Had you ever met him, or talked with him before the murder?"

"No."

"How long after the murder did you come home?"

"It must have been fifteen or twenty minutes."

"Did you hear Stanwood telling the officers what had happened?"

"You mean after I came home on the night of the murder?"

"Yes."

"No, I heard nothing. My wife told me about what had happened. She heard the sound of the shot. She was in bed. She thought at first it was a truck that had backfired. That's all I know about it."

"Did she hear the murderer running away?" asked Corning.

"You mean his steps on the pavement?"

"Yes."

"No. I think she heard the men who ran towards the car after Mr. Stanwood raised the alarm."

"If," said Corning, "she heard the steps of the murderer running away from the scene of the crime, she could have told, from the sound of the steps, whether or not the man was lame, couldn't she?"

"Perhaps; but she didn't hear any steps. I'm afraid she can't help you as a witness, Mr. Corning. I've talked the matter over with her in great detail. She knows nothing that would help your client."

"Does she know anything that would hurt him?" Corning asked.

"No. She heard the shot, that's all."

Ken Corning said: "Thank you. I'm sorry I disturbed you," and pushed his way through the door.

THE COLUMBINO was a cabaret where fairly good liquor could be obtained. An orchestra played dance music, and a half-dozen entertainers put on a varied vaudeville program between dances. B. W. Flint sat alone at a table, eating slowly, pausing from time to time to stare at the dancers or watch the entertainers.

Ken Corning stood by the hat-check stand, and watched Flint for a few minutes. He tried to find if Flint exchanged any signals or significant glances with anyone else in the room.

After his inspection had yielded him nothing, Ken Corning walked into the cabaret, and moved over to Flint's table.

Flint looked at him with keenly appraising eyes, and a face which showed no expression whatever, either of hope or surprise.

Ken Corning dropped into the chair across the table.

"Well?" asked Flint.

Ken Corning reached into his pocket and took out a sealed manila envelope. His eyes were fastened on Flint's face as he pulled the envelope into sight.

Flint looked at the envelope just as he had looked at Ken Corning, without any particular expression.

Ken Corning toyed with the envelope.

"What assurance have I," he asked, "that if I do what you want, you can do what you said you would?"

Flint's answer was prompt and pointed. "You haven't any assurance," he said, "except my word."

"But I don't know you," said Corning.

"Exactly," Flint said.

Corning studied the smoke which eddied upward from his cigarette.

"Suppose you should double-cross me?" he asked.

"How could I double-cross you?"

"That's easy enough. You could use the contents of that envelope to trap my client."

"If I wanted to double-cross you," said Flint, "I would have had detectives stationed around here. I would have given them a signal as soon as I found out you had the envelope, and they would grab you and take the envelope from *your* possession. After you pass it over to me, I have no way of connecting it with you or your client except by my testimony, and your word is as good as mine."

"If no one sees me when I hand it to you," said Corning.

"Well, no one needs to see."

"All right," said Corning. "That sounds reasonable. I'll go out and get in a taxicab and wait. You go straight down the street for two blocks and wait at the corner. I'll follow you and get out. You get in the same taxicab, look under the seat cushion, and you'll find the envelope."

"You're going to a lot of unnecessary trouble," Flint told him. "You could hand it to me here, under the table."

"No, I'd rather have it that way," said Corning.

Flint shrugged his shoulders.

"Wait until I can get my waiter and pay my check."

Ken Corning walked from the cabaret, found a taxi at the door and sat in it until he saw Flint leave the cabaret and walk swiftly down the street.

"Cruise along behind that man," he told the driver.

As the cab ground into slow motion, Ken Corning pulled the manila envelope from his pocket and slipped it under the cushions of the seat. He kept peering about, to make certain that no one was following Flint. At the corner of the second block, Flint stopped. Corning tapped on the glass and handed the driver a dollar bill.

"I'm leaving you here, buddy," he said. "That man waiting there at the corner is going to signal you."

The cab driver turned to flash Corning a single suspicious glance, but pocketed the dollar bill and grinned as he pulled into the curb. Corning stepped out of the cab without looking at Flint, turned and walked rapidly back towards *The Columbino.* Flint raised his arm and signaled the cab.

Ken Corning's roadster was parked at the curb, facing the direction in which the cab was headed. He climbed into the roadster as Flint was entering the cab, and stepped on the starter. As the cab swung out into the middle of the street, Ken Corning snapped home the gearshift and eased in the clutch. His roadster purred into traffic behind the taxicab.

Following the taxicab was an easy matter. Flint was evidently in a hurry, and had instructed the cab driver to step on it. The cab went at high speed straight down the boulevard, turned to the left, roared into speed again, and slowed as it came to the neighborhood in which the murder of Samuel Grosbeck had been committed.

Ken Corning slowed his car, switched out the lights, and pulled in close to the curb. The taxicab ahead of him swung abruptly to the right, came to a stop. Flint got out, paid off the driver, and ran across the sidewalk, up the steps which led to a porch, then across the porch.

The residence was that of Edward Jason, the foreman of the Grand Jury.

Ken Corning sat in the roadster and smoked for some fifteen minutes. At the end of that time, Flint had not left the house. Corning stepped on the starter, tossed away his cigarette and drove back to his office.

JANGLING peals of the telephone bell greeted Ken Corning as he fitted his latch-key to the door of the office. He hurried across the room, scooped the receiver to his ear and said: "Hello."

Helen Vail's voice was guarded.

"Chief," she said, "I've been trying to catch you for an hour."

"Something important?" he asked.

"Yes. I wonder if you can come over."

"Where are you?"

"At the *Monadnock,*" she said. "I've got apartment 318."

"All right," he told her. "I've got one more job to do before I get there. It'll be about half an hour."

"I'll be waiting," she told him. "Don't knock, just walk right in."

Corning took the elevator to the street and walked three blocks to an office building. On the seventh floor he entered the offices of the Intercoastal Detective Agency.

He gave his name to a young woman at the switchboard and asked for Tom Dunton.

"Third door on the left," she said. "The last office."

Corning opened the door, walked along the corridor, and entered a small office barely large enough to contain a desk and two chairs. A man of about fifty, with broad shoulders, got to his feet and extended his hand.

"Hello, Corning. Haven't seen you for a long while."

Corning shook hands, sat down, and started in talking business.

"A man named Oscar Lane," he said, "arrested for purse snatching. Bail has been fixed in the sum of five hundred dollars cash or one-thousand-dollar bond. No one has bailed him out. He's in jail."

"All right," said Dunton. "What can we do?"

"Bail him out," said Corning.

He took a wallet from his coat pocket and counted out currency. When he had finished, he pushed the pile across to Dunton. Dunton picked it up and counted it, then reached for a receipt book.

"Five hundred dollars," he said. "Who do we say is putting it up?"

"Take some name that sounds like an alias—John Jones or Sam Black, or something like that. Get a man who looks a little seedy to go in and put up the bail. He'll say that Lane is a friend of his."

"And then, what?"

"After you get him out on bail, I want him shadowed. I want to know where he goes and with whom he talks. Put enough men on the job to keep him under constant surveillance. Don't let him get away no matter what happens."

"Sometimes you can't help it," Dunton told him. "You know that. A man can always give an operative the slip."

"This is one of the times you've *got* to help it," Corning told him.

"We'll do the best we can," Dunton said.

Corning took the receipt, folded it, pushed it into his pocket, and turned to the door.

"How's the Fred Parkett case coming?" asked Dunton. "Going to get him off?"

"Maybe."

"They say it's a cinch he's going to be convicted. Some of the wise guys were telling me there was nothing to it. I told them that any case you were handling was loaded with dynamite for the prosecution. I offered to bet even money that you get him off. Was it a good bet?"

Ken Corning narrowed his eyes and looked at Tom Dunton.

"If Oscar Lane," he said, "gets out of jail and gets in touch with Dick Carr, a detective, go ahead and bet all the money you can get."

"Are you telling me this so that I'll be sure to keep Lane shadowed?" asked Dunton, grinning.

"I'm telling you that so you can win some money," Corning told him, and walked out of the office.

KEN CORNING pushed his way into apartment 318.

Helen Vail was stretched out in an overstuffed chair, with her feet on a davenport. She seemed very much at ease.

Ken Corning looked around the apartment. "Something's wrong with you," he said.

"What's wrong? Haven't I done what you told me to?"

"That's just the trouble," he said. "You haven't cut any corners yet."

"I know when to cut corners and when to do just what I'm told," she said. "Any time I've disregarded instructions it's worked out all right."

"Any time it doesn't, you're canned," he told her. "What's the dirt?"

"Mabel Fosdick's checking out," she said. "She's going somewhere. I think she's leaving for good."

"Know where she's going?"

"It's some place out of the state. I don't know just where. She's not supposed to tell anybody."

"How about the other girl, Edith Laverne?"

"She's staying here apparently."

"Thought the girls had jobs here."

"They have. But Mabel Fosdick had something offered her that will take her out of the state. She's packing up and intends to get out a little after midnight."

"What kind of girls are they?" asked Corning.

"Mabel Fosdick is on the square. I'd trust her," said Helen Vail. "The Laverne woman is different. She's one of those mealy mouthed women who are always worrying about their reputations, and all that stuff. Mabel Fosdick is right out in the open with everything she does."

"You think it's unexpected, this business of Mabel Fosdick's getting out?"

"Yes, I'm certain it is. I was commencing to get friendly with her."

"Has some man been calling here this evening?"

"Not that I know of."

"She's mysterious about it?"

"Yes, whatever it is. It's some job that has been given her, and she's been told not to say anything about what it is, or where it's going to take her."

"What's Mabel Fosdick going to do with her furniture? Is she going to take it with her?"

"The apartment's furnished. All she's got is her personal belongings. She has a big trunk, a small trunk, two or three suit-cases, and a hat box."

"You've been up there?"

"I helped her pack."

"Good girl."

"I can tell you something else—she keeps a diary."

"Now," said Ken Corning, "you're getting somewhere. That diary is what I want. Could you get a chance to look in it?"

"No, it's one of the kind that are locked and have a key. She was right there all the time and I didn't have a chance to get it."

"Where is it, in one of the suit-cases?"

"Yes."

Ken Corning looked at his watch.

"Okey," he said. "You took the apartment under an assumed name?"

"Sure."

"All right. You'd better vanish."

"What are you intending to do?"

"I don't know. What's the number of Mabel Fosdick's apartment?"

"Four nineteen. It's on the floor above."

"She's in there now?"

"Yes."

"Do you know if she's got her tickets purchased?"

"I think her tickets have been sent to her."

"What does she look like?" asked Corning.

"She's about as tall as I am; about twenty-four or twenty-five years old. She's got a gray coat with a fur collar. She's a brunette, and runs pretty heavy to lipstick. But she's a good kid and she looks it. Trim and pretty, but not loud."

"How about your clothes?" asked Corning. "Have you everything so you can put it in one suit-case?"

"Sure. That's what you told me to do."

"Okey, kid. Get that suit-case packed, and beat it. Leave me the key. I'm going up and stick around on the upper floor for a little while."

"Promise me you won't get into trouble," she said.

He smiled at her, shook his head, and walked out.

Ken Corning climbed the stairs to the floor above, spotted apartment 419, took up his station at the end of the corridor, and waited.

He waited less than five minutes when the door of the apartment opened and a trim, well-dressed young woman stepped into the corridor, pulled the door closed behind her and walked swiftly to the elevator.

Corning waited until he heard the door of the elevator cage slam shut, then moved down the corridor and bent over the lock on the door of the apartment. His third skeleton key clicked back the bolt, and he walked in.

The apartment was similar to the one occupied by Helen Vail. Baggage was stacked up in a neat pile, as though awaiting the call of a transfer man.

Corning started in on the suit-cases, and found the diary packed in the first. He made no attempt to examine the diary there, but closed up the suit-case, took the diary with him, and went back to Helen Vail's apartment. Helen Vail had gone.

Corning picked the lock on the diary, sat down and read it carefully. When he had finished reading, he put it into his pocket and went back to Mabel Fosdick's apartment and knocked on the door. There was no answer. He knocked again, and then when there still was no answer, once more opened the door and stepped into the apartment.

The baggage was gone.

Ken Corning looked at his watch, nodded and went back to Helen Vail's apartment. He put in ten minutes making certain that there was nothing left in the place which could identify Helen Vail as the tenant who had kept it for so short a time. When he had finished, he left the key on the table, walked out of the apartment, and pulled the door shut after him. The spring lock clicked into place.

THE midnight train was clicking over the switches when Ken Corning approached the slim girl in the gray coat with the fur collar.

"Miss Fosdick?" he asked.

She looked up at him speculatively, and nodded coolly.

Ken Corning said: "I want to get a little information from you. It's a matter of some importance. Do you remember the night that you went to the hockey game with Arthur Longwell, Jim Monteith and Edith Laverne?"

She spoke in a cool, collected voice. "May I ask just what business it is of yours?"

"It happens," he said, "that it's rather important. If you don't answer it might interfere with your trip."

"You're a detective?"

"I'm simply telling you that it might interfere with your trip."

She sighed. "Yes," she said, "I remember the occasion."

"Do you remember the teams that were playing?"

"Yes."

"Do you remember the date?"

"I'm not certain that I do. It was some time in the winter—in December, I think."

"Do you remember which team won, and the score?"

"Yes."

"Do you suppose it was on the ninth of December?"

"I'm sure I couldn't tell."

"Could you tell if you consulted your diary?"

She gave a little convulsive start and stared at him.

"Yes," she said, "I think so. Why?"

Ken Corning reached into his pocket and pulled out her diary.

She gasped. "Why, what are you doing with that? That's mine. You've no business taking that! You must have stolen it from my suit-case!"

"We'll talk about that a little later," he told her. "Let's look at the date in the diary and see if you can tell exactly what evening that trip took place."

She didn't open the book, but stared at him with blazing eyes.

"You had no business to read my diary," she said.

Ken Corning planted his feet wide apart, braced his body against the swaying motion of the train, and stared down at her.

"All right," he said. "Now I'm going to tell you something. Samuel Grosbeck was murdered on the night of December ninth. Fred Parkett is being tried for that murder. Jim Monteith and Authur Longwell are going to swear that they were in the vicinity and saw a man running away; that they recognized the man as the defendant, Fred Parkett; that the date was December ninth, and the hour was 10:30 p.m.

"Those men weren't there at the time. They're simply giving testimony to help convict the defendant. They knew that you could give evidence that the four of you were sitting in a box at the rink at the very moment the two men claimed to have been near the scene where Grosbeck was murdered. As a result, they're getting you out of the state."

She stared at him with an agony of conflicting expressions on her countenance.

"In fact," said Corning, "you have wondered somewhat about this position and why it was offered to you. You have known generally that Longwell and Monteith were going to be witnesses in this murder case. You haven't taken the trouble to check back and find out the date and time of the murder, and then consult your diary. I suggest that you do so now."

"They wouldn't do anything like that," she said. "They couldn't. They're not that type."

By way of answer, Ken Corning opened the diary to the date of December ninth, and pushed the open volume into her lap.

"Read it," he said. "You don't even need to rely on the diary for it. If you remember the hockey game, the records show that it took place on that particular date, and that it wasn't over until eleven fifteen—more than an hour after the time the two men swear they were at the scene of the murder."

* * *

HIS eyes red and swollen from loss of sleep, Ken Corning propped his elbow against the side of the telephone booth, and wearily closed his eyes as he listened to the squawking noises which came over the receiver.

"Did you cover the rooming-house," he asked, "where you say Lane went?"

Tom Dunton's voice showed a trace of impatience.

"Of course we covered the rooming-house," he said. "We checked every man and every woman who went in there, and shadowed them when they went out."

"And you're sure Dick Carr wasn't one of the people who went in?" asked Corning.

"Hell!" said Dunton explosively. "I guess I know Dick Carr when I see him, don't I? I tell you, Dick Carr didn't come near the place, and, as nearly as I can find out, there wasn't any other detective that did."

"Anybody that looked a little bit suspicious, or off-color?" asked Corning.

"There was only one man," said Dunton, "and that was a bird about sixty years old, with spectacles that had a black ribbon running down from them. He was clean-shaved, hatchet-faced, tight-lipped, and he looked as though he was afraid somebody was going to catch him. We followed him when he left, and he got in a car that had a chauffeur. The chauffeur drove him off."

"Get the number of the car?" asked Corning.

"Yes. We got the license number and we're looking it up . . . wait a minute, here it comes now. Here's the dope on the car. It's owned by a man named Stanwood, Harry Stanwood, of 9486 North Bronson."

Ken Corning frowned.

"Does that mean anything to you?" asked the detective as Corning continued to be silent.

"Yes," said Corning, "it means a lot. I don't know just what it means, but I think it's what I wanted to know. I'll call you back later on, maybe."

He hung up the receiver and strode out of the telephone booth. The weariness seemed to have gone from his face, and in its place was a look of keen concentration; the look which is on the face of a chess player as he contemplates the men on the board at a critical stage of the game.

Corning took a taxicab, and went to his office. The night operator took him up on the elevator. Corning inserted his key in the spring lock of the office door, and pushed it open. A paper, which had been inserted between the door and the sill, caught his eye. He picked it up.

The note was scribbled in a few words, on a single sheet of paper: *"Apparently you handed me wrong envelope. Have you another? Call GLadstone 6-4938."*

The note was unsigned. There were not even any initials on it.

Ken Corning looked at his strapwatch. It was 1:45. He sat down at the telephone and dialed the number of Helen Vail's apartment. He heard the bell ringing, and waited for several rings before he heard her voice on the line.

"Were you asleep?" he asked.

"Don't be silly," she told him. "I was lying awake, thinking up nice things to say to you in the morning for ringing my telephone at this hour."

He managed a grin, but it was a grin with his lips only. His eyes were cold and hard.

"Remember when we represented the men who were arrested in that theater war?" he said. "There were several smoke bombs that were held for a while as evidence. We have them in the office somewhere. Where are they?"

"In the cloak closet. In a big box over in the back. Why do you want them?"

"I happened to think of them for a certain purpose. If I didn't have them I'd have to think up something else."

"Are you going to get any sleep?"

"Probably tomorrow," he said.

"I thought you were going to be in court tomorrow."

"I think," he said, "the case will be continued."

He slid the receiver back on the hook, and called GLadstone 6-4938.

The sound of the ringing signal came over the telephone just once, and then a rasping, impatient voice snapped: "Hello. What do you want?"

"Corning speaking," he said. "I gave you the wrong envelope."

"I know you did," Flint's voice replied, with a certain cold suspicion in its tone.

"I've got the right envelope now," said Corning.

"Where are you?" Flint inquired cautiously.

"I'm out in the ninety-four hundred block on North Bronson. Can you meet me there in about an hour?"

"I can get there before that."

"No," said Corning, "I think an hour will be about right."

"Look here," Flint told him, "the proposition that I made you is predicated on fair play all around. You can't get what you want unless I get what I want, and I don't want any more false alarms."

"Don't come unless you want to," said Corning, and slammed the receiver back on the hook.

He went to the cloak closet, got out the box which contained the smoke bombs, carried them down to his car, and made time through the deserted streets.

The house at 9486 North Bronson was a stucco residence in a fairly exclusive neighborhood. The building was set back from the sidewalk, with a strip of lawn and some ornamental trees at the corner.

Ken Corning moved with the swift certainty of a skilful law-breaker who knows exactly what he intends to do. He walked along the shadows until he had reached a side window. A jimmy from his pocket pushed open the window. He lit a smoke bomb, tossed it inside of the house. He walked to the back of the house, jimmied another window, tossed in a second bomb, circled on the other side, and put two more bombs in the house. Then he returned to the sidewalk, where he sat in his automobile, patiently waiting.

After a few minutes dense clouds of black smoke began to pour from the windows of the place. There was, however, no sign of activity. The building remained slumbering and dark.

Ken Corning looked at his watch.

Ten minutes passed. There was a light suddenly visible in a window in the upper floor of the house. Almost at once other lights came on. These lights showed dimly as reddish oblongs of illumination through the billowing clouds of smoke which eddied about the place.

Once more Ken Corning consulted his watch.

GETTING hurriedly from his car, Corning raised his voice in a shout of "Fire! Fire!! Fire!!!", ran across the strip of lawn and started to pound on the front door with hands and fists. After a few moments, he kicked in the glass of a window, making a great noise as he did so, and once more shouted his alarm of fire.

He heard steps on the stairs, a man's voice shouting.

The lower floor was filled with pungent, thick, oily smoke. Ken Corning climbed through the window, shouting at the top of his lungs, and pushed his way through the smoke. He found a doorway, stairs which led up from a hall, and saw a faint light shining through the smoke at the top of the stairway. A dim figure loomed up out of the smoke ahead of him.

Corning shouted once more: "Fire!"

A man's voice said irritably: "What is it? Where is it?"

Corning reached forward, touched the bulk of the figure with questing fingers.

"Can you get out?" he shouted. "The whole basement is on fire! The place is going up in smoke!"

"Just a minute," said the querulous voice.

"There's no time to be lost! You've got to get out right now!" said Corning. "I've turned in the fire alarm, but the timbers may collapse at any moment."

The man on the stairs cursed and started to turn back. Ken Corning clutched at his garments.

"No, no, you can't go back there! It's fatal! You've got to come!"

The man swung a clumsy fist in an awkward blow which glanced from the side of Corning's head. Corning let loose his hold and the man ran upstairs. After a second, Corning started in pursuit.

The man reached the top of the stairs, plunged along the dimly lighted corridor, through which dense clouds of smoke were moving slowly. He entered the door of a room and vanished. Corning waited by the door of the room, crouched, tense, expectant.

Forty seconds passed and the man came running out of the room. As he reached the corridor, Corning stopped him, then swung his fist expertly to the man's jaw. The man slumped, knocked out.

Corning caught him and flung the senseless form over his shoulder. He groped his way down to the lower floor, found the front door, got it open and stumbled out into the night, with his helpless burden.

Several people were standing in front of the house, clad in

various forms of nightdress, staring with wide eyes and open mouths. A clanging gong and the wail of a siren announced that the fire department was within a few blocks of the place.

Corning ran out across the lawn to his automobile and dumped the man into the machine. He was about sixty years of age, tall and thin, with a hatchet face and thin lips. He was clad in pajamas and slippers.

One or two of the spectators crowded up close to the machine.

"Overcome by smoke," said Corning. "I'm rushing him to a hospital."

He ran around the car, climbed in behind the steering wheel, stepped on the starter and purred away from the curb.

A car was parked some fifty yards down the street and a man stood by the car, watching the sidewalk and street, then turning to stare at the residence from which the smoke was pouring.

Ken Corning slowed the car as he approached. His lights struck the man who was standing by the running-board. It was B. W. Flint.

Corning called to him: "Okey, Flint. Fall in behind and follow me."

The man in Corning's car stirred, groaned and asked an unintelligible question in thick tones. Corning pushed him back against the cushions.

He ran his car around the corner, made speed for three blocks, and then pulled to the curb. The other car, with Flint at the wheel, was right behind him. Corning switched off his lights and the motor and waited until he heard Flint's steps coming along the sidewalk. Flint drew alongside the car.

The man at Corning's side made an ineffective effort to open the door. Corning pushed him back.

"Have you got the envelope?" asked Flint.

"Come around the other side," said Corning. "I'll talk to you there."

Flint moved around to the other side of the car.

Corning spoke rapidly.

"The reason I gave you the wrong envelope," he said, "was because I didn't have the right envelope. I wanted to find out what it was all about. The general idea was that Grosbeck was killed by a stick-up. He wasn't. He was betrayed by a friend. When you thought you had the envelope you took it right to Jason, which told me what I had surmised—that Jason suspected

Grosbeck had important evidence that was to go to the Grand Jury. Jason was out when Grosbeck came to his house to see him. Grosbeck waited for Jason to come back. Somebody shot Grosbeck."

The man in pajamas struggled feebly. "What the devil's the meaning of this?" he asked.

"You were overcome by smoke," Corning told him, "and I rescued you."

"All right, I can get out now," said the man.

"Who is it?" asked Flint.

"Harry Stanwood," said Corning. "Do you know him?"

Flint gave an exclamation of surprise.

Corning continued to talk rapidly.

"Two witnesses pin the kill on Fred Parkett. There's a man named Longwell and one named Monteith. They claim they were there and saw Parkett running away from the scene of the crime. They weren't there. Those witnesses were planted. I've got an affidavit showing they couldn't have been there. It's the affidavit by one of the young women who was with them at a hockey game that didn't break up until an hour after the murder. Mrs. Jason heard the shot, but she didn't hear anyone running away from the car where the murder was committed. The reason for that is that *nobody did run away.*"

Corning turned abruptly to Stanwood.

"How about those papers, Stanwood?"

"What papers?" gasped the man, his face a pasty white.

"The papers that you took from Grosbeck's body as soon as you had killed him," said Corning. "The papers that were of such importance to the Grand Jury. The papers that were going to incriminate Dick Carr and some other detectives."

"You're crazy!" Stanwood said.

Corning smiled, and the smile was cold.

"It won't be hard to find out," he said. "The way I dope it out, Stanwood made the kill, and Dick Carr, the detective, is standing back of him. They needed a fall guy, so they picked on Fred Parkett, the ex-convict. Naturally, Stanwood wasn't going to surrender the papers until he was out in the clear. But even then he couldn't stand the gaff. He figured that he had to gild the lily and paint the rose, so he worked with Carr, and got a purse snatcher to plant some evidence on my secretary. I put some smoke bombs in his house so that he'd think the place was burning down, and I figured he'd carry his most valuable possessions with him when he went out."

Stanwood cursed and swung his fist full into Corning's face. Corning took the blow without flinching, leaned forward and pinned Stanwood's arms. Flint ran around the car and jerked open the door. The two struggling men fell to the running-board. Flint reached up with the barrel of the gun and brought it sharply down on Stanwood's skull. Stanwood lay limp.

Flint reached an exploring hand into the breast of Stanwood's pajamas.

"Here it is," he said.

"All right," Corning said. "I don't want to mix in this any more than I have to. Suppose you tell me what your connection is."

"I'm a Federal detective," said Flint. "I was in touch with Jason right after the murder. Jason suspected it wasn't a simple hold-up, but we always figured Parkett had done the job. Grosbeck had some valuable evidence, and he'd split with the gang. He was going to turn the evidence over to Jason. Jason told him to come to his residence. He'd talked with Jason over the telephone. Jason was delayed getting there, and when he got there Grosbeck was dead."

Ken Corning brushed the dust from his knees.

"How about packing him over to your car?" he said. "I don't want to figure in this part of it if I don't have to. I've got a young woman named Mabel Fosdick in the *Beechwood Hotel.* She's made an affidavit, and she's willing to tell the truth. She can give you the lever that will crack the testimony of Longwell and Monteith. They'll probably name the people higher up when you work on them."

Flint clicked handcuffs of the wrists of the unconscious figure in pajamas. He looked at Corning and his grim features relaxed.

"Do you *always* get your clients out?" he asked.

Ken Corning shrugged his shoulders.

"Sometimes," he said, "I get a break. And sometimes . . . I have to make a break."

Flint chuckled.

"All right," he said. "You take his feet and I'll take his head."

Devil's Fire

KEN CORNING pushed his way through the gawking pedestrians who still loitered on the sidewalk. They had formed in a white-faced ring about the red pool which spread along the cold surface of the gray cement, reflecting the street lights until they seemed like glowing rubies.

"Who saw it?" Corning asked.

A uniformed officer extended a long arm.

"On your way," he ordered. "It's all over now. On your way. Keep moving. Nothing more to see."

A man moved up to Ken Corning, sized him up with eager eyes.

When he spoke, his voice was whining.

"I seen it, boss."

The officer singled out Ken Corning.

"Hey, you! On your way. There ain't nothin' more to see. Keep movin'."

Ken Corning sized up the narrow shoulders, the glinting eyes, the lips that twisted back from the teeth.

"All right," he said. "What happened?"

The officer barged into them.

"You heard what I said. Get movin' an' keep movin'. Just because there's been a man hurt ain't no sign that . . ."

"I'm collecting evidence," Ken Corning told him.

"Huh? Collectin' what?"

"Evidence."

"Who you with?"

"I'm a lawyer. I'm representing the man that was arrested for the murder, George Pyle."

"You're a lawyer, representing George Pyle?"

"Right."

"Who hired you?"

"A friend of Pyle's. They told me to get here and get the facts, then to see what I could do for Pyle."

The officer's eyes showed doubt. The crowd, sensing some new diversion, surged in to a closer circle. The man at Ken Corning's elbow said for him alone: "Let's go some place where we can talk, bo."

The officer restated his command, this time in a louder voice, as though he would make himself more certain by adding to his vehemence. Ken Corning took the man's arm.

"Let's go," he said.

They pushed through the curious ring of spectators, heard in the dim distance the wailing of a siren, heard the officer, assured now of his power, ordering the curious bystanders to be on their way.

Ken Corning picked a rooming-house.

"We can go up here," he said.

"Okey, boss," the man told him.

They turned in under the illuminated sign and climbed a flight of dark stairs. A simpering landlady, well past middle age, pushed a buckram-backed book with frayed pages across an inclined desk.

Corning looked at the narrow-shouldered man.

"Got any place where you're staying?" he asked.

"No."

"What's your name?"

"Henry Lampson."

"All right. Write it. I'm staking you to a room."

The man wrote his name on the register. The broad-hipped landlady regarded him with shrewd eyes, then looked at Ken Corning.

"Something at twelve a week," she suggested.

Ken Corning peeled off two fives and two ones from a roll of bills which he took from his pocket.

The landlady took down a key from a hook and labored slowly down the corridor. The men followed. She opened a door with something of a flourish. Ken Corning pushed Lampson into the room, followed him, and closed the door.

"All right," he said, "what happened? When did it happen?"

The man looked around the room, turned to regard the closed door. His eyes slithered over Corning.

"About half an hour before I saw you in the crowd and heard you say you were hired for this guy Pyle. That's right, is it? You're the guy's lawyer, eh?"

"Yes."

"What's in it for me?"

"Nothing unless you tell the truth."

"Then?"

"That depends on what the truth is."

Lampson thought that over for a few minutes, then said: "Well, there were three or four guys walking down the street— the dead man, the man that got pinched, and a couple of others. They were ahead of me. There was some sort of an argument. I didn't pay too much attention to what it was. Then I saw there was a fight, or it looked like it would have been a fight.

"You say you're representing the guy that got the pinch, and that his name is Pyle?"

"That's right," Corning said.

"Who's the dead man?"

"A chap named Frank Glover. He draws quite a bit of water in some sections of the underworld. Go on. Tell me what happened. I'm interested in that fight business."

"Well, it wasn't really a fight. The two guys were holding your man. The one that was killed was sore, but he was keeping his hands in sight, and not making any passes with his fists. Your man, the one that you're actin' as lawyer for, was talkin' plenty. He was sore, too, and he was telling the whole cockeyed world about it. The two were holding him. He was trying to do some- thing, either to reach a gun, or to swing his fists. There was a lot of argument."

The man paused.

"All right," Corning told him. "I'm listening."

"Well, everything happened sort of quick like, then. Somehow or other this guy, that's your client, got loose from the two guys. He sort of crouched, swung to one side, and then I heard a gun go 'bang.' Your man started to run, and the other guy went down to the sidewalk. Right through the heart, I heard it was, and with lead that mushroomed."

"Go on," Corning told him, as Lampson hesitated. "He started to run, and then what happened?"

"It was a police radio car that swung around the corner. Seems like it had been somewhere in the neighborhood, and somebody telephoned an alarm in to the police. Anyway, that's the way I heard it from the guy on the car. The police car saw the man running, and they nabbed him."

"How long was that after the shooting?"

"It couldn't have been very long. The man had run about a block. It takes a guy a little while to run a block, not long."

"And the two men who were with the murdered man. What did they do?"

"They seemed to huddle there for a minute, then they went down on their knees beside the stiff. They were pulling open his shirt, taking off his vest, and doing that sort of thing. They didn't raise a yell, and they didn't try to get the man that was running. They told the cops they didn't have guns, and they wasn't running after any murderers."

Ken Corning paced the floor of the shabby room. The eager eyes of the narrow-shouldered man followed him.

"The dead man had a gun," Corning snapped suddenly. "The police found it on him. Isn't that right?"

"Sure that's right. I seen it."

"Why didn't the two guys take that gun and stop Pyle?"

"I don't know. Nobody asked them that question."

"And they found Pyle's gun?"

"Yeah. Pyle claimed he didn't do any shooting, that he didn't have a gun and all that sort of stuff, but a broad from the apartment house on the corner saw him throw something back of a signboard. The cops started prowling around and found a gun. I heard one of them say that it was the gun that killed the dead man. I don't know, only what the cops said."

Ken Corning turned to stare steadily at the other.

"How did it happen they didn't hold you as a witness?"

"Because I didn't speak my little piece. I pretended I was just a guy who had come up after the shooting."

"Why didn't you tell them?"

The man fidgeted slightly.

"Because, brother, I don't want the bulls prying around into my record, where I've been and what I've been doing."

He opened his coat. There was a leather case suspended under his arm. He snapped back a flap, pulled out steel tools which he dropped to the table. They gave forth dull, clinking noises as one of them dropped on top of the other.

Ken Corning regarded the pile with puckered eyes.
"Burglar tools, eh?"
"Sure."
"Why did you come clean with me?"
"Because you're a mouthpiece. I may need a good mouthpiece. I got a rod, too. See the point? I got a record. I ain't clean on my last rap, broke parole if you want to know. I knew the bulls would take me to headquarters for questioning if I told my little story. So I kept mum. Then you came up and started talking, and I knew you could fix it so I got a little piece of jack, maybe, and didn't get a police frame."

Ken Corning picked up the burglar tools.
"Where's the rod?" he asked.

The man who had given his name as Lampson pulled back the bottom of his coat, tugged a gun from his right hip pocket. It was a .22 Colt automatic.

"That's it, brother," he said. "You're taking charge of it from now on."

Ken Corning sniffed of the end of the barrel. He pulled back the mechanism until he could eject the loaded shell, thrust a thumb nail into the opening, holding it in such a position that it reflected light into the interior of the barrel. He studied the riflings with a thoughtful eye, sniffed of the end of the barrel again.

"Gee, you ain't trying to pin it on me," said the man, the whining tone of his voice once more in evidence.

Ken Corning raised his eyes, regarded the man over the top of the end sight on the barrel.

"What sort of gun was used in the killing?" he asked.

"Gee, boss, how should I know? The cops found the gun a good half block from where I was standin', and . . ."

"Never mind that," Corning told him, interrupting the whining flow of words. "You know all right. You were there, where you could hear everything. What sort of gun was it?"

Lampson's eyes sought the floor. His face twitched nervously.

"Honest to gawd, boss . . ."

"What sort of gun?" bellowed Corning.

The answer was so weak as to be almost inaudible.

"A .22 automatic, boss; what they call a Colt 'Woodsman.' That's why I'm going to need a mouthpiece, bad."

* * *

CORNING paced the floor of his office. Every few seconds he snapped his left arm around in front of his face and stared at the dial of his wrist-watch, then went on pacing.

A key made a metallic noise in the lock of the outer door. The bolt clicked back. Helen Vail, Ken Corning's secretary, stood straight and slim on the threshold, her eyes filled with anxiety.

"Got here just as quick as I could, chief," she said. "I didn't get the telephone message until I got back from the picture show. What is it?"

Ken Corning took out a package of cigarettes, snapped out one, offered it to Helen Vail, took another for himself. She came close to him to share the flame of the match.

"I don't know what it is," he said, exhaling cigarette smoke as he extinguished the flame of the match. "I got a telephone call about eight o'clock from a man who said he was George Pyle's bodyguard. He said Pyle had been framed, that there was a shooting out at Lincoln Drive and Beemer Street, and for me to get out there right away.

"I had the car here. I made it in nothing flat. The police had moved the body and taken Pyle to jail. I picked up a yegg who tells me his name is Lampson. He's a witness to the whole thing. He thinks perhaps Pyle did the shooting, but he's willing to shade his testimony our way if he can get a little cash. He was packing a .22 automatic. The police say it was a Colt 'Woodsman' .22 that killed Glover. A girl says she saw Pyle chuck one away. She's a peroxide blonde cashier in a cheap restaurant. She's positive as hell. I didn't get to talk with her, but I talked with the girl who shares the apartment with her.

"Frank Glover was the man that got bumped. He'd been asking for it for a long while. Sam Gilman and Shorty French were with him at the time. They say Pyle got in an argument and tried to swing on Glover. Glover used some fighting language, but didn't move his hands. They grabbed Pyle's arms. He broke away, jerked out a rod and let Glover have it, right through the heart, just the one shot. That's their story.

"The gun the cops found back of the signboard seems okey to them. It had been recently fired—one shot. I understand there were some fingerprints on it—not so awfully clear, but clear enough, and that those fingerprints were Pyle's.

"The cops did the usual routine stuff. They kept people on the move. I went to a rooming-house with this witness, Lampson.

When I came out, I went back to the scene of the shooting and did a little prowling. I found this."

Ken Corning took a jagged-edged bit of tissue paper from his pocket and placed it on the desk. The girl leaned forward, touched it with her fingertips, then recoiled.

"Blood!" she said.

Ken Corning nodded.

"Sure," he told her. "I found it lying in the pool of blood that was on the pavement. I picked it up."

"Does it mean anything?" she asked, staring.

"I don't know. It's queer. Why should a piece of tissue paper be lying in a pool of blood. It's not so very big—half an inch one way, by a quarter of an inch the other, but it's something that isn't explained; and, in a murder case, everything should be explained."

Helen Vail's lips pursed thoughtfully.

"Do you suppose that red color is due entirely to the blood-stains?" she asked. "The paper looks funny, somehow."

"I don't know that, either," Corning said.

"What you want me to do, chief?"

He shoved his feet wide apart, standing as though he had braced himself against a blow. His jaw was pushed forward, the lips clamped into a firm, straight line.

"Those damned cops won't let me talk with Pyle, and I've got to do it. I'm going to get out a writ of *habeas corpus.*"

"They won't admit him to bail in a murder case," she pointed out.

"I know that right enough," he said, clipping the words short, "but they'll let me see him. I want to talk with him."

Helen Vail jerked the rubber cover from a typewriter.

"After that?" she asked.

"After that," he said, "you're going to find out something about that girl who saw the gun flung in behind the billboard."

"All rightie. Give me elbow room while I fill out these blanks. What's his name? Just George Pyle?"

"Right," he said.

She looked up as she was pulling legal blanks from the drawer of her desk.

"How about other witnesses?" she asked.

"Plenty of them who saw Pyle running away after the shooting. They heard the sound of the shot, and looked around to see what it was all about. They saw Glover falling, Pyle running. There's no one who saw him throw the gun over behind the billboard except the jane in the apartment."

"Any question that the gun the police found is the one that did the shooting?"

"Too early to tell. But an expert can check it by firing test bullets. Those things are proven mathematically these days."

She nodded, fed the legal blank into the typewriter and started swift fingers clacking the keys with the staccato effect of gunfire.

GEORGE PYLE stared through the wire partition which stretched across the long table in the visitors' room in the jail. His eyes were red and bloodshot. His face was pale. Every few moments he licked his lips nervously with the tip of his tongue.

"Gawd, Corning, you've got to spring me on this rap."

"It's a frame-up?"

"Of course it's a frame-up! Do you think I'm such a triple-damned fool as to shoot a man down, with four million witnesses staring at me?"

"It was your gun that did the killing."

"That's a damned lie. I never saw the gun in my life."

"It's got your fingerprints on it."

"It can't have."

"That's what the experts say."

"What experts?"

"A fingerprint expert the police hired, and one that I hired."

Pyle's tongue flicked his lips. His eyes shifted from Corning's, then returned with the look of desperation of a caged animal.

"Can't you get me out of here? It's those damned bars. They leer at me all the time. I see them everywhere I turn. They're driving me nuts."

Corning shook his head slowly.

"Keep cool," he counseled. "You get yourself all worked up and they'll trap you into some sort of an admission, and then it will be all off."

Pyle sucked in a deep breath, as though he had been about to dive under a cold shower.

"Corning, can they . . . will they . . . is there any chance . . . do you suppose that they'd . . . the death penalty, you know. I wouldn't get that, would I?"

Corning's eyes were impatient.

"Listen," he said, "you're in here, charged with first degree murder. The D. A.'s going after the death penalty. There's a case against you that looks black as hell. Now quit this damned yellow yammering, and get down to brass tacks. There's only one way I can get you out of here, and that's through the front door, and I can't do that unless you use your head to think with instead of getting hysterical. Now tell me what happened."

The man on the other side of the coarse wire mesh ran an apprehensive finger around the inside of his shirt collar.

"Gawd!" he said, hoarsely.

Corning waited, steady-eyed, remorselessly patient.

After a moment, Pyle began talking in a low, mechanical voice, his eyes fastened on the battered top of the long table.

"I was walking down the street with Sam Gilman, Shorty French and Frank Glover. Frank and I were due for a showdown. He'd been chiseling. I knew it. He was prepared to sit tight and fight it out. I didn't want to do that.

"I didn't intend to discuss things until we got to Glover's apartment. I was supposed to be alone, but I'd planted three of my men in an apartment next to Glover's. They were ready to shoot the door of Glover's apartment into splinters and bust in, if they heard any sounds of trouble. And they were watching the elevators so that if any of Glover's men marched me out with a rod in my back they'd get a surprise."

Corning's voice was impatient.

"Where was your gun?" he asked.

"I didn't have any."

"Don't make me laugh."

"That's on the up and up, Corning. I didn't have any rod. I swear I didn't. That was one of the things Glover insisted on. I was to come alone and have no rod. We were to go to his apartment for a talk. What he didn't know, was that I'd been working on a plant next to his apartment for three or four months. I'd moved some of my men in, and had Tommies up there and some grenades. I'd have pineappled his joint in a minute if he'd tried anything funny.

"Well, we were walking along the street with everyone quiet-like, until suddenly, just at that place, Shorty French let a remark drop that showed me Glover had been two-timing with my girl. I saw red, I'll admit that. He could have had a regiment around him, and I'd have called him just the same.

"I tried to swing on him, and Shorty and Sam Gilman grabbed me. Glover sneered at me and asked me what I was going to do about it. I'd have done plenty if I'd had the chance. Then I managed to break away, and just as I did it, there was a bang. I swear I don't know who fired the shot, but it sounded as though it had come from right around me somewhere.

"It seemed like a half second after the shot before anything happened, and then I saw that Glover was sagging down to the ground. I knew it was some sort of a frame-up, and I guess I lost my head. I started to sprint.

"Then a cop car came around the corner, and I knew I was framed for the rap. But I didn't throw any rod behind any billboard, and I didn't have any rod on me, and I didn't do any shooting."

Ken Corning stared steadily at his client.

"You heard the shot?"

"Sure."

"It was right near you?"

"Yes."

"And you figure it must have been either Sam Gilman or Shorty French that fired that shot?"

"Of course."

"But you didn't see any gun, and you couldn't swear that either of them made even so much as a threatening motion?"

"No."

Ken Corning's stare was that of a doctor who must give unpleasant news to a patient. "Pyle," he said, slowly, "do you think any jury on earth is going to believe that story?"

Beads of perspiration glinted from the prisoner's forehead, but his eyes met those of the lawyer.

"No," he said, in a voice that was filled with terror.

CORNING stood, feet planted wide apart, eyes staring steadily at Harry Lampson.

"Get this," he said, "and get it straight. I'm representing George Pyle. He comes first. You can't drag me into your troubles, or pull a double-cross on Pyle. I'll help you out of your jam, if I can help my client by doing it. Otherwise I won't."

The man who had been so meek and appealing was now cold and hard.

"Where the hell do you get that noise about me being in a jam?

I ain't in any jam. I came clean and told you the low-down that would help your client. If I don't get a cut, I kick through with the real stuff."

Ken Corning eyed the man with evident distaste.

"Meaning?" he asked.

"Meaning that I'll switch over and tell the bulls about your man flinging the gun away as he ran, about seeing the rod in his hand just before the shot was fired."

"Like that, eh?" Corning asked.

"Like that," Lampson told him.

"Seems to me you're independent as hell all of a sudden."

"Does it?"

"It does."

The man shrugged his shoulders.

"Well," he said, "there's the dope. Take it or leave it. I'm sitting pretty."

Ken Corning walked to the window of the room. It was dingy and narrow. The lace curtain which covered it seemed indicative of the fact that the occupants of the room were usually more concerned with keeping the public from seeing in, rather than seeing out themselves.

Corning's eyes, staring down at the shadows of the street, caught the swing of heavy shoulders as a big man pushed his way into the door of the rooming-house. Another man stood, loitering in a doorway across the street. He seemed strangely immobile.

Ken Corning whirled on the man who was watching him with ratty eyes.

"What kind of a double-crossing game—?"

He had no chance to finish the question. Feet sounded in the corridor outside of the room. Heavy knuckles pounded the panels of the door.

"Jeeze," said Lampson in a strained, choking voice.

He got to his feet, scuttled across the room in an ecstasy of haste, twisted the key in the lock. A man on the other side of the door pushed it open, barged into the room.

"So," he said.

Police detective was stamped all over him, from the broad-toed shoes to the heavy neck, the accusing eyes, the thick lips that held a cigar clamped at an aggressive angle.

"Hello, Maxwell," said Corning, casually.

Maxwell held Corning with his eyes.

"You got a hell of a crust, tampering with a state's witness."

Ken Corning laughed.

"In the first place," he said, "I wasn't tampering with him. In the second place, he isn't a state's witness. He's my witness. I found him on the street after the shooting, and I brought him here. I was with him when he registered, and I paid for the room."

The detective twisted his heavy lips.

"Says you!" he grated.

He turned to Lampson. "What's the low-down?" he asked.

Lampson's voice was low, rapid and toneless, like the voice of a frightened child speaking a piece at a school entertainment.

"He came in here and told me I had to swear that Shorty French had a gun in his hand and that I seen it. He said I had to swear that the man that ran away couldn't have done any shooting, that his arms were held until after the gunshot was fired, until after Glover hit the pavement. He said, if I didn't swear that, he was going to plant a rod on me and frame me for the murder rap."

"Subornation of perjury," remarked Maxwell in a voice of rumbling accusation.

"Baloney!" snapped Corning.

"If you think it's baloney," Maxwell told him, tugging handcuffs from the back of his belt, "try and laugh this off."

Corning looked at the handcuffs.

"What the hell do you think this is?" he asked.

"A pinch," Maxwell said.

Abruptly, Corning laughed. "Gentlemen," he said, "let's not have any misunderstanding about this. Let's agree upon the date and the time; also the persons present. This is Wednesday, the eighth of the month. The hour is exactly seven and one-half minutes past four o'clock in the afternoon. There are present in this room, Henry Lampson, myself, and Thomas Maxwell, a police detective, who has just recently entered the room. There are no other persons in this room. Is that right?"

Maxwell stared with suspicious eyes at Ken Corning. Lampson looked at the police detective with the look of helpless interrogation which a tenderfoot gives to a guide in the forest.

"What the hell you trying to pull?" asked Maxwell.

"Nothing," Ken Corning told him, "except that I want to get

the time and the place established beyond dispute. Have I said anything that wasn't the truth?"

"Aw, go jump in the lake!" Maxwell growled. "You can't run a bluff on us with all that line of hooey. You're going to headquarters."

"Got a warrant?" Corning asked.

"Got enough to take you in for questioning," Maxwell remarked with emphasis. "After I get you in for questioning, Lampson here is going to swear to a charge. Ain't you, Lampson?"

"Sure," Lampson said.

"And there's no mistake or misunderstanding about the time and the place and the persons present?" Corning asked.

"Hell, no!" the detective exploded. "Have that your own way; but you're coming with me now."

"Fine," said Ken Corning with evident satisfaction. "Put those bracelets away. They don't frighten me any. You aren't going to use them, anyway, until you've got a warrant. I'll pay the taxi fare to the jail."

They walked from the room. Lampson locked the door and put the key in his pocket. Maxwell took Ken Corning's arm in a firm grip. Ken Corning laughed.

"You fellows are going to hear more of this," he said.

"Yeah, I know that line of hooey," the detective told him.

They filed down the stairs. There was a taxicab waiting at the curb. They entered it and went to the jail. Lampson scrawled a signature upon a legal blank that had already been typed. He held up his right hand and mumbled an affirmative to the oath which was administered.

"How about getting bail?" asked Corning.

"Sure," said Maxwell. "You won't have no trouble on that. We don't want to throw you in. We're just getting you where you ain't tampering with witnesses. You can get out on your own recognizance if you want."

"Well," Corning said, "let me get to a telephone, and then I'll fix up a bail bond."

"You ain't going to make application for a release *without* bail?" Maxwell inquired.

"No."

"All right then. Have it your own way. I was just trying to be nice to you. Hell, you don't have to get high hat! You're playing a game, and so'm I. I caught you off first base, an' I tagged you with the ball. There don't need to be hard feelings."

"Thanks," said Corning, sarcastically. "When I want your advice I'll ask for it. Let me get to that telephone."

He was shown a telephone booth. He dropped a coin, closed the door, and gave the number of his office. Helen Vail's voice answered the telephone.

"Listen," he told her, "this is important as the devil. You've got to have some help. Get Johnson from the Intercoastal Agency to help you. There's a rooming-house at Beemer Street near where Glover was murdered. A chap named Lampson has a room there. He's out. Get a pass key. Get into the room, put in a dictograph some place where it's concealed behind a picture or something. Run the wires into the adjoining room. I rented that room yesterday under the name of Ragland. I thought it might come in handy. Set up a plant there. Have a notebook filled with pothooks. Use an old one.

"Take this down, and put it in the notebook as the last thing that was said. . . . Ready? . . . All right. Here we go. 'And there's no mistake or misunderstanding about the time and the place and the persons present?' 'Hell no. Have that your own way, but you're coming with me now!' "

There was a moment of silence, then Helen Vail's voice over the wire: "Okey, chief, I got that. What else?"

"Just use your head," he told her, "and sit tight. I'll be there some time. I don't know when. Stick there, even if it's a week. Have meals sent in if you have to. Sleep in a chair; but don't leave that room."

"I gotcha," she told him.

Ken Corning hung up the telephone, walked from the booth.

"I'm having trouble getting bail," he said.

Maxwell shrugged his shoulders. "Any time you want to ask a favor," he said, "I'll get hold of the D. A.'s office, and they'll send a man down and agree you can go on your own."

"I," said Ken Corning, "will see you in hell before I ask a favor."

"Okey, have it your own way," said Maxwell, and grinned.

Ken Corning walked back to the telephone booth. "I'll try another angle," he said.

He got a bail bond company on the line, a company to whom he had given a fair share of business from various clients. "I'm in the can," he told them, "on a charge of subornation of perjury. It's a frame-up to blow up one of my witnesses in the George Pyle case, and give the witness a good background for switching over to the prosecution. The witness is a crook with a criminal record, and they want the publicity of getting me for subornation of perjury to make it look okey for the witness to make a switch. The bail's ten thousand dollars. I'm stalling. Wait for about half an hour, then bring over a bond and spring me. Got that? Fine."

Ken Corning hung up the telephone, waited around the jail office. Maxwell yawned, frowned. "We're not waiting all night," he said. "I've offered you an out. You won't take it. You either raise bail in the next thirty minutes, or you stay here overnight."

"It'll be here inside of thirty minutes," Corning told him.

"It's just a matter of business all around," Maxwell said, his manner propitiating.

"Go to hell," Corning advised him.

AT the expiration of the half hour, a representative of the bail bond company bustled in with the bail bond. Maxwell checked it over.

"Why didn't you want to go out on your own?" he asked. "What's the idea of all the fuss?"

Ken Corning regarded him with cold, watchful eyes. "Can you keep a secret?" he inquired.

Maxwell looked suspicious, but nodded.

"You see," Corning explained, "I wanted to get something on the police. I wanted to show that the police were framing up cases, and show that they were trying to railroad George Pyle by intimidating his lawyer and his witnesses."

Tom Maxwell sprawled out in the chair. He stretched his feet far out, slid down on the small of his back, yawned prodigiously.

"Yeah," he said, "a fat chance *you* got, under arrest for subornation of perjury."

Corning nodded.

"You see," he went on, speaking in a patient tone, as though explaining an elemental matter to a small child, "I wanted to be certain that Lampson actually went on record *under oath* before I sprung my side of the case. Otherwise, I'd have taken you into the room where my witnesses were, before we went down to the jail."

Maxwell was half way through another yawn. Abruptly, his

jaws snapped shut. His body became rigid with attention. Slowly, he hoisted his weight on his elbows until he was sitting upright in the chair.

"Witnesses?" he asked.

"Sure," Corning told him. "You don't think I'm a big enough fool to walk into a police trap with my eyes shut, do you? I had a dictograph wired into that room, and every word that was said was taken down by a shorthand reporter who sat at the other end of the dictograph in an adjoining room. That was why I was so anxious to have it straight just exactly who was present, just exactly the time and place, and who was talking. Remember that don't you?"

Maxwell came out of the chair as though it had been electrified. He stared at Corning with wide, bulging eyes. Then he strode across the room, jerked open a door, and said: "A couple of you boys come with me. We're going to make a fast ride."

He came back towards Corning, his face flushed, lips twitching.

"Damn you," he said, "you can't pull a line of hooey like that. You'll plant witnesses by tomorrow, but this is the time we call you, and call you cold. Come on. If you've got any dictograph in that room, show it to me, and show it to me now!"

Ken Corning became reluctant.

"I'm a free man now, out on bail. You can't order me around."

Maxwell laughed sneeringly, "Thought it was all a damned big bluff. But it don't make any difference what it was. You're going right back there and point out any alibi you've got, and you're going to do it now."

They loaded Corning into a police car, took him back to the rooming-house, up to the room where he had been when Maxwell had made the arrest.

"Show us," said the detective.

Corning shrugged his shoulders, walked across the room, looked out of the window, down into the darkness of the street, and said: "Go to hell!"

Maxwell's laugh was gloating. "Search the dump, boys," he commanded.

He started the search, jerking down a cheap, framed chromo. He pulled a calendar from the wall, flung it to the floor, pulled out another picture, and suddenly paused, eyes wide, mouth sagging, staring into a metallic circle.

"Jeeze," he said, "a dictograph!"

"I told you," Corning remarked, lighting a cigarette.

Maxwell pushed his way from the room, into the corridor, turned the knob on the door of the adjoining room, flung his weight against the door, and sent it banging inward.

There was a couch over near the window, on which lay a man, snoring peacefully. At a table in the center of the room, sat Helen Vail, hair somewhat rumpled, her eyes weary. About her were cigarette stubs, empty beer bottles, a litter of bread crusts from sandwiches. The room looked as though the two occupants had been there for a week.

In front of Helen Vail was a shorthand notebook filled with pothooks and straight lines. There was a receiving end of a dictograph suspended above the table.

Helen Vail turned tired eyes towards the door. The man on the couch gave one last explosive snore and sat up, knuckling his eyes.

"Johnson," explained Corning, "of the Intercoastal Detective Agency."

Johnson slid his feet to the floor, grinned sheepishly, and said: "Hello, everybody."

"Did you get it, Helen?" asked Ken Corning.

Helen Vail stared at him. "I got everything," she said.

"What's the last thing you've got?"

She thumbed back through the pages of the notebook, saying mechanically: "You mean the last thing before this last bunch of conversation when the detectives took you into the room, searching for the dictograph?"

"Yes."

She marked a place, started to read, using a toneless, artificial articulation: "Question by Mr. Corning: 'And there's no mistake or misunderstanding about the time and the place, and the persons present?' Answer, by officer, 'Hell, no. Have that your own way; but you're coming with me now.'"

She looked up questioningly.

"That what you meant?" she said. "It's the last of the conversation. The door slammed right after that and we heard you going down the corridor. I heard some words as you went past the door, but I didn't try to take them. You said you wanted only the conversations that took place inside that room."

Corning nodded.

She picked up the pages of the notebook, pinched them between thumb and forefinger, and riffled them. "There's an awful lot of stuff here," she said, *"all* the conversations, you know."

Ken Corning glanced over at Maxwell, then turned once more to Helen Vail, and said: "Never mind those, not now. You can write up your notes later and Johnson can support them with an affidavit."

Maxwell took two swift strides towards Corning. His face was flushed, the eyes glittering, veins on the sides of his forehead stood out like small ropes.

"Damn you!" he gritted. "Think you're —— damned smart, don't you?"

"I think," Corning told him, "that when the police rely on the testimony of an ex-convict to frame a charge of subornation of perjury on a reputable lawyer, and a charge of murder on George Pyle, that they'd better be damned certain they aren't going to get in over their neckties before they start rocking the boat."

Maxwell grunted a comment to the two men who had accompanied him.

"Come on, boys," he said, "there's nothing for us here."

The men filed out of the room, the door slammed. Helen Vail grinned at Corning. Johnson sighed.

"A good plant?" asked the girl, indicating the remnants of sandwiches, the butts of cigarettes.

"I'll tell the world," Corning gloated. "You must have been busy!"

"We raided the garbage pail in the lunchroom of the office building," she told him, "and we dumped all the ash trays into a paper. It took a little while to rig the dictograph, but we worked it as fast as we could. The Intercoastal had a set, so we didn't lose time there. It wasn't connected up with anything except dead wires. I was afraid they were going to test it. If they had, it wouldn't have worked."

Corning chuckled.

"It was the build-up that did it. Maxwell got such a shock that he lost his grip."

"Want me for anything more?" Johnson asked.

"Better stick around," Corning told him. "There may be something that'll turn up."

"What'll they do now?" Helen Vail wanted to know.

Corning studied his cigarette smoke.

"That's hard to tell. They *had* planned to make Lampson a star witness, to spread the news of my arrest, and the attempt to 'fix' the prosecution's witness. Now they'll have to crawl in a hole. Probably they'll let Lampson sneak out of the picture. They'll dismiss the charge against me."

"But," protested the girl, "why don't *you* be the one to bust into the newspapers with the whole story and make them see that the police are framing on Pyle?"

He shook his head.

"Because then I'd have to go on record as claiming we had verbatim reports of the conversations in that room. As it is, we made a good enough plant to bluff Maxwell. He'll let sleeping dogs lie, and wonder when and how I'm going to raise my point. It'll make them jumpy all through the case. But, if we busted into print, some of the wise guys would demand a transcription of the conversations. We could fake them, but they wouldn't be exactly right. Some smart bird would see the discrepancy, start in checking up on details, and catch us in a hell of a mess.

"I'd rather act on the sleeping dog principle and keep mum about the entire affair."

Johnson nodded.

"My agency would go as far as it did," he said, "but no farther. We couldn't afford to be mixed up in a mess if someone should start checking back on the facts."

Helen Vail suddenly gave a little exclamation, slipped open the pages of her shorthand notebook, and took out a bit of colored tissue paper.

"Lookee what I found," she said.

Ken Corning examined the piece of paper, a bit of crumpled red tissue, upon one side of which was a dark encrustation. It was about the same size as the other bit of paper he had found in the pool of blood on the sidewalk.

"Where'd you find it?" he snapped.

"Same place you found the other."

"What is it?" Johnson asked.

Ken Corning kept his eyes on the piece of paper.

"Damned if I know," he said, "but I'm going to find out."

HELEN VAIL crossed her knees and made little smoothing motions with her fingers as she pressed her skirt over the curve of the uppermost knee. "I can't get a thing on her, chief. Her name's Mary Bagley. She has a corner apartment on the second floor. She works as cashier in the Big Disc Restaurant Company's Ninth Street restaurant. She doesn't seem to have any men friends to speak of, doesn't flash around in expensive clothes, seems just like any ordinary working girl. She's positive as the very devil. Says she didn't see the shooting, but she did hear the noise of the shot, and that she looked out of the window and saw Pyle running down the street towards her apartment house. She says she saw Glover lying on the sidewalk, and the two men standing beside him.

"She saw the men stoop over and start loosening Glover's collar, and about that time Pyle was abreast of the billboard on the opposite corner of the street. She says he ran diagonally across the street, drew back his hand, and flung something that glittered just the way blued steel glitters in the light. Then he started running down the cross street, the police car swung around the corner, and picked him up. She says she got a good look at his face as he ran down the street, and it was Pyle, without the shadow of a doubt. She'll identify him anywhere. She picked him out of a line-up at the jail."

Ken Corning frowned, paced the floor thoughtfully.

"Her apartment's on the second floor?"

"Yes."

"You've become friendly with her?"

"Yes. And I know Esther Ogier, the girl who shares the apartment with her. Esther wasn't there at the time. She's ushering in a picture show and doesn't get off until after eleven every night."

Ken Corning absently took a cigarette from his pocket, tapped it on the edge of the polished silver case, lit it, exhaled a stream of smoke.

"It doesn't check," he said.

The girl stared at him. Abruptly, he whirled on her.

"You think she's telling the truth, don't you? You think Pyle did it. Isn't that right?"

"I don't know what I think," she told him. "You told me to find out certain things. I found them out. I've never talked with Pyle. I don't know his side of the story. But I do know that there's lots of witnesses. There are a half dozen different people whose attention was attracted by the shot and who saw Pyle running."

Corning shrugged his shoulders.

The telephone rang. Helen Vail lifted the receiver, said: "Hello" in a low voice. After a moment she nodded, held the instrument out to Ken Corning.

"It's the jailer speaking," she said. "He said Pyle has something important to tell you."

Ken Corning scooped the receiver up in a single motion, held the transmitter to his lips. "All right," he said, "this is Corning speaking."

Pyle's voice was low-pitched, cautious.

"You remember the thing you was asking me about—if it was mine?" he asked.

"Something heavy?" Corning inquired.

"That's it."

"All right. What about it?"

"I just happened to think how fingerprints might have got on it."

"Okey. Be careful what you say. Spill it."

"Well, I had an argument with a certain person. I had to take something away from him, something he was threatening me with. I gave it back to him, later, when I'd emptied it."

"Same general description?" asked Corning.

"Yeah, the same thing—'Woodsman,' you know. Ain't many around yet."

"Okey. Who was it?"

"His name's Pete. They call him Pete the Polack. It was a while ago and I haven't seen him since. But you can locate him through the shooting galleries. He ran a gallery for a time out at the concessions in Cedar Street Park."

Ken Corning thought for a few seconds while the telephone line made buzzing noises.

"Know anything more?" he asked.

"Nothing that'll help. I thought you'd want to know about this."

"I do," Ken Corning told him, and hung up the receiver.

He swung back in the swivel-chair, clasped hands behind his head, and fixed his eyes on Helen Vail, although by their expression he seemed to be looking through and beyond her.

"Just had a glimmer of light," he began slowly. "There were two things that seemed to tie Pyle to the shooting. First, the sound of the shot, which Pyle himself admits was close to him; second, his fingerprints on the .22 'Woodsman' which was found behind the billboard Pyle passed and which the ballistic experts say fired the fatal shot.

"Pyle has just explained, reasonably, if true, how his prints might have been on that gun, and he has given me the name of a man who should be an expert shot with that particular calibre.

"Now, supposing another man than Pyle shot Glover—and we can eliminate the two other men in the group, for they could not have placed the gun where it was found—"

Ken Corning was speaking more rapidly; there was a gleam of growing excitement in his eyes.

"Supposing another man *did* the shooting—where could he have been? He must have been in the close vicinity of that billboard and—remember, Pyle said that everything was quiet until, unexpectedly, just at that place on the street, one of the men made a remark that started the fight.

"All right. A building close to the billboard, with windows overlooking the scene of the shooting and the cross street around the corner, is that building where the ready-to-order witness, Mary Bagley, has a room."

"And her room," interjected Helen Vail softly, "is on the corner and has a window on either street."

"Exactly," snapped Ken Corning. "And I'm starting right from there." The swivel-chair made a sharp thump as he leaned abruptly forward.

"Another thing—I've examined the gun that did the killing, the 'Woodsman' .22, one of the most accurate of the smaller calibres in the hands of an expert—say a man familiar with shooting galleries. The muzzle of that gun has marks such as a friction coupling of a silencer *could* have made."

He stood up abruptly. His eyes were bright and hard. He reached for his hat.

"But," said Helen Vail, "how about the sound of the shot—right close to Pyle?"

"I think," Ken Corning said, "you and I have solved that."

"I!" said Helen Vail incredulously.

Ken Corning smiled down at her. He clamped his hat on his head. "Going out," he told her. "Don't look for me back until you see me."

"Anything Johnson can do instead?" she asked.

"I don't think so. It's got to be handled with gloves. I want to do it myself. I want to coax a couple of people into my hands right. What's the name of the apartment house where this Bagley girl hangs out?"

"The Catalina. That's the name above the door."

He nodded, strode to the door of the outer office.

"Keep in touch with things," he said. "Better have someone come in here to stick around the telephone nights. I don't know when I'll be back, and I want it so I can call in at any time and get service. Maybe that redhead that we had before can help out."

She smiled at him, a smile that was almost maternal, despite the fact that she was ten years his junior.

"And have her get things all twisted the way she did before! No, thanks! I'll have them bring in a cot, and my meals, and I'll stick around here on a twenty-four-hour shift until the case is over."

He started to say something, changed his mind, grinned at her and closed the door as he went out. He went at once to the *Catalina Apartments.*

"I want something in a corner apartment," he told the tired-eyed woman who acted as manager.

She looked at him appraisingly.

"The corner," he went on, "that's on the northeast."

She shook her head slowly.

"I don't think there's a thing."

"No vacancies?"

"None that I can rent. Three of them are vacant, but the rent's paid until the first of the month. The tenants moved out some days ago rather suddenly. One of them took some of the personal belongings he had there. The others just moved, and I haven't seen them."

"Rather strange?" asked Corning disinterestedly. There was a sudden bright gleam in his eyes.

The tired eyes surveyed him with weary caution.

"I don't know," she said. "I'm paid to rent apartments; not to speculate on the affairs of the tenants."

Ken Corning turned on his heel, walked out of the apartment house, taxied to the want-ad department of a morning newspaper and made arrangements for a quarter column ad. Then he went out to Cedar Street Park.

A thin chap with high cheekbones, thin lips and bright eyes was running the shooting gallery concession. Ken Corning paid a quarter for a gun full of shells, knocked down moving ducks, shot three times at a ball which spurted up on a jet of water, and, when he had the attention of the proprietor, said: "I want to pull a publicity stunt."

"Yeah?" asked the proprietor, the voice toneless, the eyes sharp with interest.

"Yeah. . . . Fill her up again."

The man tilted a tube of cartridges into the magazine of the repeater.

"Ever hear of a guy named Pete the Polack?" asked Corning.

The man's hand jiggled. Shells spilled to the floor. He cursed in a high-pitched whine, stooped to the floor.

"No," he said, when he had straightened.

"Used to run a concession out here," said Corning, carelessly. "I thought he'd be glad to help me. I know some friends of his."

The man slipped the loose shells into the gun, kept his eyes away from Corning's.

"Used to be a heavy guy with a mustache out here. He sold out to me. I think they called him Pete, but I ain't sure. He's been gone for a while now. I never did get to know much about him. He ain't ever been back since I bought in."

He slid the tube into place, cocked the gun and handed it to Ken Corning.

"What sort of a publicity stunt was you figuring on?" he asked.

"Going to put up a prize for the best blonde working-girl shot in the city. She's got to shoot at a regulation target. Gets one hundred dollars and a loving cup. The shots are free if she makes over a certain score, otherwise she pays. She should get about half price."

"Profits all gone now," the man said. "Things ain't gone down in this game, costs are still high. . . . Where do I come in on the free shots—the ones that go over a certain score?"

"You'll pay that in return for your publicity," Ken Corning said, knocking down a moving duck. "I'm going to give the thing a lot of space in the newspapers. It'll bring a lot of people in here, spectators."

"To see the shooting?" asked the gallery man skeptically.

Ken Corning held the trigger back against the trigger guard, worked the pump of the gun with swift motions of the forearm.

"No," he said, as the hammer clicked on an empty chamber, "to see the blondes."

The proprietor of the gallery looked at the vacant spaces in the places where the imitation clay pipes had been.

"You ain't bad with a rifle yourself, brother."

"Not so good. A little out of training," Corning told him. "A month or so would get me back so I could do something worth while. How about it?"

"What's the publicity?" asked the man back of the counter.

"I'm going to start a selling campaign on a hair-bleaching process that makes silky blondes out of brunettes and restores natural color to hair and all that sort of stuff."

"So that's why you want 'em blondes," said the man. "What's the rest of it."

"And the winner of the big prize," Ken Corning told him, "is going to be the sales manager of my company. She's going to get a lot of free publicity first. The best blonde shot in the city."

"Sounds goofy to me," the man said.

"All publicity schemes are goofy," Corning assured him; "the idea is to think up something new, so you can get the advertising. All of the logical things have been thought of already. The new things you think of are goofy."

The man back of the counter said nothing, but continued to look at Corning.

Corning took a dollar from his pocket, and slid it across the counter.

"Now listen," he said, "I don't want any misunderstanding about this. I'm going to have a bunch of blonde working-girls come in here to shoot. I'm going to have a crowd around the place. The shoot is going to be advertised as between the hours of seven o'clock and eleven o'clock tomorrow night, first come, first served. At eleven o'clock the girls who have had the two highest scores are going to shoot off the finals—and the one who's going to win that final shoot is going to be my sales manager, do you understand?"

"Just how do you mean?"

"Just what I say—she's going to win."

"Suppose the other girl should be a better shot?"

"She probably will. My sales manager can't hit a flock of barn doors."

The bright eyes watched Corning with feverish concentration.

"How the hell is she going to win if she can't shoot?"

"Because," said Corning, "she isn't going to be shooting at the target at all. She's going to be shooting at the backstop, but the target she's shooting at is going to be one that's been prepared in advance. You're going to pretend to put a plain target on the carrying wire that takes the target back, but it isn't going to be a plain target. It's going to be one that's had six shots put right through the black bull's-eye in the center of the target. Each contestant is going to fire six shots. Naturally, my girl's going to win. She's going to have the highest score."

"A frame-up, eh?" said the man.

"Of course it's a frame-up," Corning told him impatiently.

"I've got to get some coin out of it, then," the man told him.

"How much coin?" Corning asked.

"Fifty bucks, and the shots have got to be paid for at full price."

"You'd be getting rich," Corning protested.

"The hell I would," the man said. "In the first place, you ain't going to have over a dozen girls to compete—not if they have to pay for their own shots if they don't make better than a certain record. There ain't a dozen women in the city who know how to handle guns. You should know that yourself. Watch a woman come to a shooting gallery. She never does it unless there's some man who drags her in, then, most of the time, she shoots with her eyes closed."

"All right," Corning told him, wearily, "have it your own way. I can't be bothered with a lot of details."

Corning opened a bill fold and took out five ten-dollar bills.

"My name's Steve Richey," he said.

The man on the other side of the counter extended his left hand for the money, placed his thin, feverish right hand inside of Corning's palm.

"My name's Ted Fuller."

"The shoot," said Corning, "starts tomorrow night at seven o'clock and lasts until eleven. There'll probably be a crowd. My girl is going to show up for her qualifying shoot just a little before anyone else gets here. We'll fake the qualifying target, and it's up to you to see that she wins."

"Don't worry," Fuller said, pushing the money into his pocket, "she'll win. It may look kind of raw, but she'll win."

"I don't give a damn how raw it looks," Corning told him. "I want the publicity."

* * *

CORNING found a rooming-house which suited his purpose, at 329 Maple Avenue. He registered under the name of Stephen Richey, then he rang up his office and heard Helen Vail's voice over the telephone.

"Listen," he told her, "you had a blonde friend who used to come into the office once in a while. I've forgotten her name. She was the kind that would photograph well. I think her name was Marian, but I'm not sure."

"That's right," Helen Vail told him, "Marian Sharpe. She's a good scout."

"All right," Corning told her, "I want her. I want her to go to a rooming-house at 329 Maple Avenue, and ask for Stephen Richey. That's the name I'm registered under. I'll be waiting for her. Think you can get her?"

"Sure; she's out of a job and needs money."

"Okey," Corning told her. "Now here's another one. You'll notice that all of the newspapers are carrying an ad in the 'Help Wanted—Female Department' announcing a competition to determine the best shot among blonde working-girls in the city. I want you to see that Mary Bagley has her attention called to that ad."

"Want me to suggest that she try for the prize?" Helen Vail asked.

"That's exactly what I don't want," he told her. "I simply want you to see that her attention is called to the ad. Then, if she decides she's going to try to win the prize, I want to know it. But I don't want you to bring any pressure to bear on her. Think you can do that all right?"

"Sure. I can find that out all right."

"Okey. Now if she decides to go into the competition, let me know here at this rooming-house. The telephone number is Plaza 6-7931. You can simply ask for Mr. Richey and they'll put me on the line. I've already got the girl spotted so that I won't need you to point her out."

"You want to know right away?" asked Helen Vail.

"Just as soon as you can find out."

"Okey, I'll call you back."

Corning had dinner, read the evening newspapers, and was sitting in silent concentration, staring at the curling smoke from his cigarette, when there was a knock at the door. He opened it, and encountered the laughing blue eyes of a twenty-five-year-old blonde, who said, all in one breath: "I didn't delay any, but came right over just as soon as Helen told me that you had a job for me."

"Come in," Corning told her.

She walked into the room, sat down on the chair which he placed for her, and watched him with eyes that were no longer smiling, but were keenly attentive.

"What is it you want?" she asked.

"Can you shoot a gun?" Corning inquired.

"Just a little bit. I could probably kill a husband if I had to, but I couldn't hit any smaller game."

Corning reached for his hat.

"All right," he said, "you're going out and learn."

He took her to several shooting galleries, giving her instructions in the holding of the rifle. Then he took her to Ted Fuller's shooting gallery.

"This," he said, "is Marian Sharpe, the woman who's going to win the contest tomorrow night."

Ted Fuller's bright eyes surveyed the young woman in swift appraisal.

"Let's see you shoot," he said.

"Nix on that noise," Corning told him. "She can hit the back-stop and that's all that counts."

"It's going to look like a fake," Fuller said. "A good shot can tell by the way a person holds a gun whether they're holding on a target or not. Then, the paper target always makes a little jump away from the back-stop when a bullet hits it. . . ."

"What the hell do I care how raw a deal it is, or what it looks like?" said Corning. "Let the loser squawk all she wants to. I'm going to get the publicity, ain't I?"

Fuller shrugged his shoulders.

"I was just telling you, brother," he said.

"All right," Corning said, "I don't want you to tell me anything. All I want you to do is listen."

"Go ahead," Fuller told him, "I'm listening."

"We're going to fake up a couple of targets right now," Corning said. "Straight bulls'-eyes. Six shots and six dead centers for the target we use in the finals, and not quite so good a group in the one that represents the qualifying shoot."

"Listen, brother," Fuller said, "you've got to fix the thing up so it doesn't look quite so phoney; otherwise . . ."

"I thought you were listening," Corning said.

"I am," Fuller replied, "but you'll be listening about this time tomorrow night."

Ken Corning picked up a rifle.

"Put up a couple of targets," he said. "I want to fix up the fakes, and put 'em good and close. I don't want to waste shots."

IT was nine thirty when Mary Bagley came into the shooting gallery of Ted Fuller.

"This the place where the contest is going on?" she asked, taking a newspaper clipping from her purse.

Fuller nodded. "Meet Mr. Richey," he said, "the guy who's running the show."

Ken Corning stepped forward and bowed. "You wish to enter as a contestant?" he asked.

She nodded.

"Fill out this blank," said Corning, handing her a printed blank and a pencil.

Mary Bagley filled in her name, address, occupation, and looked at Ken Corning with cold, hard eyes.

"Is this on the up-and-up?" she asked.

"Sure it's on the up-and-up," he said.

"And there's a cash prize of one hundred dollars?"

"That's right," Corning told her. "And a loving cup."

"I'm not so strong for the loving cup," she said, "but I can use the hundred."

"All you've got to do to get it, is to win," Corning said. "Just sign the application blank showing that you're to be governed by the rules of the contest, as established by the manager."

"What are the rules?" she wanted to know.

"Simply that you shoot a qualifying target any time between now and eleven o'clock tonight. At eleven o'clock, the two best targets are picked out, and there's a final test in which six shots are fired by each contestant. Then the prize is awarded."

"Now listen," she told him, "if I shoot in this thing, I'm likely to win, so I don't want any misunderstandings."

"There won't be," said Corning, handing her a gun. "If you don't make a certain score, you have to pay for your own shots. If you go above that score, I pay for the shots."

The girl picked up a rifle, squinted down the sights, raised and lowered the hammer in order to get the pull of the trigger.

"Any practice shots?" she asked.

"No practice shots," he told her.

"All right, put up the target."

Ted Fuller clipped a pasteboard target on the carrier, looked at Corning significantly, and by a swift flip of his wrist, sent the target down the long, dark tunnel, until it finally came to rest against the back-stop, with a diffused electric light showing the target in bright illumination.

The gun snapped to the girl's shoulder. She shot with both eyes open. The six shots came belching forth from the gun in rapid succession. She laid down the gun and turned to Corning.

"All right," she said, "pay for the shots."

Fuller pulled on the carrier wire, which started the target fluttering back towards them.

"Wait until I see the target," Corning said.

Fuller held up his hand, caught the target as it came along the wire, gave it a single swift glance, then turned to Corning and grinned.

"Pay for the shots," he said.

Ken Corning flipped a coin on the counter.

The girl looked at her wrist-watch.

"The final is at eleven o'clock?" she asked.

"That's right," Corning told her.

"I'll be back," she said.

A crowd of curious spectators that had formed in a semi-circle around the back of the shooting gallery opened to let the girl through as she went out.

Ted Fuller moved over towards Ken Corning, handed him the target.

"You're going to have trouble," he said, out of the side of his mouth.

Ken Corning said nothing, but slipped the target into the pile of targets.

The crowd grew in size.

Two uniformed policemen appeared to hold them in line. Fuller did a rushing business in between times, the gallery echoing to the sound of shots. Toward eleven o'clock another policeman appeared. The three officers kept the crowd back.

At ten fifty-five, Mary Bagley returned to the gallery.

"Who shoots off the finals?" she asked.

"We don't know yet," Corning told her. "It isn't eleven. Somebody may show up in the next five minutes."

Mary Bagley shrugged her shoulders.

"I don't know who I'm going to shoot against," she said, "but I'm going to be in at the finals."

Corning stood with his watch in his hand. At precisely eleven o'clock he slipped it back into his pocket.

"All right," he said, "pick out the two best targets, Fuller."

Ted Fuller's thin, restless hands pawed through the pile of targets. In the background, five or six young women with blonde hair, and of various ages and sizes, surveyed each other with silent hostility. Back of them surged the crowd of spectators.

"These two," said Fuller, pointing to Mary Bagley and to Marian Sharpe.

"All right," said Corning, "let's shoot off the finals."

Fuller clipped a target on the carrier.

"You shoot first," Corning said to Mary Bagley.

She looked at Marian Sharpe with keen appraisal, then turned and picked up the gun.

"All right," she said.

Once more she shot with both eyes open. The spectators surged forward, against the line which had been extended by the police. The unsuccessful contestants stared with a disdainful scrutiny.

Mary Bagley shot more slowly this time, but her shots were spaced evenly and regularly. As she snapped back the pump mechanism of the rifle she did it with a forceful regularity which punctuated the interval between shots. They were as evenly spaced as if timed.

As she fired her sixth shot, she set down the gun on the counter, turned to Corning.

"This other jane uses the same gun and the same sights," she said. "Understand?"

Corning nodded affably.

"Certainly," he said.

Ted Fuller flipped his hand and brought back the target. As he handed it to Corning and Mary Bagley, and as they leaned forward to study it, Ted Fuller put the new target on the carrying mechanism. He stood so that his body shielded the target from the gaze of the spectators, then he sent it scurrying and fluttering along the long, dark tunnel, until it came into position at the back of the tunnel, against the back-stop, full in the field of light.

By the time Mary Bagley looked up from a contemplation of her target, Marian Sharpe was shooting.

Mary Bagley watched with wary eyes; saw the manner in which the girl slid back the repeating mechanism; saw the almost imperceptible wince as the gun was fired. Her eyes became scornful and her lip curled.

The girl fired the sixth shot, set down the gun, and looked at Ken Corning. There was something pleading in her eyes.

Ted Fuller stepped back and gave the wire a quick, sharp pull. The wire rolled over the pulleys, and the target came fluttering back. Ken Corning was careful to wait until it had reached a point almost directly in front of Mary Bagley, before he brought it to a stop. He stood in full view of the spectators, unclipped the target, then whistled. He pushed it towards Mary Bagley.

"Look at that!" he said.

Mary Bagley looked at it with eyes that slowly widened.

Ken Corning raised his voice.

"Miss Marian Sharpe," he said, "wins the prize of one hundred dollars and the loving cup."

"I," said Mary Bagley, slowly and distinctly, "will be a dirty name!"

Corning passed over the ten ten-dollar bills to Marian Sharpe, and glanced significantly at the crowd, then started to applaud. The crowd caught the hint and broke into a spattering chorus of applause. Before it had finished, Mary Bagley was standing in front of Ken Corning, her eyes blazing.

Her first words were snapped out before the applause had finished, and the crowd, sensing the purport of her remarks, became instantly curiously silent.

"What kind of a skin-game is this?" she demanded. "That target's a fake and you know it! There isn't a shot in the world that could shoot that kind of group at that distance, and hold the gun the way that broad held it. She damn near closed her eyes every time she fired. That target was a frame-up!"

Corning shrugged his shoulders and turned away.

"You signed the application blank," he said, over his shoulder, "and said that you agreed to abide by the rules of the contest and the selection of the winner. Miss Sharpe has been selected as the winner."

"Baloney!" blazed the girl. "You can't pull a stunt like that. I'll have you arrested!"

Corning kept his back to her, but took the arm of Marian Sharpe, and piloted her through the crowd.

ON his way to the rooming-house on Maple Avenue Ken Corning stopped to telephone the police.

"Listen," he said, "I don't want my name used in this and I don't want anybody to know who I am. I'm just giving you a tip. You can take it or leave it, but I've got a room in a rooming-house at 329 Maple Avenue. There's a couple of guys in a room on the same floor who have made a dicker with a fellow to give them some counterfeit money and a bunch of dope. I heard them make the deal. They're going to make a delivery some time within the next hour. The room is number 49, and there's a closet in that room. The guys are out now, but if you can get a couple of men to hide in the closet, you can catch them right when they make the delivery. But don't ever let on that you had a tip, or they'll know who gave it to you."

He slammed up the telephone, took a taxicab to his rooming-house, but did not enter at once; instead, he went across the street and stood lounging in a shaded doorway, watching.

Within a matter of ten minutes, a light coupé slowed down and pulled in to the curb. Two tall, square-shouldered men pushed their way purposefully from the coupé, and entered the rooming-house. The coupé moved away.

Corning waited another five minutes, then went up the stairs of the rooming-house, unlocked the door of his room, went in, sat down, turned on the light, and started to read a newspaper.

Fifteen minutes passed, while Corning smoked and read. Then there were steps in the corridor, and peremptory knocks on the door.

"Come in," said Corning.

The door pushed back. A squat, heavy-set man with black mustaches stood glaring at him. Behind him, and slightly to one side, was Mary Bagley.

"This the guy?" asked the man.

"That's him," said Mary Bagley.

The heavy-set man pushed his way into the room, waited a moment until Mary Bagley came in, then kicked the door shut.

"You're the guy that put on the shooting contest," said the heavy-set man.

"Who are you?" asked Corning. "And what business is it of yours?"

"Never mind," said the man. "I came here to see that this jane gets a square deal. That thing was the crudest kind of fake, and you know it. You can't pull anything like that and get away with it. I've been in the shooting gallery business myself, and I know just how it was done. This winner was picked in advance. She didn't even shoot at the target, but shot at the back-stop. The target was a frame-up all the way through. The whole thing was put on ice. . . ."

"You," said Ken Corning, speaking in a cool, calm voice, "seem to know a hell of a lot about it. If you know so much about how that was done, maybe you can tell me what these are."

He reached his hand in his pocket, took out a wallet. From the wallet he took two pieces of torn paper.

"Know what these are?" he asked.

The man stared with black, glittering, hostile eyes.

"What the hell do I care what they are?" he asked.

"They're bits of red tissue paper that are stained with blood," Ken Corning explained.

The black eyes lifted from a contemplation of the torn fragments of paper, to stare glittering menace at Ken Corning.

"They are," went on Corning, "bits of paper from the torpedo which was exploded to make it seem that the shot which killed Frank Glover was fired from the group of men who were near Glover at the time he fell.

"The real shot was fired from a .22 automatic in Mary Bagley's apartment. You fired the shot, and then slipped out and placed the gun back of the signboard. Mary Bagley posed as a witness."

The glittering black eyes became ominous, with a slight reddish-brown tint suffusing the pupils.

"I don't know what the hell you're talking about," said Pete, the Polack.

"Oh, yes you do," said Ken Corning slowly. "That's the reason that all of the tenants in the corner apartments were moved out. You didn't want anyone to hear the sound of the shot. I figured you were back of it because it took an expert shot to fire a single shot from the window of that apartment, and be certain Glover was killed. The other men were your accomplices. They baited George Pyle into losing his temper, then were careful to hold him in such a position that he was out of the line of fire, but so that you could shoot to one side of him, and make it appear that the bullet had come from his general direction.

"You thought there was a chance you might be looked for, because it was your gun. Pyle had left his fingerprints on it when he took it away from you and you had carefully preserved those fingerprints. But I figured Mary Bagley for your friend, and knew that if she had been your friend, she'd have hung around your shooting gallery and learned how to shoot pretty well. I also figured that if she got a raw deal she'd be pretty likely to hunt you up to champion her cause, so you've walked into my little trap."

"You can't prove a damned thing!" said Pete.

Corning shrugged his shoulders.

"I can raise a reasonable doubt in front of a jury," he said, "so that they won't convict Pyle, and I rather think they'll convict you."

Pete's right hand suddenly flicked to his shoulder. There was a glitter of motion, and Ken Corning found himself staring into the black muzzle of an automatic.

"Well," said Pete, "I'm not so sure that you're going to keep in good health, myself. You look unhealthy to me."

Corning stole a glance back to the closet door.

Nothing happened.

Little glittering lights played across the dark surface of the eyes which bored into his.

"Don't, Pete!" said the girl in a hissing voice. "You can't get away with it."

"The hell I can't!" said Pete.

"Not here! Not here. Take him for a ride."

The lights continued to play about the eyes, but a look of cunning came over the face.

"That," said Pete the Polack, "isn't a bad idea. Get your hat, guy, and start walking out. Walk easy and natural."

Ken Corning got his hat, started for the door. Pete the Polack moved up close to him. Corning reached for the knob of the door.

"Never mind," said Pete. "The broad will open the door. Go ahead, Mary."

The girl pulled the door open. Pete moved close to Ken Corning. Ken Corning started through the door, scooped out his right arm, caught the girl about the waist, and flung her back against the man with the gun.

Pete cursed, jumped to one side. Corning side-stepped before Pete had the gun free. He fired. The bullet ripped a hole in the side of Corning's coat as it went past. The girl screamed, dropped to the floor.

Corning lashed out his right fist. The girl cursed, rolled over, grabbed Corning's left leg and sunk her teeth into the calf.

Pete the Polack reeled backward under the impetus of the blow, but flung up the gun again. Corning tried to kick his foot loose from the grip which held it. The girl clung to him tightly, her arms locked around Corning's leg.

There were swift steps in the corridor behind Corning. A voice shouted: "Stick 'em up!"

Corning ducked. Pete fired. The girl's grip weakened. A gun behind Corning roared booming reverberations. Pete flung his weapon slightly to one side, fired again. Corning was conscious of someone behind him stumbling, lurching against the plastered wall, then slowly slumping downward with fingers scraping along the plaster.

Corning leaped over the girl's kicking legs, faced Pete the Polack. He saw the gun coming up, lashed out with both hands, trying to catch the hand which held the gun. Pete jumped back, and Corning flung himself forward in a tackle. He heard the roar of two shots fired in rapid succession, felt the jar of lead thudding into the huge torso, heard Pete groan, felt him sway, then heard a peculiar sputtering noise as blood bubbles came to the lips of the man and broke. The form went limp in his arms.

Ken Corning turned and straightened. One of the plain-clothesmen stood in the room, his face twisted with hatred, an automatic in his hand.

"The dirty —— killed the squarest dick that ever walked in shoe leather!" he said.

Mary Bagley sat up and screamed. The plainclothesman grabbed her wrist, dragged her across the floor. Pete the Polack made gurgling noises and tried to talk.

"I think," said Corning, "he wants to make a confession. You'd better listen."

"I don't give a damn *what* he confesses to!" the officer said.

"He killed my pal. If my bullet hasn't killed him, he's going to get the death penalty."

"Well *I* care," said Corning. "This man killed Frank Glover."

A look of infinite weariness took the glitter from the hard black eyes. The head nodded. More blood sputtered from the lips, and the eyes glazed.

"Grab that girl!" said Corning. "She can give us the whole story."

Mary Bagley got to her knees, stared at the face of Pete the Polack.

"My God, he's dead!" she screamed.

IT was one o'clock when Ken Corning got Helen Vail on the telephone.

"You can go home now," he told her. "It's all over."

"What happened?" she asked.

"A frame-up," he said. "Glover's own bodyguard wanted to get rid of him and take over his lay. They wanted to frame the crime on Pyle whom they also wanted out of the way. They worked the frame-up and exploded a torpedo at the same time a crack-shot plugged Glover from Mary Bagley's apartment. That was Pete the Polack who had his own grudge against Glover and jumped at the chance. They'd decoyed the radio car into the neighborhood by a fake call. Pyle was framed all the way along."

"Was that why you pulled the shooting gallery stuff?" she asked.

"Yes. It was a thousand to one chance, but I had to get Mary Bagley's boy-friend out in the open and just where I could work on him."

"Any action?" asked Helen Vail.

"A little," he told her. "I gave the cops a tip that should have had them in my room. They got the numbers mixed and got in the wrong room. It wasn't until the shooting started that they got into action. Pete plugged one of the dicks right through the heart."

"Did you get a confession?" asked Helen Vail.

"Yes, from the girl. After Pete fired the shot he knocked the silencer off the gun, ran down stairs, and when he saw Pyle go by, planted the gun behind the billboard and disappeared."

"You coming back to the office?" she asked.

"No," he told her. "I'm going out and hunt up Lampson. He'll tell the truth now."

"You mean about the crime?"

"No. I mean about the frame-up they tried to work on me."

"He won't dare to talk," she told him. "Not with his record."

Ken Corning laughed grimly.

"When I get done with him," he said, "he won't dare to keep silent. These fellows started this funny business and now I'm going to start fighting the devil with fire."

"Be careful your fingers don't get burned," she warned.

"I," he told her, "am the one guy in this hookup that's got asbestos gloves."

Blackmail with Lead

KEN CORNING stopped at the battered table, which ran the length of the jail room, and looked through the coarse wire screen into the face of Sam Driver; a face that was twitching nervously.

"If I'm going to be your lawyer," said Ken Corning, "I've got to have all there is to know about your case."

Sam Driver fidgeted uncomfortably in the chair on the other side of the screened partition. He acted as though he could already feel a current of electricity coursing through the chair, burning the life from his body.

"Listen," he said, "don't you s'pose you could cop a plea?"

Ken Corning shook his head.

"I sounded out the deputy D. A. They want first degree or nothing and they won't make any promises about the death penalty. That's up to the judge."

"Jeeze," said Driver, "that's no break at all."

"You will have to give me the true facts if we're going to get anywhere," Corning told him.

Driver looked furtively around and then leaned forward and spoke rapidly, the words coming from the side of his lips.

"I wouldn't have killed Harry Green for a million dollars," he said. "We was buddies. We'd batted around together a lot. He'd give me the shirt off his back, and I'd give him my last dollar.

"We'd had a little run of luck. The cards had been breaking better for us, and we had this old flivver. We stayed at the auto camp and used the car together. I don't know where Harry went that night. He was out on a game somewhere, but he didn't have the car. I had the car. I drove it up to visit some relatives of mine on Hampshire Street.

"It was dark when I got there, and I stuck around and had a

175

few drinks. Then I came out and got in the car and started out towards the automobile camp. I guess I was a little bit crocked. Anyway, a car drove up alongside, and a couple of dicks started to shake me down. They said my headlights was glaring, and I was driving funny. They looked the car over for booze, and found Harry Green's body in the back."

"How did it get there?" asked Corning.

"I wish I knew, boss, honest to gawd I do! It wasn't in there when I started out with the car, I know that."

"All right," said Corning, wearily, "what about the money?"

"That's another funny thing," said Driver, lowering his eyes and shifting about in his chair nervously. "I had about five thousand bucks on me. It was in crisp new bills. The bulls claim that I got that from Harry Green; that that's why I croaked him. Why, listen, I wouldn't take any money from Harry. . . .."

"I've heard all that before," Corning said. "How did you get the money?"

"I won it fair and square, in a poker game."

"All right, you've got to produce the people who sat in that poker game."

Driver placed his hand to his face, started tugging nervously at his mouth with the tips of his fingers.

"I can't do that," he said. "They were friends of Harry's, but strangers to me. Harry introduced me to the club and I got in the game. They wouldn't admit sitting in a poker game; not with a murder rap."

Ken Corning drummed silently on the table, with the tips of his fingers. His steady eyes bored into the cowering optics of the man on the other side of the screen.

"Get this, Driver," he said slowly, "and get it straight. Unless you can give me the truth on that case, and I can make something out of it, you're going to get the death penalty."

Driver's lips quivered. He held them with his fingers for a moment. His eyes were shifty with panic.

"All right," he said, "give me a chance to think things over a bit. Maybe I can work out something."

"You've got to have something that you can tell a jury," said Ken Corning slowly. "Something that the jury will believe; something that is going to sound logical, in spite of all the cross-examination a District Attorney gives you. In short, Driver, the only thing that will work is the truth."

"But I told you the truth."

"It doesn't sound like it," said Ken Corning grimly.

"To you, or to a jury?" asked Driver.

"Neither to me nor a jury," Ken Corning said slowly.

Driver wet his lips nervously with the tip of his tongue, said nothing.

"Do you," asked Ken Corning, taking a notebook from his pocket, "know a woman by the name of Ella Ambrose?"

Sam Driver nodded his head slowly.

"Yes," he said, "she lives out there near where the folks are, on Hampshire Street."

"What does she know about the case?" asked Corning.

The eyes of the prisoner sought his face, and, for the first time during the interview, became steady.

"Search me," he said. "She can't know anything about it."

Corning nodded.

"Yes, she knows something about it. I can't figure just what it is, but it's something that she thinks is important. She wants me to come down to the house, after dark tonight, and not to let anyone know I'm coming. She sent me a message."

Driver shook his head and made a simultaneous gesture with his shoulders and the palms of his hands.

"You better go see her," he said. "Maybe she knows something, but be sure it's something that's going to help me. If it ain't, get her out of the country."

Corning suddenly snapped a swift question at the prisoner.

"Driver," he said, "what did you do with the gun that killed Harry Green?"

For what seemed like three long seconds, Sam Driver sat with sagging jaw, and looked as though someone had slapped him in the face with a wet towel. His eyes bulged, and the muscles of his throat worked convulsively. Suddenly he said all in one breath: "Jeeze, boss, I never saw any gun. For gawd's sake, don't you go getting an idea like that through your head. How would I know what happened to the gun?"

Ken Corning got to his feet.

"That," he said, "is just a mild sample of what the District Attorney is going to do to you on cross-examination. You've got to answer the questions better than that, or you'll get murder in the first."

* * *

WIND tugged at the skirts of Ken Corning's overcoat as he stood on the dark street corner and strained his eyes at the shadowy houses, trying to see the numbers above the doors.

He moved forward, out of the circle of illumination cast by the street lamp, and became conscious of motion in the darkness.

He whirled and stood tense.

A lad of about twelve years of age came out from behind a board fence. He was leaning against the wind, and his cap was pulled down low against the tug of the gale. The light from the corner showed a young-old face, with shrewd, peering eyes, and a much frayed coat that was originally several sizes too large.

"You're Ken Corning, the big lawyer?" the boy asked.

"Yes, I'm Corning."

"My mom, she was afraid you couldn't find the place, so she sent me to wait around," said the boy.

"Who is your mother, lad?"

"Mrs. Ambrose. She's the one you're goin' to see."

Ken Corning nodded his head. "All right, son," he said, "let's go."

The boy remarked in a swiftly nervous monotone, "We'd better cut through the alley. Mom's afraid somebody may be watching the place."

"Why should they watch the place?"

"I don't know. Mom told me not to talk nothing over with you, just to bring you to the house."

The boy slipped through the gate in the fence. "Watch your step when you get around here," he warned. "There's a bunch of tin cans over there on the side."

He moved unerringly, following some path which was invisible to the lawyer's eyes. All above was smelly darkness. Houses fronted on the narrow street; houses that were cheap and unpretentious, yet were palaces beside the hovels which were scattered around the backs of the lots. All about were the sounds of human occupancy; low voices which carried through the flimsy walls of mean structures, the raucous blasts of a cheap radio which sounded from a living-room where comparative affluence announced its presence in strident tones.

The shadow grew deeper and Corning's guide was but a blotch of black moving against a dark background. Abruptly he paused.

"This is the place," said the boy, and started beating lightly with his knuckles on a door.

"Who is it?" asked thin, tired tones from the interior.

"It's me, Mom."

"Did *he* come with you?"

"Yeah. Open up."

A bolt rasped back on the inside of the door, then, as the door swung open, an oblong of dim light from an oil lamp silhouetted the broad hips and shoulders of a heavy-set woman who hulked in the doorway.

"Come in," said the woman.

Ken Corning stepped into the dark room. The woman pushed the door shut.

"I couldn't understand," said Corning, cautiously, "why you didn't come to the office."

The woman placed a finger to her lips, looked over at the boy. "Frank," she said, "you run over and see if Jimmy won't let you stay with him for a while."

The boy turned the knob, held the door against the wind, slipped out into the night.

KEN CORNING stared at the woman. She was in the early fifties. Adversity had stamped its mark upon her, and her face had set in lines of whining defiance, as though she had learned to cope with the world by aggressively protesting her rights with shrill-voiced insistence. Her features were heavy, the eyes small and sharp. The lower jaw was full and determined, but the upper part of the mouth seemed pinched, with a high, narrow roof.

"You're defending Sam Driver?" she said.

Ken Corning nodded.

"Why didn't you come to the office?"

"Because they got the place watched."

"Who has?"

"I d'know. Maybe the police."

"Why have they got the place watched?"

"I spoke out of turn," she said.

"To whom?" Corning inquired.

"The cop on the beat. I told him that I didn't think Sam Driver was guilty, and that I knew some stuff that would give him a break. The cop told me I'd better keep out of things that didn't concern me. Right after that, men started to stand around in front of the house. They waited in automobiles, and poked around, as though they had business, but they didn't fool me any. They were dicks, watching me."

"All right," said Ken Corning, "what do you know?"

She leered at him shrewdly.

"There's got to be something in it for me," she told him.

Slowly, Ken Corning shook his head.

"All the money that Sam Driver has," he said, "is held by the law, on the theory that it belonged to Harry Green, the man he's charged with killing. If I can get him acquitted, naturally he gets that money back. I'm going to take most of it for my fee. There'll be some left for him and some for expenses. If he wants to make you a present after the case is over, that's up to him."

She twisted her fingers together and looked at Corning with avaricious eyes that took in every detail of his tailor-made clothes.

"Seems like it's going to be pretty soft for you, if you get him off. Seems like I'd oughtta have some cash."

"No," said Corning, "they'd ask you about that when you got on the witness stand. If you told them I'd given you a single nickel, they'd make it appear I'd bought your evidence."

"I wouldn't have to tell them," she suggested.

"You won't get anywhere with that line. And it doesn't listen well. If you know anything, go ahead and tell me."

She twisted her fingers for a moment, then suddenly broke into speech.

"All right," she said. "I know Sam Driver, and I know his sister-in-law well. They've got a place here on Hampshire Street. The man's got a job, and they've got a radio 'n everything."

"Yes," said Corning. "What of it?"

"Well, Driver used to come and visit them. Sometimes he'd bring Harry Green with him. More often he'd come alone. He drove a flivver, and kept it parked out in front of the place when he was inside. I got so I knowed the flivver.

"The night of the murder, I knew that Driver was inside, at his sister-in-law's, hoisting a few. I was going uptown, and I saw a man walking up and down the sidewalk, and I figured I'd wait until he got out of the way, before I came out into view.

"I seen a new model Cadillac car come down and stop side of Driver's flivver. Guys got out that had on evening clothes. You could see the white of them in the light that came from the street lamp. There were two of them. I saw them pull something from the Cadillac and put it in the flivver. It was something heavy."

"Could you see definitely what it was?" asked Corning slowly.

"No. But it was heavy."

"How do you know the car was a Cadillac?"

"It was a Cadillac," she said, doggedly enough, "a new model Cadillac. I keep up on automobiles because my boy talks about them all the time. He knows every new car that comes out."

Ken Corning looked at her searchingly.

"You don't look like the type of woman who would be interested in a Cadillac automobile."

"I knew that new model Cadillac."

"All right. Then what happened?"

"Then," she said, "they went around to the headlights on Driver's automobile and started doing something to them with a monkey wrench or something. I thought they were car thieves that was stealing the headlights, but they were dressed too good for that."

"Go on," Corning told her.

"That's about all. I got to thinking things over, and I thought you'd ought to know."

"Got the license number on the Cadillac car?" he asked.

She shook her head rapidly.

"No," she said, "I . . ."

There was the sound of peremptory knuckles banging on the door.

"Open up!" said a gruff voice. "This is the law."

She looked in swift consternation at Ken Corning.

"You double-crossed me," she said.

Corning shook his head. He was on his feet, standing over in a corner of the room, shifting his eyes from the face of the woman to the door.

The door quivered, then banged open, shivering in the wind.

Three men pushed their way into the room. The last man shoved the door closed, and the oil light flickered and danced in the wind.

"Well," said Corning, "what's the trouble?"

The man who had been the first into the room looked at Corning.

"Nothing that concerns you, buddy," he said. "It's something that concerns the woman. She's been selling hooch."

"I have not!" said the woman.

The detective grinned.

"Got a warrant?" asked Ken Corning.

The man's voice was scornful. "Of course I have," he said.

"But I haven't been selling any booze. I haven't got any booze. I don't know anything about . . ."

"Look around, boys," said the man who was in charge.

"I think," said Ken Corning, "that I'll have to take a look at that warrant."

"Sure," said the officer, with elaborate sarcasm. "Go right ahead and look at it all you want to. Read it and weep."

He took a folded paper from his pocket, passed it to Ken Corning with exaggerated courtesy.

Corning looked at the search warrant, which was duly issued and in regular form. One of the men had gone to the closet, and was bending over, sending the beam of a flashlight to the dark interior. Suddenly he called: "Okey, chief, here it is."

The woman started to cry.

"I didn't mean anything," she said. "Just some stuff that I kept there to take when I wasn't feeling good. I never sold any and I never gave any away. I'm a poor widow woman, with a little boy to support, and . . ."

The man in charge grinned at Ken Corning, then turned his eyes to the woman, and interrupted her wailing excuses.

"Get your coat on, sister," he said. "We've got a car waiting outside."

Ken Corning pulled his overcoat up around his neck.

"I'll be seeing you boys later," he said, and pushed his way out into the windy night.

IT was two hours later when Ken Corning arrived at the jail with a writ of *habeas corpus* and a fifteen thousand dollar bail bond, issued by a company that knew him and accepted his guarantee. Ella Ambrose was delivered into his custody.

She climbed into the car, sat at his side, and said to him: "Did you get me out?"

"Yes," he said.

"Did they dismiss the charge?"

"No, I had to get a writ of *habeas corpus* and get you out on bail."

"Thanks," she remarked, after a moment.

"I want you to go to my office and make a statement," he told her.

"Sure," she told him, with ready loquaciousness. "But I've got to get back and find out about my boy. Maybe he came back and went to bed, or maybe he stayed over at his friend's house."

"All right," Corning told her. "I'll take you home first if you want."

"I wish you would."

He pushed the car into speed.

"Then you can come back to the office with me, and give me a statement," he said.

"Yes," she remarked in a colorless tone of mechanical acquiescence.

"About this Cadillac car," said Corning. "Do you suppose . . ."

"Of course," she said, "I couldn't be *sure* it was a Cadillac."

"Could you see what the men were carrying?"

"No, I couldn't really swear that they carried anything. I saw a car stop, and then the men got out."

"But you're certain they carried something over and put it in Sam Driver's automobile, is that right?"

"No, I'm not certain of it, I think they did."

"What makes you think they did? Didn't you *see* them?"

"No, I can't swear that I saw them. That is, I saw them moving around, and then, after I read about the case in the papers, I got to thinking that that's what they *might have done.*"

"Two men?" asked Corning.

"Yes, there were two men."

"In evening clothes?"

"Well, they probably had on evening clothes. I can't be certain about that."

"I see," Corning told her, and lapsed into silence. He drove her to her house, held the door open for her.

"You're going to wait for me to go back and make a statement?" she asked.

"No," he said gravely, "I don't think I'll need a statement."

"Thanks a lot," she said, "for what you did in getting me out."

"Not at all," he told her.

When she had vanished into the shadows about the cheap houses, which clustered together in the lot like freight cars in a railroad yard, Corning savagely snapped his car into gear, and drove furiously, until he came to an all-night drug-store where there was a telephone.

He put through two calls.

The first was to his office, telling Helen Vail to get a taxicab and go home. The second was to the office of the company that had written the bail bond at his request.

"On that Ella Ambrose bail on *habeas corpus,*" he told the bonding company, "I've lost interest in the case. I wish you'd pick up the defendant and get a release of the bail bond."

The voice at the other end of the line chuckled.

"Sorry, old man," it said, "but there's been a note come through, that the case is to be dismissed and the complaint withdrawn."

"I see," said Ken Corning, and hung up the receiver.

JOE VARE, private detective, sat in Ken Corning's office, and looked across at the lawyer.

"I don't get you," he said.

"It's simple," Corning told him. "Go to the Cadillac agency, get the list of new car deliveries, check the people carefully, find out if one of them *might* be the sort to have had some connection either with Sam Driver or with Harry Green."

Vare twisted a half-smoked cigar thoughtfully, rolling it with his thumb and forefinger.

"Driver and Green were bums?" he said.

"You might call them that."

"Think they'd have friends who drove new Cadillacs?"

Corning leaned forward.

"Get this, Vare," he said. "This is a murder case, and the Cadillac car is a lead. In a murder case I run down *all* leads, no matter how shaky they look." Vare got to his feet and grinned at the attorney.

"Okey," he said. "I'm on my way."

As the detective left the office, Helen Vail slipped through the door, closed it behind her, and said softly: "There's a Mrs. Brown out there, who wants to see you about the Driver case."

"All right," said Corning, "let's take a look at her."

Helen Vail held the door open and nodded. A woman of approximately thirty or thirty-one years of age, modishly attired, came into the office, and regarded the attorney from wide, brown eyes. She wore a brown, tight-fitting hat, brown dress, brown shoes and stockings. Her clothes gave the appearance of well-tailored wealth.

"Sit down," said Corning, as Helen Vail gently closed the door. The woman dropped into a chair.

"What can I do for you, Mrs. Brown?"

"Nothing," she said. "I think *I* can do something for *you.*"

He raised his eyebrows.

She opened her purse and took out a roll of currency, which she held in her gloved fingers.

"I'm going to be frank with you," she said.

"Yes," said Corning, "go ahead."

"You're representing a man by the name of Sam Driver, who is accused of murder?"

"Yes."

"I don't want Mr. Driver to know that I came to you."

"Does he know you, Mrs. Brown?"

"Yes," she said. "You see, I used to know Sam Driver in the old days—that was a long time ago. Our roads separated. We went different ways. He went his way and I went mine. He went down and I went up."

"All right," he said. "Go on."

"The District Attorney hasn't got much of a case against Driver. It's largely circumstantial evidence. You've beaten the prosecution once or twice in some spectacular cases. They're afraid of you. If you'll have Driver think up some good story about a fight and a killing in self-defense, the District Attorney will let Driver plead guilty to manslaughter. But if the man stands trial, he's going to be railroaded."

"What makes you think that?"

"I don't know. I know there are powerful influences at work against him, that's all."

"Where do you get your information?" asked Corning, watching her closely.

"About what?"

"About the District Attorney's office, for instance, and the powerful influences."

She shook her head, and the brown eyes softened into a twinkle as she regarded him.

"You have your professional secrets," she said. "I have mine. I'm just telling you."

"Well, then," he said, "tell me some more."

She looked down at the tips of her gloved fingers, suddenly raised her eyes, and, with an expression of utter candor on her face, said: "If he doesn't plead guilty, they're going to give him the death penalty."

"Why?" he asked.

"For lots of reasons. There's politics mixed up in it, and you know what politics are in York City."

"Yes," he told her, "I know. But why should politics be mixed up in the killing of a hobo?"

"That's something else again," she replied. "You're frightfully inquisitive for a lawyer."

"Well, what am I supposed to do?"

"Take this money. Use it as an additional fee. I don't suppose you got much from Sam Driver. Go ahead and work out a good story with him. It's got to be a good story with a self-defense angle to it—something that the District Attorney's office can give to the newspapers to keep the people from making a very strong protest when they accept a plea of manslaughter."

"Who handles the publicity?" asked Corning, still watching her narrowly.

"You fix up the story," she said. "Your client will spill it to a newspaper reporter or the District Attorney."

"Suppose he makes a statement that constitutes an admission to the killing, and then you're wrong about what the District Attorney is going to do?" Corning asked.

"I'm not wrong."

"That's what you say. I can't risk my client's life on the strength of your unsupported word."

She bit her lip for a moment.

"I hadn't thought of that," she said, slowly.

She looked down at the tip of her brown shoe for a few moments, then straightened and pushed the money across the desk towards Ken Corning.

"I think I can figure out a way so it will be all right," she said.

Ken Corning regarded the roll of bills.

"I can't take money from you," he said, "to do what *you* think is best for my client. I've got to do what *I* think is best."

"I understand that. But I know you wouldn't take the money from me, unless you were going to play fair."

Ken Corning reached out and took the money.

"Just a moment," he said, moving towards the outer office, "and I'll get you a receipt."

Ken Corning pushed his way through the door, closed it behind him, and nodded to his secretary.

"Helen," he said, in low, swift tones, "put on your hat, go down on the elevator and stand in the lobby of the building. When this woman comes out, tail her. See where she goes. Let me know as soon as you find out."

She slid back her chair from the desk, and was reaching for her hat as Corning turned back towards the private office. He had a blank receipt form in his hand.

"You'll have to give me your full name, in order to get a receipt," he said to the woman who called herself Mrs. Brown.

"I don't want a receipt," she said.

Ken Corning shrugged his shoulders.

The woman got to her feet, smoothed down her skirt, and smiled at him.

"I think we understand each other," she said.

"I'm not certain that I understand you," he told her.

"Oh, well," she said brightly, "I think I understand you—perfectly."

She was very trim and straight as she marched from the office, closing the door gently after her.

SEVERAL minutes passed, and Corning heard the door of the outer office open and close. He remembered that Helen Vail was out, and got to his feet, walked across his private office, and opened the door.

A tall, well-groomed man, with cold eyes and a smiling mouth, said: "You're Ken Corning?"

Corning nodded.

"I'm Jerry Bigelow," said the man, and shook hands.

As he saw there was no look of recognition on Corning's face, he added: "The man who runs the column entitled 'Inside Stuff' in *The Courier.*"

Corning ushered him into the inner office, and the man sat down in a huge leather chair, crossed his knees, and tapped a cigarette on a polished thumbnail.

"I've got orders to mention your name in my column," he said.

"All right," said Corning with a grin. "Are you going to pan me, or give me a boost?"

"That's up to you," said the columnist.

Corning raised his eyebrows.

"You know," said Bigelow, "I like to give the inside facts a little bit before the public gets them. I like to give it a touch of spice, and give the impression of being very much in the know."

Corning nodded once more, silently, warily, his eyes half slitted as they watched the man who had called on him.

"Now," Bigelow said, still smiling with his lips, but his cold eyes fastened on the smoke which curled upward from his cigarette, "there's been some talk going around town about you. They say that you have busted a lot of precedents, fought the political ring that's supposed to be running York City, and are making a lot of money."

Ken Corning said nothing.

"I just thought," remarked Bigelow, "that if I should write up a little sketch for my column that you had whipped the big boys into line, and they were going to give you a break from now on, it might do you some good."

"What are you getting at?" Corning asked.

"Well," Bigelow said, "you're representing a bum and a panhandler who's got a murder rap on him, Sam Driver. The prosecution has got a dead open-and-shut case on him, but there's been a rumor going around that you've got the D. A.'s office a little jumpy because you've managed to get some acquittals in cases they thought were dead open-and-shut."

"Well?" asked Corning.

"Well," said Bigelow, "there's talk that the District Attorney doesn't know exactly what to do in this Driver case. He's got some circumstantial evidence, but it doesn't show very much. If Driver should come out and change his story, and admit that he did the killing, but claim that it was done in self-defense, because he found out that Green had been mixed up in some pretty shady stuff that Driver didn't approve of, there's a pretty good chance the District Attorney would figure he didn't have enough evidence to go on with a murder case, and he might let Driver get a plea of manslaughter."

"What makes you think the D. A. would let Driver make a manslaughter plea?" asked Corning.

"Just a little inside stuff," Bigelow told him. "Of course I keep my ear pretty close to the ground."

"Okey," said Corning. "Then suppose I *don't* have Driver put up a self-defense story, and take the rap for manslaughter. Then what's going to happen?"

The smile left Bigelow's lips, his cold eyes fastened directly on Ken Corning.

"I've got orders," he said, "to mention your name. If you did something that was pretty clever, I could write it up and give out the dope that you had been taken in on the inside. If you passed up a chance to make a clever play, and did something dumb, I'd probably have to write that you weren't such big-time stuff after all; that you'd let a fast one slip through your fingers because you couldn't use the old bean."

Corning got slowly to his feet.

"All right," he said, "I guess you've said all you were supposed to say, haven't you?"

Bigelow pinched out the end of his cigarette, dropped it into an ashtray, regarded Corning thoughtfully, and then said slowly: "Yes, I guess I have."

He started to walk from the office, but turned at the door.

"Let me know, will you?" he said. "Because I'm anxious to get your name in my column."

"Don't worry," Corning told him, "I'll let you know."

The telephone was ringing when Corning closed the door of his inner office, behind Bigelow's departing figure. He scooped the receiver to his ear, and heard Helen Vail's voice.

"Listen, chief," she said. "I followed her to a private automobile—a coupé. I picked up a taxi and tailed her. She got away, but I got the license number of the automobile before she gave me the slip."

"Did she know she was being followed?" asked Ken Corning.

"I don't think so, chief. It was just a bum break in the traffic."

"All right," said Corning, "what about the license number?"

"I telephoned in to the police registration department," Helen Vail said, "and got a friend of mine on the line. I didn't tell him, of course, what I wanted to know for. He gave me the registration."

"All right," said Ken Corning, "what was it?"

"The car," said Helen Vail, "is registered in the name of Stella Bixel. She's the widow of the man who was killed by the burglar in the country cabin last fall. You may remember the case . . ."

"Okey," said Ken Corning, crisply, "that's good work, Helen. Come on back to the office."

*   *   *

CORNING looked across his desk, into the speculative eyes of Edward Millwright, the expert on handwriting, fingerprints and questioned documents, whom he had asked to come in to see him.

"Can you," he asked, "get access to the police files, or to the Bureau of Criminal Identification records?"

The handwriting expert squinted his eyes thoughtfully.

"I *have* done so," he said, "on cases where I was working with the police, and once or twice on cases where I had uncovered some evidence which the police thought would be of value."

"Could you get somebody else to look up some information for you and pass it out?"

"I might."

"All right," said Corning, "here's another question. I understand that recently they're taking fingerprints of bodies that go through the morgue."

The expert nodded.

"I am representing," said Ken Corning, "a man named Sam Driver, who is accused of the murder of Harry Green, a gambler, panhandler, and general bum. I don't think anyone ever claimed the body of Green. I think it was finally buried, after an autopsy, at county expense. The body went through the morgue, and I think fingerprints were taken."

"All right," said Millwright, "what do you want me to do?"

"I want you," said Corning, slowly, "to find out what's funny about the case."

"How do you mean?"

"There's something funny about the case—something that I don't know anything about. I don't think it's anything connected with Sam Driver, so I think it's something connected with Harry Green, the murdered man. I want you to get those fingerprints and check them."

"I could get the fingerprints," said the expert, "the records of the morgue are open. But I'm not so certain about checking them; not the way you want them checked, anyway."

"Don't you know some peace officer who could wire the classification in to some of the central identification bureaus?"

"I might work that, yes."

"All right, do that; and furthermore, I wish you to check up the fingerprints with any police bulletins that may be floating around, on unsolved crimes."

"In other words, you think there's something fishy about this man, Green, is that it?"

"I don't know," Corning said slowly, "but I'm going to find out. There's something funny about the case, and pretty powerful influences are bringing pressure to bear on me, to make me handle it in a certain way."

"Why should powerful influences be mixed up in a case involving a hobo?" Millwright wanted to know.

"That's what I want to find out," said Corning.

Millwright nodded, got to his feet.

"With any kind of luck," he said, "I can let you know inside of twenty-four hours; otherwise, it'll just be a slow and tedious process, with the cards stacked against me."

He was shaking hands with Millwright, when Vare, the private detective, came into the room.

Vare waited until the door had closed behind Millwright, then sat down and pulled a list from his pocket.

"Well," he said, "I got a list of all of the Cadillacs that have been purchased in the last year. That is, of course, those that were purchased from the agency here in the city, or those that were registered as being owned in the city."

"Does it give us anything?" asked Corning.

"Not a thing," Vare said. "It was a crazy proposition thinking that it would. As I understand it, you figure Sam Driver may be hooked up with somebody who bought a Cadillac. Driver's a hobo, a crook and a murderer. The list of the fellows who bought Cadillacs reads like a social directory. Everybody on this list has got some social position, except the three fellows who have stars opposite their names—they're bootleggers."

"Well," said Corning, "a bootlegger may have some connection with a murderer."

Vare grinned.

"Try to uncover it," he said. "Those birds work pretty fast and play 'em pretty close to their chest. Try to nose into their business, and see what happens."

Ken Corning's forefinger slid down the list. Abruptly it came to a stop and he looked at the detective.

"I notice," he said, "that Harrison Burman bought a Cadillac."

Vare nodded.

"Burman," he said, "is the owner of *The Courier*. That's the paper that stands in with the big shots. It comes pretty near running the town."

"Wait a minute—wait a minute!" said Corning. A strange light of excitement was growing in his eyes.

He grabbed a pad and wrote names on it, which Vare could not see—names set in the form of a circle with short lines leading from one to the next.

In order as he scribbled, they were:

Green—Driver—Mrs. Bixel—*The Courier*—Jerry Bigelow— George Bixel—Harrison Burman. The name Burman completed the circle next to that of Green.

Ken Corning crumpled the sheet, looked at the private detective and grinned.

"Do you remember," he asked, "a murder case that took place last October, a chap by the name of George Bixel?"

"Sure," Vare said. "I remember something about the facts of the case. There was quite a bit of comment about it at the time. It was one of those lonely mountain cabins, and a crook pulling a hold-up, trying to get Mrs. Bixel's jewelry. Her husband came in and tried to hold the guy for the police. The guy shot him and escaped."

"Harrison Burman was up there in the cabin at the time, wasn't he?" Corning asked.

Vare looked at the attorney, and his forehead puckered into a frown.

"What the hell are you driving at?"

"Nothing," said Corning. "I'm just asking you about the case. You should remember it fairly well. It seems to me there's a reward out for the murderer, or there was at one time."

Vare nodded slowly.

"All right," said Corning, "what are the facts, as nearly as you can remember them?"

"Bixel and his wife went up to the cabin," said Vare. "It wasn't Bixel's cabin. It was a cabin they had secured from a friend somewhere. In fact, come to think of it, I think it was a cabin Burman had hired or owned, or something. Anyway, Bixel and his wife went up there and asked Burman to come up and join them for a week-end.

"While they were there," he went on, "a yegg got into the

room one night when Mrs. Bixel was dressing, and tried to stick her up for her jewels. George Bixel happened to come into the room. He grappled with the yegg, and Mrs. Bixel screamed. Burman was outside somewhere. He came in on the run, just as the shot was fired that killed Bixel, and the crook turned the gun on Mrs. Bixel. Burman struck at the crook and jiggled his arm so that the shot went wild. Then Burman tried to grab the man, but the man jumped to the window, took a shot at Burman, which missed, and jumped out and ran away. The police found the gun where he'd left it by the window."

"Fingerprints on the gun?" asked Corning.

"Yes, fingerprints on the gun, and the police were able to trace it by the numbers, and I think they managed to identify the man who had pulled the job. He was an ex-convict; one who had been paroled. I can look it up in just a few minutes and let you know."

"All right," Corning said. "Look it up and telephone me."

"Anything else?" asked Vare.

Corning shook his head.

"Go get that information," he said, "and let me know as soon as you can. That's what I'm after right now."

Vare nodded and left the office.

Ken Corning got up from behind his desk and started pacing the floor. He paced back and forth for almost twenty minutes, and then the telephone rang. Vare's voice came to him over the wire:

"Got all the dope on that case, Corning," he said. "The convict's name was Richard Post. He's got a long criminal record, most of it for petty stuff. He was paroled from the pen on a charge of forgery, and two weeks after his parole, pulled this hold-up in the mountain cabin."

"Have the police got out dodgers for him on this Bixel murder?" asked Corning.

"Oh, sure," said Vare. "I've got one of them here in the office."

"Gives fingerprints and everything?"

"Yes. Gives his criminal record and a photograph—front and side."

"Thanks," said Corning, "I think that's all," and hung up.

He put through a call to Millwright, the handwriting expert.

"Millwright," he said, "the police have got a dodger out on a convict named Richard Post. He's wanted for murder. The dodger has got his fingerprints, taken from the jail records; also front and side photographs. I wish you'd hunt up that dodger and check it with the fingerprints of this man, Harry Green, who was murdered."

"I can do that for you in just about five minutes," Millwright said. "I've got the fingerprints from the morgue records, and we keep a file of the police dodgers."

"Okey," said Corning, "I'll hold the phone."

He held the receiver to his ear, lit a cigarette, and had smoked less than one-third of it, when Millwright's excited voice came to his ears.

"Got it!" he said. "And it's a good hunch."

"The same man?" asked Corning.

"The same man. There can't be any doubt about it; the fingerprints check. The man that was murdered is the man the police have been looking for, under the name of Richard Post. He's the one who murdered George Bixel in a hold-up in a mountain cabin."

"All right," said Corning, "that's all I wanted to know."

"What do you want me to do with the information?" asked Millwright. "Pass it on to the police? They'll be interested to know that the Bixel murder case is cleared up."

Corning chuckled.

"The reason that I got you to work on this thing," he said, "instead of a man who had any police affiliations, is because I wanted to control the information, once I'd secured it."

"What do you want me to do with it?" asked Millwright.

"Lock it up tight in a safe and then forget it's there," Ken Corning said slowly. "When I want to use it, I'll ask you about it. Until then, sew it up in a sack."

Millwright's voice was dubious.

"That," he said, "is plain dynamite. It's going to get out sooner or later."

"All right," Corning said, "let's make it later. Forget that you know a thing about it."

He hung up the receiver, and grinned triumphantly.

CORNING threaded his way through the narrow alleys where the little houses were crowded close together. He found the one where he had called on Mrs. Ambrose, and after searching in vain for a bell button, resorted to his knuckles.

There was no answer.

He pounded again. After a minute or two, the door of an adjoining shack opened, and a hatchet-faced woman, with sharp black eyes, stared at him.

"Are you in charge of these houses?" he asked.

"Yes, what do you want?"

"Is this the house occupied by Mrs. Ella Ambrose?"

"She's gone."

"Where did she go?"

"I don't know. She packed up all of a sudden, and got out inside of an hour. I thought maybe somebody was dead or something. She wouldn't tell any of us anything. But she paid her rent when she left."

"Is that unusual?" asked Corning.

"It was with her," she said. "She was away behind with her rent. She paid it all up."

Corning stood, thinking, for a moment, then said:

"I'd like to rent this house."

"All right," she said, "it's for rent if you've got the money. It's cash in advance, and no wild parties. This is a respectable place, tenanted by people that are trying to get along."

Corning pulled out his wallet. "I'll pay a month's rent in advance."

"You'll pay two months' rent in advance," she said, "I've had enough trouble with these houses."

Corning paid the small sum demanded as rent, pocketed the receipt, received the keys to the place, and returned to open the door.

The place was furnished as he had seen it last. All that had been taken were the personal belongings of Mrs. Ambrose. The rooms still held that peculiar musty smell of stale cooking. There was the same rickety furniture with its faded upholstery, trying bravely to put up a bold front.

Corning prowled about for fifteen or twenty minutes, then locked the door, pocketed the key, returned to his car, and went to his office.

Helen Vail stared at him curiously.

"You're going to put on a one-act skit," he told her.

"What about?"

"You remember the Mrs. Ella Ambrose that we got out on *habeas corpus?*"

"Sure I do."

"All right. She's moved away."

"Suddenly?"

"Yes."

"I take it Santa Claus came down the chimney and gave her a big wad of coin and she moved away without leaving an address."

"That's exactly what happened," said Corning. "And it just occurred to me that the person who played Santa Claus for her doesn't know her personally."

He tossed the key to the little shack on the desk, and said: "Get some of the oldest clothes you can find. Get your hair all snarled up and let your face go to seed. Take a little grease paint and make lines around your eyes."

She grinned.

"Then," he said, "go down to the place on Hampshire Street, where there's a bunch of shacks clustered together in the back part of the block. It's way out in the sticks. I'll give you the address. It's on a rent receipt somewhere." He fished around in his pocket until he found the rent receipt, and tossed it over to her.

"Then what do I do?" she asked.

"Then," he said, "you pretend that you're Mrs. Ella Ambrose, and put on an act. I've got to write it out. Bring your book, and I'll dictate the things I want you to say. The first thing we've got to do, however, is to make a decoy note."

"What do you mean?"

"Write," he said, "in an angular, feminine handwriting a note addressed to Harrison Burman. It will read as follows:

" 'I got to thinking things over, and I don't know where I stand. I know well enough who's back of the whole business. I'm going to talk with you before I go away and stay away. After I started away, I got to thinking things over. I've got a boy, and it ain't fair to him, so I figured I'd come back. You've got to come down to my place and talk with me personally. I'll be expecting you this evening. When you do that, I'll be satisfied, but I ain't going to do no wrong with a boy to bring up. Yours respectfully. Mrs. Ella Ambrose.' "

"Think he'll fall for that?" asked Helen Vail, looking at her shorthand notes with puckered eyes.

"I don't know," said Corning. "If he doesn't fall for that one, I'll think up another one. But I think this will do the work. Write it without any punctuation and don't use many capitals. Make it look illiterate—like the sort of letters we get from cranks."

Helen Vail set to work.

After the letter was finished and mailed, Corning spent some time giving careful instructions to his alert secretary and having her repeat them back to him until he was satisfied.

HELEN VAIL sat in a dilapidated overstuffed chair in Mrs. Ambrose's former home. She wore stockings that were shapeless, with runs in each stocking. Her dress was ill-fitting and had evidently been dyed by unskilled hands. The color was a nondescript black which seemed to have been unequally spread over brown, with the brown peeping through in places. There were deep lines etched about her mouth and her eyes. In the dim light, she seemed twenty-five years older than her real age. She was patiently embroidering.

Knuckles sounded on the door.

"Come in," she called.

The door pushed open, and a big man with a curiously white face, stood on the threshold.

"Mrs. Ambrose?" he asked.

"Come in," she said, in a thin toneless voice of great weariness.

He closed the door behind him.

"I'm Harrison Burman," he said slowly. "I got your letter."

Helen Vail sighed. It sounded like a sigh of weariness, but it was of intense relief. The man did not know the real Ella Ambrose and had taken her at her word.

"All right," she said. "Come in and sit down. I want to talk with you."

Burman's tone was cautious. "You want money?" he asked.

"No. I just want to put my mind at rest."

"All right," he told her irritably, "go ahead and put it at rest. You probably know that you're double-crossing me. You're not living up to your bargain. You had promised to be in Colorado by this time, and to stay there."

Helen Vail acted her part perfectly.

"I can't help it," she said, in that same lifeless tone which is the unconscious badge of those who have given up the struggle.

"I'm a mother with a boy to bring up and I want to bring him up right."

"Well," rasped Burman, "what is it you want?"

"I know a lot more than most people think I know," she said.

"Have you got to go into all that?"

"Yes," she said, "into all of it."

"Then go ahead and get it over with."

His hands were pushed down deep into his coat pockets.

Helen Vail kept her eyes downcast and spoke in the same weary monotone.

"I knew Sam Driver," she said, "and Driver talked to me, and I knew Harry Green, who wasn't Harry Green, but was Richard Post, a man wanted for murder."

"Sure," said Burman irritably, "we know all that. That's why you got the money to get out of the country. If it hadn't been for that, you wouldn't have had a cent."

"I know," she said, in that patient monotone of weariness. "And I know something else. Harry Green didn't kill George Bixel. You paid him to take the rap. You got caught with Mrs. Bixel. George Bixel, her husband, caught you, and you shot him.

"I guess you had to do it to keep him from shootin' you. Maybe you're to blame. Maybe you ain't. That's what bothers me. I got that on my conscience and I can't sleep. You didn't think I knew about it. You thought I just knew about planting Harry's body in Sam Driver's car. But I knew everything about what had happened. Sam Driver didn't know it, because Harry never told him. Harry told me all he knew and Sam told me all *he* knew. So I knew everything.

"There you was out with another man's wife and mixed up in a shooting. She and her husband hadn't taken that cottage at all and have you come up to join them. You and the woman had taken that cottage and the husband found you. You was a big publisher and you couldn't afford to get mixed in a scandal, even if you could prove that you had to kill him to keep him from killing you. So you paid Harry to take the rap for murder and get out. You made him do it. But Harry spent the money, and then he wanted to get more, so he came back and got more.

"First, you tried to scare him by saying you'd let him get tried for the murder and then he scared you by telling you to go ahead and his lawyer would show up what happened. There was a lot of things, I guess, that had to be kinda shaded over. Things that you didn't want the authorities looking into too much, about how long you'd been up there and how long Mrs. Bixel had been up there and how long her husband had been up there.

"So Harry Green got to bleeding you for money. You couldn't stand it. You had an argument or a fight with him and shot him. But you knew where Sam Driver was, because Harry Green had told you where he was. Harry tried to make you think that Sam Driver could be a witness for him if you ever pinched him on the murder rap.

"Well, you had somebody that helped you and you put Harry's body in Sam's car and then you fixed the headlights so Sam would get pinched. You knew Sam was an ex-convict and nobody'd believe him. But you did a slick stunt. You put lots of money in Harry's pockets; then, if anybody did know the truth, it would look like Harry had been to your place and got the money and somebody had killed him afterwards. You figured either that Sam Driver would find the body and take out the money and try to beat it—as he did—or else, if he didn't find the body until after he'd got pinched, the money would make it look like Harry Green had been to your place and gone away, in case anybody suspected what the truth was."

Burman's face was the color of bread dough, pasty and lifeless. He stared at her with glassy eyes and a mouth that sagged.

"You're absolutely crazy," he said, "you can't prove a word of it!"

"Maybe not," she said, "but, with what I know, and what Sam Driver knows we could come pretty near proving it. And I could prove that you and somebody else took Harry Green's body and dumped it into Sam Driver's car, because I seen you. I seen your Cadillac car and I know it. And I seen you. You had on evening clothes when you did it."

Burman stood staring down at her with eyes that were cold and malevolent, lips that quivered.

"What do you want?" he asked.

"I want to know that you acted right," she said. "If you did, I can shield you. But if you didn't, I can't."

Burman spoke swiftly, persuasively.

"Look here," he said, "some of your facts are right and some of them are wrong. Green didn't tell you the whole truth. Green had broken into the place and tried to hold up Mrs. Bixel. I came into the room just in time and smashed Green over the head. It knocked him out and I put him in a closet.

"Then Bixel showed up and was going to shoot me. I had the gun that I'd taken from Harry Green and I shot first, that's all. When Green regained consciousness, I put it up to him that he could either take five thousand dollars in cash and dust out, or that I'd turn him in for murder and frame it on him anyway. I was desperate and I had to do it. You can understand that. The killing was in self-defense, but I had another man's wife with me and I'd killed her husband. A jury would have been hostile."

Helen Vail's voice maintained its tone of dreary weariness.

"You ain't justified yourself yet. It ain't right to have Sam Driver framed for this other murder. You had no right to kill Harry Green. You're a rich man. You could have kept on paying him money and it wouldn't have hurt you. You've got to let Sam Driver go free."

"I can't do that," he said irritably. "I've fixed it up so he can get a break. He can take a plea for manslaughter."

"Maybe the District Attorney wouldn't agree to that," said Helen Vail, in her assumed voice.

"Sure he will," said Burman. "I can get anything I want. I am a political power here and I can fix things up. I've already got word to his lawyer. All you've got to do is to get out and stay out, and things will be all right."

"Would Sam go to jail on that manslaughter charge?" asked Helen Vail in a slow, apathetic voice.

Burman cursed.

Helen Vail shook her head wearily.

"No," she said, "I've had this on my conscience and I guess I've got to tell Sam Driver's lawyer; it ain't right not to."

Burman's hand dug deeper into the right-hand pocket of his coat.

"All right," he said, "if that's the way you feel about it, it's your own fault. If you'd lived up to your bargain and done what you promised to do, you wouldn't have got into this."

"Into what?" she asked, looking up from her embroidering.

"Into this!" snapped Burman, and jerked an automatic from the pocket of his coat.

Helen Vail flung herself to one side with a stifled scream. The door from the kitchen exploded outward, and Ken Corning shot across the room in a low-flung football tackle. Burman wavered for an instant with indecision, and indecision was fatal. Ken Corning struck him with the force of a charging bull. Burman crashed to the floor.

The gun slipped from his fingers, skidded halfway across the room and slammed against the side of the wall. Corning felt the weight of the man rolling over on him, squirmed to free himself, heard a chair crash to the floor. His hands dug into the collar of the man's coat. He was conscious of a tugging strain at his arms, then the coat fell in folds over his face. He kicked the garment from him, rolled to his hands and knees, and was in time to see Burman plunge through the door, into the night.

Ken Corning retrieved the gun and dropped it into the pocket of the coat Burman had left behind.

"Good work, kid," he said.

Helen Vail stared at him with her eyes wide and round.

"What'll he do now?" she asked.

"God knows," he told her. "But the situation has got to come to a head now. He knows that we know. He was afraid the woman knew too much, so he used his influence to get her pinched on a liquor charge. She was peddling it, and he must have had detectives watching her. Once he had her in jail, it was easy to get her not to talk in return for squaring the liquor case."

"How much did the woman really know?" asked Helen Vail.

"Perhaps not much," Corning said slowly. "I put two and two together, and doped out what must have happened."

Helen Vail was staring at the tip of her shoe, her face pensive.

"What's the matter, kid?" asked Ken Corning. "Was it asking too much of you?"

"No," she said, "I was thinking of that Mrs. Bixel and her laughing brown eyes. I hate to see her dragged through this."

Ken Corning's eyes narrowed.

"Let's go up to Burman's house," he said slowly, "and see if we can reach some kind of an agreement."

THE roadster slid to the curb in front of Harrison Burman's residence.

"You sit here," Corning told Helen Vail.

Her lips clamped in a firm line, her face still smeared with the make-up, her hair covered with the wig, the girl shook her head determinedly.

"Nothing doing," she said. "If he gets a chance, he'll kill us both, to silence us."

"Not now," Corning told her. "Down there at the shack, when he lost his head, he would have killed you. He's driven almost crazy. But he'll show some sense now."

"Just the same," she told him, "I'm going in there with you, or you're not going to go."

He stood for a moment, staring at her.

He started to say something, but a woman's scream knifed through the silence of the night.

"It came from the house," said Helen Vail.

Her lips had scarcely finished with the last word, when a pistol shot sounded from the house.

Ken Corning started to run towards the front steps.

"Don't!" screamed Helen Vail. "Don't go in there until you know what's happened! Keep out of it, chief, please."

Ken Corning continued to run, and Helen Vail flung herself from the automobile, gathered her ragged skirts about her, and sprinted after him.

The front door of Harrison Burman's residence opened. A woman rushed out of the house, leaving the door open. She headed down the steps, apparently running in blind panic, and without seeing the two figures who were coming up the granite stairs which led to the front porch.

Ken Corning flung out his arms and caught her in midflight, swinging her around and holding her, despite frantically beating hands and kicking feet.

Abruptly the woman ceased to struggle and stared at Ken Corning with eyes that were wide and round, a face that was white as chalk.

"You!" she exclaimed.

"Mrs. Bixel," Corning said, "tell me quickly—what happened?"

She stared at him for a moment in wordless tension, as though she had great difficulty in readjusting herself to the outer world. Then she said: "Harrison Burman shot himself."

"Any servants?" asked Corning.

She shook her head, tried to say something and, instead, made only a throaty noise.

Corning turned to Helen Vail. She answered his unspoken

question with a nod. Together, they piloted the woman down the
stairs and into the automobile.

"You're sure he's dead?" asked Corning.

She nodded, wordlessly.

"Did he leave any confession, or anything that would incriminate you, in connection with shooting your husband in that
cabin?"

She stared at Corning with alarm manifest in her eyes.

"You're among friends," Corning told her.

"No," she said, in a low voice. "There was no confession; no
writing."

Ken Corning drove her to his office. Together, he and Helen
Vail quieted her and gave her coffee mixed with brandy. Later
they drove her to her home.

IT was twenty-four hours later that Ken Corning called *The
Courier* and got Jerry Bigelow on the line.

"You're always anxious for the real inside dope, Bigelow," he
said, "and I just wanted to mention that if you thought the public
would be interested in the real inside facts surrounding the suicide of Harrison Burman, they would be able to hear them when
the evidence is brought out in Sam Driver's trial."

"Now just what does that mean?" asked the columnist, in a
cool voice.

"It means just what I said," Corning remarked. "It means that
I know the identity of the man called Green, who was murdered.
It means that I know how he met his death. It means that I know
what happened up in that cabin in the mountains when Bixel was
killed."

"And you mean that will come out at the trial?" asked Bigelow.

"It will come out at the trial."

"If there isn't any trial will it come out?"

"If there is no trial," said Ken Corning, speaking slowly and
distinctly, "the facts will never be known—that is, the real facts."

And he slid the receiver back on the hook.

Next morning, when he read his paper, he noticed with satisfaction that Jerry Bigelow, in his column given to gossip of the
town, and the inside facts back of many of the political moves,
made a prediction that the case against Sam Driver, accused of
the murder of Harry Green, would be dismissed; that the District

Attorney had relied upon circumstantial evidence which had not worked out exactly as anticipated. The columnist predicted as "hot inside stuff" that a dismissal of the case was contemplated.

Ken Corning carried the newspaper to his office, slid it over to Helen Vail.

"I saw it already, chief," she said. "What does it mean?"

Ken Corning grinned at her.

"It means," he said, "that the widow of Harrison Burman is in charge of the policies of the paper, and, therefore, has a great deal to say about the political activities of York City. It also means that we haven't, as yet, discovered who the gentleman was that helped Harrison Burman put the body of Harry Green in the automobile belonging to Sam Driver."

She looked at him with sudden consternation.

"You mean to say it was Jerry Bigelow. . . ."

Ken Corning shrugged his shoulders and walked on to his inside office. From the door he called back to her: "Never speculate about a closed case. There is always a live one coming along that will keep us busy."

And then the door softly closed and the latch clicked.